Going Deep

A thrill shot through Brynn's stomach as Jones lifted her more easily than Mike had ever done. His strength made her feel tiny and vulnerable. She lifted her arms in a high vee and held the position. 'Go Trojans!' she cheered out of habit, a smile on her face. Both the cheer squad and the football team broke out in applause.

Brynn looked down at him and found that he was looking straight up at her crotch. With her legs spread and him holding her feet, there was nowhere to hide. Her shorts blocked his view of anything too personal, but her pussy lips clenched just the same. From her point of view she could tell he wasn't unaffected, either. The front of his shorts was tented around his swelling cock. Her balance rocked. Much more of this and she'd do something she might regret.

Other books by the author

Tiger Lily

Going Deep
Kimberly Dean

BLACK LACE

Black Lace books contain sexual fantasies.
In real life, always practise safe sex.

First published in 2004 by
Black Lace
Thames Wharf Studios
Rainville Road
London W6 9HA

Design by Smith & Gilmour, London
Printed and bound by Mackays of Chatham PLC

ISBN 0 352 33876 8

Prologue

Her stomach was doing flip-flops. Brynn clutched her books to her chest and tried to get her nerves under control. She took a deep breath, but it didn't help. Then again, nothing was going to help. It was the first day of classes.

A gust of wind caught her hair, and her hand flew up to try to keep it in place. It was silly, really, how much time she'd spent in front of the mirror this morning. She'd just wanted to look the part. It had taken a dozen different outfits and at least that many hairstyles before she'd been satisfied. She'd been going for a strategic balance – successful, professional, and definitely respectable. The long walk in from the parking lot was quickly chipping away at that façade.

'Ah!' she cried when the relentless Texas wind found the side slit of her skirt.

Her hand dropped from her hair to try to spare her modesty. With only one hand available, though, she couldn't hide much. Instead of staying below her knee, her skirt was flapping up to mid-thigh and beyond. She caught a student staring at her legs, and her face turned red. This was exactly what she hadn't wanted to happen.

With one hand clutching her books and the other battling her skirt, she hurried to the Clausen building. She entered through the double doors and tried to regain her composure as she looked around. Students milled about, some eager for the start of new classes, others begrudging the fact that summer was over. She remembered the start-of-semester nerves all too well.

They were assaulting her now – only, this time around, they were magnified ten times over. Returning to college hadn't been an easy decision. In fact, it had been the toughest decision of her life.

She let out a calming breath and glanced at the piece of paper she'd tucked between two books. Room 255. She straightened her shoulders and headed to the stairs.

A low wolf whistle had her turning around sharply. It was the same student who'd been eyeing her legs outside, only he was joined by a group of friends. They all wore letter jackets with a big T on the left breast.

Varsity football players.

Great, she thought, rolling her eyes. Why did it always have to be football players?

Ignoring them, she started up the second flight of stairs. They followed closely behind her, and her self-consciousness reared its head. Her gaze dropped down quickly, but she was relieved to see that her skirt was respectfully in place. Wouldn't that have just been perfect? To start back at the university with her skirt around her waist?

Nothing like an old scandal to get the gossip mill churning.

Behind her, the pack was talking. Lewd comments hit her ears and her grip on her books tightened. She'd dealt with enough football players in her time to know that she needed to nip this in the bud.

'Need help finding your classrooms, boys?' she asked when she came to the second floor landing.

The one who'd spotted her outside took a step closer and looked down at her. 'I need help finding your number, baby.'

'Try 255,' she said coolly. She turned sharply on her

heel and headed down the hallway until she found her classroom. She was appalled when he hurried around her and held the door open for her.

'That's my room, too.' He winked at her. 'I'm Scott Jetson, but you can call me Jets. I haven't seen you around here before. Are you a transfer?'

'No,' Brynn said. She smoothed her hair back into its French twist and lifted her chin. 'I'm an instructor.'

She left Mr Jets standing at the door with a stunned look on his face. With her spine straight, she walked to the front of the room. Conversation amongst the students stopped as her heels clipped noisily across the hard wood floor. Her heart was pounding in her ears, but she forced a calm expression on her face as she dropped her stack of books onto the desk.

It was time to plunge into a new phase of her life.

'Welcome to Computer Science 101,' she said in a clear voice. 'I'm Professor Montgomery. Shall we get started?'

1

He was staring at her breasts.

Brynn's air caught with surprise, but a tiny little thrill ran through her system. Professor Hawthorn? No, he couldn't be staring at her body. It would be totally inappropriate. She'd respected the man since ... well, since *forever*. She had to be mistaken.

She shifted in her chair, uncomfortable with the direction of her thoughts. She couldn't let her mind wander like that. New faculty orientation was important. University policy might be the driest subject on earth, but she needed to listen to what the man was saying. After all, he wasn't Professor Hawthorn anymore; he was Dean Hawthorn. *Dean.* As in, *her boss.*

But his gaze was definitely on her breasts.

She went still when she realised his eyes were following every sway, jiggle and bounce. Her nipples tightened under the attention, and his pupils dilated.

There was no mistaking that reaction. He was looking at her. Sexually.

She discreetly lifted her notebook to hide her chest and glanced around the room to see if anyone else had noticed. Fortunately, everyone seemed to be concentrating on the organisation chart displayed by the overhead projector.

'I'm sure you all received this in your information packages,' the dean said, 'but I'd like to point out a few changes.'

Brynn crossed her legs and tried to rein in her crazy

thoughts. Hawthorn had been her World History instructor when she'd been a student at Southern Trinity, and she'd been nervous about running into people who might remember her. Maybe she was projecting. That had to be what was happening.

But what if it wasn't? What if he remembered the reason why she'd left the university? Would he think that gave him licence to look at her like that? Like a tiger ready to pounce?

'And our new registrar is Dr Robinson,' he said, oblivious to the thoughts bouncing around in her head. 'Claude, would you stand up so everyone can see you?'

Instead of looking over her shoulder like everyone else, Brynn looked at the dean through the curtain of her lashes. Darren Hawthorn, with those sexy thin lips and even sexier English accent. She'd had the hugest crush on him. He was older now, but he'd aged well. His hair was greying at the sides, but his cobalt-blue eyes were just as sharp and intense.

And those blue eyes were looking at her breasts again.

'Ms Montgomery, did you have a question?'

Brynn's eyes widened when she realised she'd lifted her hand to twirl her hair. 'Well, yes, actually I did,' she said breathlessly.

'What is it?'

Her question. What was her question?

'I was wondering about student athletes,' she said after a moment's hesitation. There was a reason why she'd attended this session. 'I have several in my classes, and I need to know the university's policy on grades and absences.'

'That's an excellent subject for discussion.' Hawthorn turned to the rest of the audience and made a sweeping gesture with his pointer. 'I'm sure many of the rest of you find yourselves in a similar situation. Our athletes are students first. We require regular attendance at classes and students must maintain their grade point average to be allowed to participate on their athletic teams.'

Brynn raised her hand. Her brain was finally kicking into gear. 'What if they're not attending? What are we supposed to do then?'

The pointer stopped waving and hung uncertainly in mid-air. 'You should discuss the matter with the team coach.'

'What if he doesn't respond to my calls and email messages?'

The dean's eyebrows drew together, and he pushed the telescopic pointer together. For the first time in over an hour, he looked her in the face. 'It sounds as if you're having a specific problem we should discuss after the meeting. Do you have a few moments to spare?'

Alone with him? 'Of course.'

'Wonderful,' Hawthorn said. He turned to face the rest of his faculty. 'Are there any other questions?'

Brynn tried to let the muscles in her shoulders relax when his attention was diverted elsewhere. Those cobalt-blue eyes were powerful, especially now that she suspected the thoughts going on behind them. She sat quietly for the rest of the session and worked on getting her nerves under control. By the time the meeting broke up and Hawthorn moved across the room to speak with her, she had nearly regained her composure.

'Thank you for taking the time to meet with me,' she said when he lowered himself into the chair beside her.

'I'll always have time for you, Brynn,' he said with a smile on his face. 'I've been meaning to drop by your office to tell you how happy I am to have you back at Southern Trinity.'

So he did remember her. Her stomach did a nice little plunge. 'I'm happy to be here.'

He settled his elbows onto the arms of the chair and steepled his fingers together. It was a gesture she remembered well. 'So tell me, how are things going?' he asked. 'Are you adjusting well? I understand this is your first time teaching.'

Her hand toyed with her necklace out of nervous habit. It drew his attention back to her chest, so she quickly put her hands in her lap. 'I'm slowly getting into the swing of things. You'd have to ask the students, though.'

'I have.' He smiled when he saw the surprise on her face. 'No need to worry. You're quickly becoming one of the most popular instructors in the computer science department.'

A sense of satisfaction uncoiled in Brynn's stomach at the unexpected feedback. It was so hard to try to read her students. Sometimes when she looked out at their faces, all she saw were blank stares. 'That will probably change after Friday,' she said with a smile. 'I'm giving my first quiz.'

He chuckled. 'Students are a finicky bunch.'

'Yes, they are.'

'You always were.'

He ran his finger down her forearm, and she went still inside.

'So tell me about this problem you're having,' he said. 'Which of our athletes is skipping your class?'

His face turned serious, and her warm body suddenly felt neglected. He'd gone from leering admirer to Dean of Students so fast, it left her confused. And that touch. What had that been?

'It's JJ Stone,' she said as she twisted her necklace into a knot.

'The football player?'

She nodded. 'He's missed nearly two weeks of class, and I'm not quite sure what to do about it.'

Hawthorn reached into his pocket and pulled out a pen and notepad. His dark eyebrows drew together as he considered the implications. 'This isn't good news. Players must attend class or face stiff penalties. The National Collegiate Athletic Association's rules are quite clear.'

'I'm aware of NCAA's stance. That's why I need your advice. I don't want him to get thrown off the team. I realise he's one of our top players.'

'Have you talked with Coach Jones?'

Her toe began tapping rapidly against the floor. She tried not to look as perturbed as she really felt, but she didn't think she was succeeding. Coach Jones. The man was impossible to reach. How was she supposed to tell him that one of his players was in trouble if he couldn't be bothered? 'It's been difficult to get in touch with the man.'

Hawthorn ran a hand through his salt-and-pepper hair. 'That's understandable. It's the heart of training season, and he's still trying to round up those last recruits. I believe he's been in Abilene the last few days.'

The dean tried to be discreet, but his gaze was now stuck on her legs.

Brynn tried uncrossing them, but that didn't help. She was wearing a straight skirt, but she'd given up on the conservative look. She was petite, and long skirts made her look stumpy. The shorter the skirt, the longer her legs. She'd been willing to make the trade-off. At least she knew she had her male students' attention during her lectures.

With Dean Hawthorn, though, it wasn't the same. Drawing his attention had other implications which she hadn't yet decided were good or bad. She tried inconspicuously to tug her skirt down, but it remained lodged at mid-thigh. 'How ... How would you suggest I get in contact with the coach?' she stuttered.

The dean folded his notebook and tapped it with his pen. 'He should be at practice this afternoon. I'll leave him a message that you're looking for him.'

A call from the dean. That might light a fire under the man. Brynn smiled politely. 'I would appreciate that.'

She stood to leave, but Hawthorn waved her back into her chair. 'Hold on, Ms Montgomery. While we're on the subject of football, I'd like to talk to you about something else.'

Brynn sat. She felt that familiar thrill in her stomach when he smiled at her again, but it was quickly followed by a shot of uneasiness.

Oh boy, was she in trouble. This man was her boss. With her history, she simply couldn't get involved with him. There'd be talk.

This time around, she couldn't let there be any talk.

'It's the cheerleading squad,' he said with a dejected look on his face. 'They need some help.'

Her eyebrows lifted. Whatever she'd expected him to say, that wasn't it. 'We're only a few weeks into the semester. I'm sure they'll be fine once the season starts.'

'They haven't been fine for the past four years.'

Her mouth dropped open, and she quickly closed it. The last four years? When she'd left, they'd been a top ranked unit. Why, they'd won three trophies at competitions during her senior year. She couldn't help the pang of disappointment that struck close to her heart. 'What happened?'

'Graduation. Injuries. The loss of Mrs Vestry. You

name it, everything that could go wrong has gone wrong.'

'Mrs Vestry?'

'Retired.'

'Then who took over her position?'

'No one. We haven't had a cheerleading coach since she left.' The sly smile returned to his face. 'Until now, I hope.'

Brynn's stomach twisted. She knew what he was asking, and it was a lot. 'Oh no, I couldn't. I'm over my head with coursework as it is. I'd love to help out, but I simply can't.'

'I thought once a cheerleader, always a cheerleader.'

'Well, of course. We are in Texas.' He'd hit the right button if he was questioning her commitment. Cheerleading was huge in Texas. Cheerleading was *life* in Texas.

'You were captain of the squad two years running.'

'That was ten years ago.'

His gaze ran over her figure unhindered, and he didn't even try to hide his appreciation. 'You look like you should be out there on the fifty yard line. I bet you can even still do the splits.'

Her fingers toyed with the hem of her short skirt when his smile told her he was picturing her in the uncomfortable position right now. 'I try to stay up-to-date by teaching at camps over the summer,' she said uneasily.

He lifted an eyebrow, and she felt herself weakening. She was new to the faculty, and she needed to make a good impression. 'I might consider being an assistant.'

He shook his head. 'The alumni are starting to complain. We need to make drastic changes, and you're perfect for the job.'

'I could help you find someone. I know a lot of people still involved with the sport.'

'We don't have the resources to pay for a full-time coach. We'd like you to take on the position part-time, in addition to your class work. Of course, we'd compensate you accordingly.'

Brynn could see how Hawthorn had risen up the university ranks so quickly. He was nothing if not tenacious. 'I'm sorry, but I can't take on the time commitment. It's my first semester here. I'm sure you understand.'

'I understand that you'll do what's best for the university,' he said enigmatically. He put his hands on the arms of the chair and pushed himself up. He was even more authoritative looking down at her. 'Don't give me an answer now. Attend the game with me on Saturday, and we'll talk about it some more.'

Brynn's stomach twittered. It sounded almost as if he were asking her on a date. 'I don't know.'

He reached up to straighten his tie. 'That wasn't a question, Ms Montgomery. I'll pick you up at six. Kickoff is at eight o'clock under the lights. We'll go to dinner first.'

He wasn't going to take no for an answer. Brynn pushed herself to her feet. She didn't know what concerned her more – the fact that he wouldn't accept her refusal to take on the squad or that she'd just been coerced into a date.

What would people think if they saw her at a Southern Trinity football game? Was there anyone around who could remember back that far? And what about the dean? What was he expecting of her?

'Do you like Italian food?'

She smoothed her skirt as the gears in her brain whirred. 'That would be fine.'

'I'll see you for our interview on Saturday then.'

'Yes, our *interview*.' She nervously plucked at her necklace. She needed time to think, and she couldn't do that while he was staring at her that way.

'I'd better go find Coach Jones,' she said as she backed away to the door. 'Thank you again for seeing me.'

'Seeing you is always a delight. Let me know how things go with JJ.'

Brynn held her stomach as she walked down the hall to her office. The butterflies inside were doing loop-the-loops. Dean Hawthorn, football, and cheerleading. Why did it feel like the fates were lining up against her?

He had to know what the combination had done to her before. Was this some kind of test? Was he trying to get a reaction out of her?

Or was he just horny?

The butterflies in her stomach jumped on a roller coaster. The idea wasn't all that unpleasant. That long ago crush certainly hadn't gone away. If anything, the man was even more intriguing now.

She walked into her office and closed the door behind her. If only she didn't have to worry about the past. All her hard work would be for naught if she jumped in bed with the dean a few weeks after taking the job. She'd come here to restore her reputation.

She pushed herself away from the door. Maybe she was getting herself all worked up over nothing. Maybe all Hawthorn wanted was an interview. She'd know for sure on Saturday. It would be here soon enough, and that brought her back to her original concern: JJ Stone. The dean had made it very clear that it was her responsibility to get Coach Jones' attention, not the other way around.

She picked up the phone and dialled the man's number from memory. As always, her call was put straight through to voice mail. She let out a sigh and hung up without leaving a message. She didn't want to confront him on the football field, but he'd left her no alternative.

She straightened her shoulders. She'd worry about Hawthorn later. Right now, Jones was in her sights. He'd ignored her long enough. It was time he gave her the attention she was due.

The mid-day sun was bright and the temperature was still warm for fall when Brynn marched out to the practice field. She lifted her hand to shield her eyes as she looked over the team.

She couldn't help but smile. The sound of clashing pads and the scent of sweating men took her back. She'd started cheering at the age of eight at peewee football games and, although the players were bigger, nastier, and smellier, everything else was the same. She felt at home here on the sidelines. She just hadn't realised how much she missed it.

She watched as the offensive coach called out a play. The linemen took their stance, but she winced when the right guard moved before the snap of the football. The coach started yelling, and she decided to move on. Another group of players was running tires, and yet another was taking on the tackling sled. Her eyes widened when a big, snarling guy slammed into the sled and moved it back five feet with hardly any effort.

It didn't look as if the Southern Trinity football team had lost its edge. If anything, they looked sharper. And bigger and faster.

She saw Scott Jetson come to the sideline for a drink of water. 'Jets,' she called.

He looked up and his eyes widened. 'Professor Montgomery. What are you doing here?'

Her student looked bigger and tougher rigged out in full football gear. The pads widened his shoulders and the tight pants made her aware that this was no boy. This was a man.

She quickly looked away. 'I'm here to speak with Coach Jones. Could you point him out to me?'

He took a drink before turning back to the field. 'That's him over there talking with JJ.'

She glanced over to where he indicated and felt a kick in her gut. That was the coach?

The tightness in her belly moved lower, and she had to press her thighs together to ease the ache.

Wow.

Coach Jones was a hunk. And a total jock. He was dressed like his players in shorts and a ragged old T-shirt, and the workout had made him just as hot and sweaty. His brown hair was wet, but she could still see the blond highlights it had picked up from so many hours in the sun. He stood with one hand nonchalantly holding a football as he gestured towards the field. His receiver stood listening to every word he said.

JJ. The receiver. She'd come here for him, but for the life of her, she couldn't remember why. Her brain was frozen on his coach.

Just looking at the man was making her mouth water. His shorts, in particular, were riveting her attention. They were long and loose, as was the style, but they hung very nicely on his backside. Slowly, she forced her gaze upward. His T-shirt had seen better days. He'd ripped off the arms, and there were enough holes and tears in the material to make her wonder how it all held together. It was frustrating to catch glimpses of the tanned skin and rippling muscles beneath.

She could see his arms, though. Her fingers itched

when she saw his tattoo. If the rest of his body matched his arms, she just might have to forget all her rules about not getting involved with a co-worker.

She rubbed her damp palms on her skirt. She needed to talk to the man, and there was no better time than the present. 'Thanks, Scott,' she said as she moved onto the field.

'Hey,' he called. 'Be careful.'

Big bodies were running everywhere. Grunts and groans surrounded Brynn as she hurried towards the coach. She felt like a lamb let loose in the lions' den as she wove her way between tough, swearing men. Her heels sunk into the soft ground as she hit mid-field, and she nearly didn't get out of the way as a fullback went rushing by.

'I'm sorry. I'm sorry,' she said over and over again. Finally, she made it across the field to where the receivers were practising.

'JJ, you're fast, but you need to be quick,' she heard the coach say. 'When you make that cut, it needs to be sharp. Otherwise, you're not going to lose your defender. You need to be open to take that pass.'

JJ's facemask went up and down as he nodded. 'OK, coach.'

'Try it again.'

Brynn stopped to watch her student run the drill. The quarterback took the snap, and JJ took off like a shot. He ran fifteen yards down the field, made a fake, and took a quick left. Apparently, it wasn't quick enough. The defensive player stayed with him every step of the way and knocked down the quarterback's pass before it could reach his hands.

'Damn it, Stone, what did I just tell you?' Coach Jones barked. He tossed his clipboard on the ground in disgust.

Brynn summoned her nerve. Now was as good a time

as any. She wasn't happy with JJ and neither was his coach. 'Mr Jones,' she called.

He ignored her.

'Sharp, it needs to be sharp,' he said to his player, gesturing with his hands.

She tried again. 'Could I speak with you, Coach Jones?'

'Get back over here and try it again.'

'Coach!'

'Keep your panties on, lady,' he finally yelled over his shoulder. 'Can't you see I'm busy here?'

Brynn's jaw dropped. Her dreamy thoughts dissipated, and she remembered how the man had patently ignored her for two weeks. He might be sexy as sin, but he was also an arrogant jerk!

JJ trotted back across the field. She waved to get his attention, and she saw his eyes widen underneath his helmet when he spotted her. He quickly gave her his back, and fume nearly poured out of her ears.

'Watch me, Stone,' Jones said, ignorant of the by-play. 'Try to see the difference to what you're doing.'

Brynn had started to march up to the coach to confront him directly, but she stopped in her tracks when he took off at full steam. She planted her hands on her hips and let out a frustrated growl. How was she supposed to catch him if he kept avoiding her?

'Coach J –,' she yelled.

His name died on her lips. There was something about the way he moved. She couldn't take her eyes off of him as he ran the pattern.

The fluidity of the way he ran ... His speed ...

He made the cut and turned to face the quarterback. She got a good look at his face when he caught the ball against his chest.

Oh God!

She took a hurried step back.

It couldn't be.

Jones. It was one of the most common names out there. It had to be somebody else, somebody who looked like him.

But it wasn't.

She turned on her heel and blindly headed off the field. She came up short when the same fullback nearly careened into her again. He ducked around her, and this time she didn't even bother to apologise. Her legs just began churning. She needed to get away fast.

Cody Jones.

Dear God!

Her feet had just hit the track that circled the field when she heard somebody behind her.

'Hey, you. Lady!'

She nearly started running.

'Blondie! Get your ass back over here. You can't come out here, interrupt my practice, and expect to just leave.'

Her heart was pounding as she rushed into the tunnel leading to the exit. Escape was the only thing on her mind until strong fingers wrapped around her arm and yanked her to a stop.

'Hey! Didn't you hear me yelling at you?'

She couldn't avoid him when he turned her around.

'Who the hell –' He took one look at her face. 'Fuck me!'

Brynn wished a hole would open up in the ground and just swallow her. This couldn't be happening.

'Brynn Montgomery,' he said in a low voice. 'What the *fuck* are you doing here?'

She cringed at his harsh language. He seemed about as happy to see her as she was to see him. It had been a long time – ten years, to be precise. She could have gone another ten years without having this miserable encounter.

She tried to concentrate on the reason why she'd come to the field in the first place. 'I need to talk to you about JJ.'

He just looked at her blankly.

'I've left you several messages.'

'You're Professor Montgomery? *You?* You're shittin' me!'

Her teeth clamped together. 'You don't need to be crass.'

He let out a snort and caught her by the chin. He forced her to look at him, and her cheeks heated when she saw the look in his eyes. Anger, surprise, and – as always – lust swirled in the dark depths. 'Still a prude, Brynn?'

She tore her chin out of his grip and took a step back. He followed her until her back was up against the concrete wall. He loomed over her, and her heart began to thud in her ears. She'd come here with a purpose. Concentrate on JJ. 'We need to speak about JJ's coursework.'

'What about it?'

'He's a student of mine.'

'I got that.'

'He's been skipping classes.'

That got Cody's attention fast. His eyes narrowed and the muscles around his mouth tightened. 'Want to run that by me again?'

'He's missed two weeks of class straight. I've been trying to get in touch with you to discuss the matter.'

'Well, why didn't you say so?'

'I did!'

'No, you didn't. Your bitchy little messages just ordered me to call you.'

She was upset enough as it was. He didn't need to call her names – not when he was the one in the wrong.

'Is that why you didn't call me back? Because I told you to?'

'I don't take orders from anyone. Or have you forgotten that, Brynnie?'

Her lips flattened. She wasn't going to get into this with him. 'Well, let's talk about it now. JJ, that is.'

One of his eyebrows lifted. 'OK. Talk.'

His dark eyes were smoky when she finally looked at him, and her stomach took a nosedive to somewhere around her toes. He'd always looked at her like that. Always. She hadn't been able to handle it then, and she couldn't handle it now.

She tried to edge away from him, but her shoulders pressed firmly against the wall. She let it bolster her. 'According to the team rules I was given, your players must attend class. If they fail a course, NCAA rules state that they –'

'I know what they state. What class are you teaching?'

Her teeth clenched. She'd made that very clear in the ten or so messages she'd left. 'Computer Science 101.'

'That doesn't make any sense. Hell, Jetson can't stop talking about that class.' His dark eyes sparkled. 'Of course, most of what he talks about are his chances of getting into your drawers.'

That was it. Brynn tried to sidestep away, but he caught her by the waist and pulled her back.

'Hold on,' he said.

The hand at her waist didn't let her go. Instead, his fingers moved in a caress that made her stomach clench.

'JJ!' he yelled back to the field. 'Get your ass over here. You've got some explaining to do.'

Brynn's breaths were coming heavily. His thumb had slipped under her lavender sweater and was on her skin.

He was touching her.

It might look innocent, but she knew better. He knew how his touch affected her. She blocked the memory from her mind, but she couldn't block her response to his touch. The tiny circles it was making clouded her head.

And he knew it. He took a step closer. With his height advantage, he could see straight down her cleavage. She hadn't realised how low the neckline of the sweater was cut when she'd put it on this morning.

She took another deep breath and smelled his sweat. He was hot, wet, and big. He was pure male, and he was making sure she knew it.

'Hey, Coach,' JJ said as he trotted up to them. He held a paper cup of water in one hand and his helmet in the other.

Cody backed away, and Brynn's chest heaved. Air. She needed air.

'Professor Montgomery tells me that you've been missing class.'

JJ hesitated. Brynn could almost see the gears turning in his head. He knew he'd been caught, but he wasn't ready to admit it. Instead, he kicked his cleats against the ground and started making patterns in the dirt. 'I was there.'

'The first week,' she countered. She was happy to finally be getting to the subject. Once they got through this, she could move on. And away. To her car. To another town. Another state.

'Yeah, so?' the kid said.

'*So?*' Cody said sharply.

JJ paled under his dark skin. He reached up and ran a hand across his smooth-shaved head. 'I don't need to be there, Coach.'

'Yes, you do,' Cody and Brynn said in unison. She looked at him sharply, but then backed down. He should be the one to handle this. If he wanted to keep his player on the team, let him get through to him. It wasn't her job. None of this was her job.

Cody planted a fist on his hip. His other hand was still plastered against the wall beside her head. Brynn realised that if she wanted to escape from his overwhelming presence, now was the time to do it.

She knew just as well that he wouldn't let her. He hadn't moved more than two feet away from her since he'd figured out who she was. It didn't matter if JJ was there or not. He wasn't letting her get away.

'If you want to stay on this team, your butt will be in that class when it's supposed to be,' Cody said. He glanced at her. 'When is that?'

'Monday, Wednesday, and Friday at ten.'

'You hear that? Monday, Wednesday, and Friday at ten.'

'But Coach –'

'What is it about this that you don't understand, Stone?'

'But it's boring!'

Brynn's breath caught, and her mouth dropped opened. The accusation hurt.

Cody pointed directly at the young man's face before she could say anything. 'Apologise.'

'I didn't mean –'

'You're already on my shit list. Apologise before I get *really* pissed off.'

JJ kicked at the ground and a puff of dirt lifted around his foot. 'I'm sorry, Professor Montgomery. I didn't mean it that way. I just already know all the stuff you've been covering.'

The excuse didn't ease her hurt feelings, but she couldn't accuse him of not giving her honest feedback.

Dean Hawthorn obviously hadn't interviewed all her students. It was just hard to hear that she was failing when she was working so hard. 'If that's the case, why are you taking the class?' she asked.

'It's a pre-requisite for C++ programming.'

Her mouth twisted. 'I'll be teaching that next semester.'

He shrugged. 'Maybe I'll like it better.'

'And maybe you better shut your mouth,' Cody warned.

Brynn's fingers clenched into fists. 'You'll have to get through 101 first, JJ.'

'Which means attending class,' Cody added.

'Yeah, yeah. I get what you're saying.'

'I'm not sure you do. If you don't pass the class, not only will you not get into programming, you'll be off the team.'

'But Coach!'

'They're my rules, and they're NCAA rules.' Cody pointed to the field. 'And if you don't think I'm serious, think about it some more while you're doing wind sprints. I want ten sets of them. Now.'

JJ's shoulders dropped, and he started to whine. He stopped, though, when he saw the determined look on his coach's face. 'Yes, sir.'

He left at a jog, and Brynn watched him go.

'I'll be damned,' Cody said softly.

'Surprised to hear that my class is boring?'

He ducked his head so he could look her straight in the eye. 'Don't take it personally. Stone's a computer freak. He fixes my laptop all the time.'

'Then what?' she said defensively. 'What did you get out of that conversation that I didn't?'

'The kid's gay.'

'What?' Her head snapped towards the field. JJ touched the twenty-yard line before turning around to head for the end zone. 'Gay? Why do you think that?'

Her heels clunked against the wall when Cody planted his hands on either side of her head again and leaned in. He looked pointedly at her cleavage. 'He didn't steal a look at your tits once.'

'Cody,' she gasped. She couldn't help it. She reached up and covered her breasts with her hands.

That didn't deter him at all. In fact, it seemed to turn him on. She could tell by the way he shifted his weight uncomfortably.

'With that skirt up to your pussy and your boobs swinging all over the place, the guy should have at least looked. Jetson sure does. You'll never catch him missing class.'

Brynn winced. She wanted her students to be talking about computers, software, or coding – anything but how boring or, at the other end of the spectrum, how hot she was. She focused on a point somewhere over Cody's shoulder. 'Does it make a difference?'

'Hell, no. I don't care how he keeps his fingers sticky as long as he keeps catching the ball.'

She closed her eyes when he caught a strand of her hair and began twirling it around his finger. He was standing so close, she'd gotten an intimate view of the tattoo on his left arm. It was barbed wire – a symbol of danger. She knew enough to heed the warning.

'I just don't get it,' he said softly. 'Gay or not, if I had a professor that looked like you, my butt would be in that seat every day.'

Focus on JJ. Focus.

'Do ... Do you think he'll start coming to class?' she asked.

'Oh, he'll be there.' Cody's hot gaze ran across her

face. He was still staring at her like he couldn't believe she was there. 'I'll want weekly reports on how he's doing.'

'I'll email you.'

He grinned. 'Still running, Brynn?'

You bet she was. She hadn't run the last time, and she'd regretted it.

She ducked under his arm and winced when the move made him pull her hair. He let go at the sound of pain, and she quickly moved away from him. She didn't care if he thought she was a coward. She hadn't known he worked here.

And she'd thought running into Hawthorn had been bad!

She needed to regroup. This changed things. It changed everything. 'There's a quiz on Friday,' she said. 'Make sure all your players are there.'

She turned and walked down the tunnel to the exit. Her back was ramrod straight, but her knees were so shaky, she didn't know if they'd last that far.

'You got away last time, baby,' Cody called after her. 'Now that you're back, though, you're going to have to deal with me.'

'Not if I can help it,' she said under her breath. She turned the corner and sagged against the wall.

Her legs simply wouldn't hold her weight anymore. She bent over and braced her hands on her thighs. She took deep breaths to try to centre herself, but she listened carefully. One footstep down that tunnel and she'd find a way to move.

She concentrated on just breathing. That alone was a major accomplishment. Seeing him again had knocked the wind right out of her. Finally, she pushed herself away from the wall. She froze, though, when she heard his voice softly echo down the corridor.

'And Brynnie?' he said. 'You can forget what I said about your panties.'

Her entire body stiffened.

'You know you can take them off for me anytime you want.'

2

Saturday night arrived sooner than Brynn would have liked, but the game and its familiar atmosphere pulled her in. The sights and sounds took her back: the clean smell of the autumn air; the sound of the announcer's voice; the taste of Kettle Korn! How could she have forgotten?

The stands were packed, but Dean Hawthorn had prime seats right on the fifty-yard line. It was a clear night, and the stadium lights lit up the field like a stage. The Southern Trinity Trojans were steadily working their way down the field. The game was exciting, but Brynn's attention was split between the players, the cheerleaders, and the dean. As if that wasn't enough, her focus kept drifting to the sidelines of the field.

Cody Jones.

She shook her head. Fate had a sick sense of humour.

She'd been avoiding him all week. Seeing him again had rocked her world and, like it or not, she'd taken to hiding until she could figure things out. She'd just never expected to see him again. Ever. If she'd known he was at Southern Trinity, she never would have taken the job. A good portion of her week had been spent considering whether she should resign now.

But she couldn't. She needed the paycheck, and she needed to get past this. What had happened between her and Cody Jones was ancient history. If he'd just let it go, so would she.

Her fingers toyed with her necklace. She doubted that

he was going to forgive and forget, though. That last comment of his had certainly said otherwise. His words had thrown her. So had his look, his touch.

Unwillingly, she glanced at him again. He looked just as good as he had the other day. He stood on the sidelines dressed in khaki pants and a blue Trojan team shirt. A clipboard in one hand and headphones on his ears kept him fully in charge of the game. And make no doubt about it, he was in charge.

Of all the men on the sidelines, he was the one with an almost kinetic energy simmering around him. His players respected him, as did his assistant coaches. He knew what he was doing, and he was very, very good at it. Even Dean Hawthorn had sung his praises over dinner.

Brynn glanced at her boss out of the corner of her eye. He was in deep discussions with one of the university's biggest donors, and it gave her a chance to study him. She still wasn't quite sure if she was on a date or simply an interview. He'd kept her off balance the entire evening.

On the one hand, he'd been the perfect gentleman. He'd picked her up at her apartment and had taken her to a nice sit-down restaurant. Their conversation had centred on the university, her classes, and the cheer squad. It had been an almost perfectly acceptable business dinner.

Almost.

She just couldn't help but notice all the intangible things that said it was anything but professional – like the way his hand had slipped to her ass when he'd helped her out of the car. He'd managed to touch her at least twenty times since then, whether it had been to brush an imaginary speck of lint off her shoulder or to hold her wrist as he looked at her watch. Her body was slowly becoming accustomed to his touch, and intuitively, she knew that was his intent.

Because, while his touches had been subtle, his steamy glances hadn't. She'd only caught him looking her in the eye once over the entire meal. The rest of the time, her breasts had been the main attraction. She was still waiting for her nipples to relax. Thank goodness she'd brought a light jacket to the game, or the donors would be wondering what, exactly, Dean Hawthorn was doing with his newest professor.

So when it came right down to it, Cody had her stressed, Hawthorn had her confused, and the cheer squad had her appalled.

'You've been staring at them for nearly a full half,' Hawthorn said, making her jump. 'What do you think?'

Brynn settled into her seat and tried to pay attention. Out of everything that was assaulting her senses tonight, the cheer squad was hardly a blip on her radar screen. That said something right there. Cheerleaders were supposed to capture a crowd's attention, hold it, and then throw it back to the team.

'I see potential,' she said, choosing her words carefully. Potential was relative, after all. It might be easier to start over with an entirely new squad.

'Potential? Really?' The dean edged closer, trying to catch a glimpse of what her cheerleader's brain saw.

'Of course. It's obvious that they all have experience. The whole team just needs to polish up its moves and get in sync.' She looked at him, and he gestured for her to continue. She looked back down at the squad and fought not to grimace at their poor spacing. 'The tumblers are fine, when they're used, but their routines need updating and they need to incorporate the male cheerleaders more. Where are the lifts?'

'Oh well, that may be my fault,' Hawthorn said,

clearing his throat. 'We banned all stunts until they could get proper coaching.'

Brynn bit the side of her cheek. She'd just stepped into that trap rather conveniently. 'Who's the captain?' she asked.

Hawthorn's attention focused on the little blonde in front. 'That's Hannah Stiles, one of our most active students.'

'She's very good.' She was the one bright spot, in Brynn's opinion. The girl had energy, dance skills, and presence. The problem was, she was so bright, she made the entire squad look unbalanced. 'It's too bad we don't have more like her.'

'It's funny you should say that. She's always reminded me a lot of you.'

Brynn glanced at the dean. 'How so?'

'Well, there are the looks, of course. You're both blonde and curvaceous.'

Hawthorn's gaze did a comparative sweep, and Brynn was momentarily taken aback. He was looking at Hannah like she was a Playboy centrefold. Had he looked at her that way when she was a student, too? Was she just now noticing something that had been there all along?

'She's also similar to you in temperament,' he continued. 'She's always striving to do her best. You're both afflicted with the classic good girl syndrome, I'm afraid.'

The knowing look in his eyes made Brynn's cheeks flare, and she hurriedly turned her attention back to the field. Her gaze was drawn like a magnet to Cody, and her entire face turned bright red. He'd always called her 'Goody Two Shoes' – like there was something wrong with it. He'd liked taunting her, flustering her, and basically getting under her skin. Apparently, Hawthorn liked to use the same tactics.

'Ah, love, don't be embarrassed. It's quite appealing, if I must say.' He ran his hand down her back, and she sat up straight when he squeezed her bottom.

She couldn't do anything, though, not while she was sitting in the midst of the university's biggest donors. He knew the bind she was in, but he just laughed and patted her ass softly before removing his hand.

Brynn ran a hand through her hair and concentrated on the cheerleaders. 'When was the last time they got new uniforms?' she asked. The style they were wearing was at least five years out of date and very unflattering.

He rubbed his chin consideringly. 'I'm afraid I don't know the answer to that question.'

'Is there money in the budget? If you want to do this, you should do it right.'

His cobalt-blue eyes sharpened. 'Does that mean that you're considering taking on the position?'

'It means that they need new uniforms,' Brynn said with a smile.

Her head was telling her a strident 'no'. She didn't have time to take on a cheer squad – not when she was still adjusting to her new job. Her heart, though, was screaming at her. The squad, *her old squad*, needed help badly, and she missed the sport. Coming here tonight had only emphasised how much.

'I believe something could be arranged.' Hawthorn nodded his head almost imperceptibly at the man he'd just been speaking with.

Brynn glanced back. The elderly gentleman seated behind them was obviously wealthy. His clothing and the Rolex on his wrist made that very clear. His attention, though, was on the game, not the cheerleaders.

She leaned towards Hawthorn, but her spine went rigid when his arm circled her shoulders. 'He . . . uh . . .'

'Yes?'

She couldn't think. His face was inches from hers. 'The man,' she said dumbly.

'Mr Clausen?'

She blinked. 'Clausen?'

'As in the Clausen Building where you teach computer science.' Hawthorn threw her a wink. 'Henry's grandfather made a generous donation to get that building started. If we let him know your connection, I'm sure he'd be inclined to reach into his pocket.'

Brynn shook her head. 'I think he'd be more apt to donate to the football programme.'

'Look again.'

The opposing team had just called a timeout and the cheer squad lined up for a quick routine. Instead of watching the painful display this time, she kept her gaze over her shoulder. Henry Clausen's rapt attention was on the women in the short skirts.

'He was one of the first to complain about the decline in the cheerleading programme,' Hawthorn said. He leaned even closer to whisper in her ear, and she flinched when his nose brushed against her cheek. 'He is somewhat of a dirty old man.'

Brynn's stomach fluttered. Was he the only dirty old man in the stands? She thought not.

The crowd suddenly surged to its collective feet. She jumped from surprise, but used the distraction to pull back from Dean Hawthorn's embrace. She quickly looked down at the field. Her eyes widened when she saw JJ Stone going out for a pass. He made a quick cut, just like she'd seen Cody teach him, and his defender stumbled.

'Go, JJ!' she screamed. She'd been a cheerleader too long for instinct not to take over. She leapt to her feet and her fingers clenched together as she waited in suspense. The quarterback finally saw his open man and let the football fly. It hit JJ right on the numbers and he wrapped the ball into his arms. His feet flew as he turned and headed down field. 'Run, JJ, run!'

The crowd went crazy when he crossed the goal line.

'Touchdown, Southern Trinity,' the announcer's booming voice called out.

Automatically, Brynn turned to her boss to give him a high five. Instead, he caught her in a bear hug. Their bodies pressed together from chest to knee, and she felt the evidence press against her belly.

She was on a date.

'Coach the cheerleaders, Brynn,' he said into her ear. 'We need you.'

Her knees turned to spaghetti. She looked down at the field and saw the cheerleaders doing leaps and shaking their pompons. The roar of the crowd, the brisk fall air, the smell of popcorn in the stands, and an interested, sexy man – it all added up until she couldn't refuse. 'Will you give me full control?' she asked.

'So you like being in control, do you?'

Her cheeks turned pink.

'You won't get it from me.' He gave her a steady look, but then pulled back before anyone could label the embrace inappropriate. 'You'll have to run things by me, but I promise I won't stand in your way.'

Brynn bit her lower lip. She hoped she wasn't accepting more than she could handle. She glanced one more time at the sidelines. 'All right,' she said. 'I accept.'

'Wonderful!' He dropped back into his seat and clapped his hands. 'We'll announce you at Coach Jones' donor luncheon next week. You can make your first appeal for new uniforms there.'

Coach Jones? Brynn felt as if she'd just run smack dab into a brick wall.

She hadn't thought things through clearly. If she were to work with the cheer squad, she'd be forced into closer contact with him. The football coach had nothing to do with the cheerleaders, of course, but they'd be at the same events and proximity wouldn't be her friend.

'Luncheon?' she said weakly. 'Maybe I should think about this some more.'

'Nonsense. You've said yes, and I'm going to hold you to it,' Hawthorn said gleefully. 'Let me just speak with Mr Clausen. I'm sure he'll spread the word for us.'

Southern Trinity won its first game of the season by a score of 28–7. Brynn gathered up her seat cushion and empty bag of Kettle Korn when the time on the scoreboard ran out. She was still worried about working more closely with Cody, but thoughts and ideas for the cheer squad were already running through her head. It had been a long night, though, and she was ready to go home.

When she turned to Dean Hawthorn, she saw he was still speaking with Mr Clausen. She let out a quiet sigh. The man was a regular windbag. She'd been introduced, and it had taken her half an hour to escape. She didn't want to get caught again, and she didn't want to stay in the stands for too long.

Cody hadn't seen her, and she wanted to keep it that way.

She glanced down at the field. He was taking off his headset and handing it to a student assistant. He ran his fingers through his hair and smiled at whatever the student said. The smile cut right through her.

In all the time she'd known him, she'd rarely seen him smile like that. He was too intense, and where she'd been involved, things had been anything but funny.

She shivered, even though the fall air wasn't yet all

that crisp. Turning, she made her way to the men's side. 'Excuse me, Dean, but I think I'll head out to the car.'

He looked at her, but she could see he was in the middle of something important. Instead of breaking off the conversation, he reached into his pocket. 'Here, take the keys. I'll be along shortly.'

Brynn smiled at Mr Clausen, but quickly ducked out. She watched her way as she climbed down the stadium steps. She tossed the popcorn bag into the trash and joined the dwindling crowd as it made its way out to the parking lot.

Dinner at the restaurant had taken longer than they'd expected, and even though Hawthorn had a special parking permit, they were at the back of the lot. She wove her way through the parked cars as engines fired up and cars moved into the slow line to exit. The streetlight at the end of the lot was burning low, and her steps moved faster.

She spotted the silver Cadillac and hurried to it. She hit the button on the remote keyring and the doors unlocked and the interior light blinked on. Her fingers wrapped around the handle to the passenger's side door and swung it open. She jumped sharply, though, when a hand reached over her shoulder and firmly pushed it shut again.

Cody saw the scream developing and clamped his hand over Brynn's open mouth when she spun around to defend herself. He caught her wrist before she could hit him with her seat cushion. 'Don't do that,' he said. 'I heard enough screaming during the game.'

He felt the tenseness in her body change.

'Cody?' Her wide eyes looked him over quickly and then scanned the parking lot. 'What are you doing?'

'You've been avoiding me all week. We need to talk.'

'Talk?' She batted his hand away, and the fear on her face was quickly replaced by irritation. 'You scared the daylights out of me.'

'The daylights?' he said, a laugh choking his throat. 'What are you, seventy years old?'

'Stop it,' she snapped. She rubbed her hand over the goose bumps on her arm. 'You should know better than to sneak up on a woman in a dark parking lot.'

He saw her sidestep coming and stopped her with a hand at her waist. His fingers wanted more, but he settled for tangling them in the belt loop of her jeans. 'Sneaking up on you is the only way I seem to be able to get close.'

Her eyes rounded, but she pressed her lips together and said nothing.

'You haven't been returning my phone messages,' he said. He let his thumb rub over the point of her hipbone. 'Every time I show up at your office, you're gone.'

'Oh really?' she said sardonically. 'How does it feel?'

He winced. 'OK, I guess I deserved that.'

He'd admit that he'd been avoiding her earlier in the week, but he'd been busy getting ready for tonight. He hadn't had the time to go hold the hand of some new professor who didn't know how the system worked.

Of course, if he'd known that Professor Montgomery was Brynn Montgomery, he would have been more inclined to do a little hand-holding or whatever else kind of holding she'd allow.

Damn, he thought for the millionth time. *Brynn Montgomery!*

His hungry eyes soaked up the sight of her. She'd knocked him for a loop when she'd shown up at practice the other day. He'd been so pole-axed, he'd had to turn the rest of the session over to his assistants. To be honest, he still wasn't quite right in the head. He was having a hard time believing she was really here.

'What do you want?' she asked as she toyed with her necklace. 'Shouldn't you be with your players?'

He caught her hand and held it in his. She tried to pull away, but he just wove his fingers through hers and held on. 'I've got assistants who can take care of that. I need to know why you're here, Brynn.'

'I came to see a football game.'

'You know what I mean,' he growled. His fingers dug into her jeans and he moved closer until their toes were nearly touching. 'What are you doing at Southern Trinity?'

Her gaze flickered away, and she started to fidget as he stared at her.

'I thought we'd been through that,' she said.

'I know that you're teaching Comp Sci 101, but why here?'

'I needed a job. The Internet company I was working for downsized me, and Trinity offered me a position.' She flipped her hair over her shoulder and her chin came up. 'I didn't know you were here.'

He tried not to let the sting from that arrow show. 'Would you have taken the job if you did?'

Her lips pressed together tightly, but she didn't answer.

'What happened to you, Brynnie?' he asked as he leaned in closer to her. 'Where did you go after you left school? You left here so fast, I couldn't find you. I tried, you know.'

Dots of bright colour lit up her cheekbones. She jerked away from him so fast, he didn't have time to catch her. 'Goodnight, Cody,' she said as she reached for the door handle again. 'Congratulations on your win tonight.'

She managed to wedge the door between their bodies, but he caught her arm and her seat cushion fell uselessly to the ground.

'Hold on, hold on,' he said as he planted his hand on the door window again. There was no way she was going to avoid him tonight. That little encounter on the practice field hadn't satisfied him at all. It had been like getting a tiny bite of chocolate cake before the entire piece was ripped away.

He wanted more.

Gently, but firmly, he pulled her away from the car and closed the door. This time, he leaned against it so she couldn't get in.

'Did you enjoy the game?' he asked. He caught her by the hips and tugged her closer. 'I saw you up there in the stands.'

She stood uncertainly between his spread legs and eyed him carefully. 'It looks like you've got a good team this year,' she said after a point.

He slid his hands into her back pockets and nudged her closer. Her hands went to his wrists, but she couldn't dislodge his touch. He curled his hands around her rear end and savoured the feeling. 'We were Division III national champs last year.'

'Really?' She quickly tamped down on her instinctive excitement. 'I didn't know,' she mumbled.

He let his gaze run over her face. If possible, she was even more of a knockout than the last time he'd seen her. Of course, during their last encounter he hadn't exactly been looking at her face.

'Our goal is to repeat this year,' he said, struggling to get past the picture in his head.

'Well, I wish you luck.'

She didn't seem to know where to put her hands. He had more than a few ideas, but she settled with crossing her arms over her chest in a defensive gesture. His teeth gritted with frustration, but he had to be careful not to spook her again. She was as skittish as a wild animal when it came to him.

Simple conversation seemed to be working, though. His hormones hadn't allowed for anything so subtle back when they'd been students. In fact, his hormones were having a hard time slowing down now. Her curves filled out that black sweater perfectly, and with his hands cupping her ass, he could hardly think. She wasn't standing still, either, and that didn't help at all.

'Cody,' she said softly. 'Please take your hands off of me.'

He heard the edge in her voice, so he let her go. She hooked her hair behind her ear and it was all he could do not to dive his fingers into the blonde strands and grab hold.

'I'd like to get in the car now.'

'No. Stay.' He couldn't help it; he reached back out and caught her hand. 'Talk with me.'

'Talk?' she said with a strained laugh.

'Just talk,' he promised. He didn't know if he'd be able to keep it, but what the hell? He quickly searched his brain for a safe topic. 'How do you like teaching?'

She rolled her neck and looked up at the stars. 'It's OK.'

'I never thought you'd come back here.'

'Neither did I,' she admitted quietly. She looked at him. 'How long have you been here?'

'Three years.'

Her teeth bit her lower lip. 'That must have been right after you blew out your knee.'

He was momentarily stunned. 'I didn't know you were a fan of professional football, Brynn.'

'You were good, Cody.'

The soft admission caught him right in the gut.

'I was sorry to see your career end that way.'

'So was I.'

The intimate conversation under the dark night sky was doing things for him. She was doing things for him. Just holding her hand wasn't enough – not with the way his cock was stiffening.

'Coaching's not so bad, though,' he said, trying to keep his body under control.

'You came home, too.'

'Yeah, I guess I did.'

She toyed with the gold necklace that shone so brightly against the black sweater and his gaze went to her breasts.

'Did you keep in touch with anyone from the old days?' she asked.

The question was like a two-by-four right between the eyes. The hot feeling in his stomach gelled like lava. 'No,' he said through a throat that felt like gravel. 'Did you?'

Her eyes flared at his sharp tone. 'How could I after what you did?'

'I did?' he said, his own temper piquing. 'Think again, baby. That was a joint effort. You certainly didn't try to fight me off.'

'You made sure of that, didn't you?'

'Damn straight, I did,' he growled.

Enough with the small talk and baby touches. They were finally getting to the heart of the matter. He gave a solid tug on her hand and caught her hard against his body. His eyes bored into hers. A question had been eating at him for ten years. 'Have you seen him since that night?'

'No!' Her hands pushed at his shoulders.

'Good,' he snarled. 'Then it was worth it.'

Her eyes widened when his head tilted and dipped. Before she could let out the cry that was on the tip of her tongue, he had it in his mouth. She went rigid against him, and he used her momentary vulnerability to his advantage. Slowly, he dragged his tongue along the wet, rough surface of hers. She groaned at the forced intimacy and the sound rang in his ears.

'Two good things happened that night,' he said with his mouth still on hers. 'I made you come, and I got you away from that bastard.'

He didn't know which boast offended her, but her defensive shields came crashing down. She hadn't succeeded in pushing him away, so she arched her body, trying to buck him off of her. The move only ground her crotch against the zipper of his pants, and his cock surged.

'Oh yeah, Brynnie,' he grunted. 'Just like that.'

'You son-of-a-bitch,' she panted as she tore her lips away.

He gave her a hard smile. He had to be getting to her for her to use such language. Even as she cursed him, though, her hips were jerking against him.

'You like me that way.' He turned with her in his arms and pushed her back against the car. He rocked hard against the notch at the top of her legs until her fingers were biting into his shoulders.

'I never liked you.'

'Yes, you did. You just wouldn't admit it. That was the problem.'

And it had been a big problem – one that had almost driven him out of his frickin' mind.

He saw the veins in her neck fluttering with every beat of her heart, and he knew she was right there with him. His tongue sought out that twittering vein and coated it with long, wet licks.

He wedged his hand between their bellies and began searching for the tab of her jeans. 'You wanted me, Brynn. You were just such a Goody Two Shoes, you were afraid of it.'

Her hands slapped at his shoulders. 'Don't call me that!'

'Goody Two Shoes?'

She turned her head away from his kiss.

'I guess you weren't after I got through with you,' he said into her ear.

She gasped when he worked her zipper down and thrust his hand into her panties.

'I turned you into a naughty girl that night.'

It was a tight fit with her body lodged between him and the car. They were connected from lips to breast to thighs. His hand could barely wiggle down her belly, but he wasn't moving away from her. No way. No how. He'd waited years to get at her like this.

Her belly sucked in on another gasp when his fingers reached her curls. 'You needed it and you wanted it, Brynn,' he said. 'Just like now.'

He kissed her again and gave a sharp tug on the blonde curls between her legs. She let out a cry and her body shuddered. He used the opportunity to lodge his hand between her legs. He cupped her pussy, and she went right up onto her tiptoes.

'I didn't deserve what happened,' she argued. Her hands wrapped around his arms, and her fingers bit into his biceps.

'Afterwards, no,' he agreed. 'You didn't deserve that.'

'Then why did you –'

'I didn't.' He kissed her temple. 'I didn't.'

He set his fingers to exploring as he watched her face. Her eyes were closed tight, and her teeth bit hard into her lower lip. Purposely, he let his thumb drum across her clit. Her eyes flew open and her jaw dropped. He did it again, and she came alive in his arms, clawing at him like a cat.

He dropped his forehead against hers. 'Spread your legs, Brynnie.'

'Damn you, Cody,' she groaned.

He looked at her steadily until, still on her tiptoes, she timidly widened her stance.

It opened her pussy to his invading hand, and he grunted in conquest. He locked his other hand on her ass as he let his fingers do the walking. He poked and prodded into all the nooks and crannies as her body shook.

'I hate you,' she whispered.

'Then hate away, baby. I could live on hate like this.'

He ran his finger around her opening, and she let out a high-pitched whine. He tightened his grip on her ass and held her still. Carefully, he pushed one finger into her. She closed around him like a hot wet fist.

'Jesus,' he muttered. 'Why are you still so fucking tight?'

'Don't,' she whispered fiercely. 'Don't talk to me like that.'

He let out a short laugh. 'I've got my finger jammed up your pussy, but you've got a problem with my language?'

He pulled back to look at her. She was no longer innocent, but she was still a prude. Challenging her sexual morals was one of the things that turned him on the most. And it turned her on, too. She just couldn't bear to admit it.

'Please,' she said.

'Since you ask so nicely,' he said. Watching her closely, he pulled his finger out. He rimmed her again, and her lip turned white where her teeth caught at it.

She let out a sharp cry when he began working two fingers into her.

'Sorry, Goody,' he said, 'but you are fucking tight.'

He wiggled both fingers until she took him up to the first knuckle. 'And fucking hot.'

Her breath caught when he pressed harder and both fingers slid in to the hilt. 'And fucking wet. I can feel you dripping on my wrist.'

'Cody,' she cried.

'Don't fight it,' he said. He leaned into her and whispered in her ear. 'Enjoy it.'

He let his thumb play with her as his fingers began scissoring inside her. When he moved to kiss her, her arms came up to wrap around his neck. Her hips had just started rocking under the tutelage of his hand when he heard a noise behind them.

'Shit,' he bit out as he tore his mouth away from hers. Quickly, he looked over his shoulder. 'Goddammit!'

Dean Hawthorn was headed straight across the parking lot for them. Cody hated to do it, but he pulled his fingers out of their new warm home. 'Are you with him?' he asked hurriedly.

She looked up at him with a glazed confused look in her eyes.

'Brynn,' he whispered. He pulled his hand out of her panties and shook her gently. 'Did you come here with Dean Hawthorn?'

He looked back and cursed when he saw the man was only fifty feet away. He quickly wiped his hand on Brynn's ass and reached for her zipper. He'd just gotten her back in order when he heard the dean's voice.

'Coach Jones? Is that you?'

He turned and used his body to block her. She needed a few more moments. 'Dean Hawthorn. Hello. How did you enjoy the game?'

'Splendid. Just splendid.'

Cody went still when the man held out his hand. He furtively wiped his fingers on the side of his pants again, but they were still sticky with Brynn's juices. Hopefully, the dean wouldn't notice. He gritted his teeth and quickly shook his boss's hand.

'Your defence looked especially good tonight,' Hawthorn said. A strange look crossed his face, but he was a born diplomat. Without a word, he reached for the handkerchief in his back pocket.

'Sorry about that ... uh, liniment,' Cody said with a cough.

'No problem. It's all part of the game.' The dean glanced up as he cleaned off his fingers. 'I see you've met up with Ms Montgomery. I'd forgotten that you two knew each other from your college days.'

Cody's shoulders stiffened. He didn't care what people thought of him, but he did care what they said about Brynn. He watched the dean carefully. Had he seen anything? If he had, how much? 'We were just getting caught up.'

Hawthorn just nodded. 'Did she tell you that I've convinced her to take over the cheerleading squad?'

Cody glanced over his shoulder. 'No, she didn't tell me that,' he said contemplatively.

Brynn's face was chalk-white, but her eyes were clear. Clear and icy. When she looked at him, he could feel the bite in his ass.

'The squad needs someone with experience to coach them.'

'She's certainly qualified.' The picture of Brynn in her cheerleading outfit had his brain racing and his cock twitching.

She saw the look in his eye and knew what he was thinking. Quickly, she moved out from behind him and crossed her arms over her chest. 'I think I might have been too hasty when I agreed to take on the additional work, Dean.'

'Nonsense,' Hawthorn said, overriding her. 'You agreed, and I didn't just spend twenty minutes with Mr Clausen to test out my hearing. He's decided to be the lead donor for new cheerleading outfits. You can't back out now.'

'No, you can't back out, Brynn,' Cody quickly threw in. If she took on the cheerleaders, she couldn't avoid him. And after the way her pussy had just latched onto his fingers, he wasn't going to allow that to happen anymore. 'You made a promise.'

He knew that would get her, Goody Two Shoes that she was. She scowled at him, but he let it bounce right off. All was fair, after all.

'Mr Clausen's donation could be quite generous,' Hawthorn said as he stuffed his handkerchief back into his pocket. 'We're not only talking about new uniforms, there will most probably be new equipment, too.'

Cody fought back a smile. The dean might be English, but he sure knew his way around Texas cheerleaders.

'New megaphones,' Hawthorn pressed. 'New gymnastics mats for practice.'

'I need time to think about my decision.'

'Pompons?' Cody asked.

'Of course.'

'Oh, come on now, Brynn. You know how much everyone likes your pompons.'

'Enough! Both of you,' she said, face aflame with colour. 'I'll do it.'

'Wonderful, a new cheerleading coach for Southern Trinity,' Hawthorn said. He rubbed his hands together. 'Our boosters will be so happy.'

'Not to mention every other male in the stands,' Cody

said as he turned to open the door. He reached to help Brynn in, but she jerked her arm away.

'Quiet,' she hissed. She threw a wide-eyed look at Hawthorn, but he was already circling the car to the driver's side. 'You stay away from me, Cody Jones.'

'Stay away? Now Brynnie, you know I've never been able to do that.' He picked up her seat cushion from the ground and let his hand rub against her thigh when he set it in her lap. 'But you and pompons? Just try to keep my booster away.'

3

Brynn felt the music pumping through her veins. Her body picked up the rhythm and went with the flow. 'Five six seven eight,' she counted. 'Keep those arms stiff, Karen.'

The redhead snapped to attention as she went through the dance movements. Brynn followed suit. Her hips rocked and rolled with the beat, but her eyes were trained on her squad. The routine they'd been practising all week was finally coming together. 'Step, ball change, step, knee, down, kick, together.'

She watched with growing pride as the team synchronised their movements. She'd only been working with them for a short time, but they were stepping up like pros. They were still a long way from being a competitive squad, but a little guidance was going a long way.

'Swivel hip, hip, turn, and punch.'

Brynn took the position next to her captain and joined in as the music hit a crescendo. It felt so incredibly good to just move. Her old job hadn't allowed any time for such 'trivialities', but she hadn't realised how much of herself she'd blocked off when she'd given up cheerleading and dancing. They weren't trivial or frivolous to her; they were her form of true expression. She could feel her body coming alive for the first time in years. Her heart was pumping and her muscles were contracting. Her breaths were coming faster as the music enveloped her.

The tumblers took their place in front of the dancers and took a running start. Emily went one way, but Jimmy – Wow! Was that kid a find. Brynn watched as he did a series of backflips down the field, ending in a back layout. 'Go, Jimmy!'

'Pivot turn, feet together, hold . . . and *smile*.'

The entire squad broke out in cheers when the music ended.

'That was fantastic!' Brynn called. Her lungs worked hard as she tried to get enough oxygen. 'Take a break and get some water. It's warm out here today.'

The team went to the water cooler, but she picked up the bottle she kept ever-present at her side. The cold liquid felt soothing going down her parched throat. She wiped the back of her hand across her damp forehead and tried to catch her breath.

Her cheerleaders were sweating as much as the football team practising on the field behind them. She took another long gulp of water, and noticed that Cody was working with Jets on defence. Once again, he was wearing a T-shirt that had seen better days. Slowly, she licked her tongue over her dry lips. Why did he even bother?

'Coach?'

She snapped to with a start. 'Yes? Oh, Hannah. What is it?'

The blonde cheerleader took a dainty sip of water out of her Dixie cup. 'You said you wanted to talk to me.'

'I did?' Brynn ran a hand through her hair. 'Yes, I did. Would you be interested in choreographing some new routines?'

'Me?'

'You are the squad captain. I assume you've done choreography work before.'

Hannah nodded and smiled. It was obvious she was

happy just to be asked. 'I made up most of the routines for my high school squad. What are you looking for?'

Brynn took another drink. 'I'm tired of watching you guys twiddle your thumbs when the band is playing. We've got routines for the school song and the fight song, but I want a generic routine we can jump into at a moment's notice. You know, something fun.'

Hannah's smile broadened. 'Are you saying what I think you're saying?'

'I want stunts.'

'Yes!' Hannah screeched, bouncing up and down on her toes.

Brynn tried to tone her down. The squad wasn't ready for a full out competitive routine. She just wanted to get them started cheering at the collegiate level. 'Keep it simple. Basic lifts – maybe an easy pyramid. We'll start small and grow as the season moves on. I'll work with you, but with my Comp Sci class, I don't have time to choreograph it all.'

'Oh, I love you soooo much. It's been embarrassing to watch all the other college teams stunting when we're not allowed.'

'Well, no more. From now on, we're a squad on the rise. Before you graduate, I swear you'll have a competition trophy.'

The blonde practically beamed. 'I'll do anything I can to help.'

'Great. It's that kind of enthusiasm that I need.'

The cheerleader couldn't seem to stand still. 'It's just so exciting, all these changes that you're making. Is the rumour about new uniforms true?'

Brynn reached for her ponytail and caught the stray strands of hair back into the rubber band. She couldn't help but roll her eyes. Fundraising. That was the one part of this job she didn't like. 'I'm going to try to get the boosters to pitch in some money tomorrow at Coach Jones' luncheon.'

Hannah turned and followed Brynn's gaze across the field. 'Could I help you with that, too?'

Brynn's head snapped to the side. 'With Cody?'

Hannah's eyebrows drew together. 'With the fund-raising. Some of us were talking about having a car wash.'

Brynn's embarrassment made her yank too hard on her ponytail, and she winced. 'Mm,' she nodded. 'That would help a lot.'

Fortunately, Hannah didn't seem to notice. She was too busy being responsible and tossing her empty Dixie cup into a trash bin. 'I can call around to see if I can find a company to donate the water and space.'

Brynn looked at her captain with a bemused smile on her face. Being a Goody Two Shoes *was* a good thing. 'Hannah, if you could do that, I'll make you captain of the year.'

She looked over the cheerleader's shoulders and saw that the rest of the squad was standing around talking and stretching to keep their muscles warm. Break time was over. 'We'll talk about it some more tomorrow.'

She set down her water bottle next to her gym bag and wiped her hands on her hips. 'Everyone gather around,' she called more loudly.

She waited until her team was close enough to hear. 'I want everyone to know how happy I am with the progress you've made. Your dancing and tumbling have really improved, but now, I think it's time for us to get down to business. Is everyone here ready to do some serious cheerleading?'

A chorus of cheers responded, and she nodded in agreement.

'How many of you have performed stunts before?'

Nearly everyone's hand went up in the air.

'How many bases do I have?'

All of the male cheerleaders raised their hands except one. 'That's OK, Jimmy. I want you out front tumbling anyway. Any spotters?'

Again the guys lifted their hands, but more of the women signalled than she would have expected.

'Flyers?'

Only three women, Hannah included, raised their hands. Brynn clicked her tongue. She would have liked to have at least four, but she'd work with what she had. 'All right,' she said. 'You all seem to have experience, but we're going to start with the basics. We always have to think of safety first.'

Quickly, she divided the squad into smaller teams consisting of one base, one flyer, and two spotters. 'Rule number one,' she said, 'No practising on cement or gravel surfaces. Rule number two: no lifts without spotters. Rule number three: no lifts if I'm not around. Everyone got that?'

Nods went through the group.

'All right, then let's get started.' She looked at her male cheerleaders. The best way to teach was by example, and she'd been a flyer since she was ten years old. 'Who wants to be my base?'

Every single male hand went up, including Jimmy's. Brynn couldn't help but chuckle. 'OK, OK. You're a funny group of guys. Steve, why don't you come up here and –'

'I'll do it.'

Her spine stiffened at the low voice so close behind her. Turning, she found Cody and nearly half his team. Only he wasn't looking at her. His arms were crossed over his chest as he looked challengingly at her male cheerleaders. 'Excuse me?' she said.

'I said I'd do it.'

Planting her hands on her hips, she let her gaze take in his big, sweaty body from his dripping hair down to his well-worn tennis shoes. They'd co-existed on the practice field until now, but she felt as proprietary of her practice sessions as he did about his. How dare he come over here and try to tell her how to do her job?

She let one eyebrow lift. 'You can't,' she said succinctly.

Jets let out a snort, but quickly covered it with a cough when Cody shoved him by the shoulder.

'If anyone's going to make you fly, it's going to be me,' he said in a low voice.

This time, half the football team let out whistles and catcalls.

Brynn wiped the perspiration from her brow and tried to tell herself that her speeding pulse was a result of the workout she'd just put herself through. She knew better than to let him goad her like this. 'Grow up, Cody. This is a sport that requires professionalism – and it is a sport.'

'I could lift four of you.'

'It's not all about strength, Bam Bam.'

More hoots and laughter followed her as she turned and walked back to her squad. She didn't hear Cody coming until he caught her by the arm.

'OK, that sounded like a challenge to me. What do I need to do?' He surprised her by smoothly moving behind her and wrapping his hands around her waist.

Lycra and spandex didn't provide much insulation to his touch. It burned on Brynn's skin and her stomach sucked in sharply. She caught at his hands and looked over her shoulder. 'No way. It takes balance and trust.'

'You think I don't need balance for football?'

She just looked at him.

His gaze sharpened. 'Are you saying you don't trust me?'

'What do you think?'

His fingers suddenly bit into her waist, and he dropped his head so nobody else could hear. 'I think you wouldn't have let me get as far as I did on Saturday night if you didn't trust me.'

Brynn took a quick step forward. There was no way she was going to let him lift her. She hadn't been lying. It took a lot of trust between cheer partners for them to do the skills that most impressed the crowd. She and her old partner, Mike, had had that trust because they'd both been serious about the sport. When Mike had touched her, it had been all business, whereas with Cody, his hands on her always meant ... well, *business*. 'No,' she said bluntly. 'It's dangerous if you don't know what you're doing.'

'So teach me. Isn't that what you're here to do?'

His gaze pinned her, daring her.

'Come on, Coach. We've all seen your trophies displayed in the Southern Trinity banquet room.'

Brynn's eyes widened when she recognised the voice, and she gaped at Hannah. Out of everyone in the group, she'd thought that her conscientious captain would support her the most.

'Yeah, come on, Coach Montgomery,' Jimmy said with a toothy smile. 'Show us what you've got.'

'Come on, Brynnie,' Cody said into her ear. 'You know you want to do it. You spent more time in college in the air than on the ground.'

She shook her head. 'Someone could get hurt.'

'I promise it won't be you.'

The comment slashed right through her. She looked at him sharply and saw the look in his eyes. Last time they'd been at this university, she had been the one who'd gotten hurt. Not physically, but emotionally, she'd been wrecked.

'I promise,' he said firmly. He turned her around so they were both facing her squad and put his hands at her waist. 'Like this, right?'

Brynn's stubbornness took root. So many people looked at cheerleading as a popularity contest where all you had to do was smile pretty and shake your booty. In Texas, though, it was a sport with a capital 'S'. The gymnastic skills alone took strength, balance, and athletic ability. If he thought this was so easy, let him try it. She settled her hands over his at her waist. 'Steve and Mark, come over here to spot. The rest of you watch and listen.'

She turned her head to talk over her shoulder. 'We're going to start by sponging up.'

'Sounds nasty. I'm in.'

She ground her teeth together. The cocky jock. She knew just how to bring him down a peg. 'It means that you'll give me a three count and toss me straight up in the air.'

She looked back at her squad. She knew she should start with a beginner's move like a chair, but there was no way she was going to sit on Cody's hand. Not in front of everyone. Not when she still hadn't shaken the feel of it between her legs since Saturday night. 'We'll start with a half-elevator.'

'What the hell is that?' he grumbled.

'On your mark, we'll sponge up – I'll jump and you give me a toss and flick me straight up at the end. Catch me by my feet and, once I've stuck it, just hold me there.'

'Catch your feet?'

She let one eyebrow lift. 'Not up to it?'

He wasn't a man who could turn down a dare. 'Count of three?'

She nodded and stared forward, centring herself. She couldn't believe she was doing this. She was letting Cody Jones touch her after she'd made herself promise never to make that mistake again, and he had no cheer experience. She must be out of her mind, but she refused to be the one to back down. Her weight went to the balls of her feet, and her knees flexed.

'One, two, three,' he counted.

She gave a small hop, landed, and launched herself straight up. He didn't give her a big enough boost, though, and she only made it as high as his waist before gravity started pulling her back to earth. His hands wrapped around her waist like a vice before she could fall.

'Let me down,' she said as she gasped for air with her feet dangling off the ground. He clutched her against his chest, and she could feel the strength in his arms, his chest, and his legs. It was only when she felt herself melting against that strength that she started kicking her legs like a two-year-old. 'Put me down!'

He finally lowered her, and she took a big gulp of air. 'All right, squad, that brings up a point. Don't be afraid to throw the flyers up there.'

'This is dangerous,' Cody muttered.

'Did I not tell you that?' She caught his hands and put them at her waist again. 'You're the one who wanted to do it.'

She bit her lip when she saw the concentration that settled onto his face. She'd only seen him look like that on the football field.

Or the parking lot outside it.

She took a quick swipe at the sweat on her forehead and forced herself to concentrate. It had been at least ten years since she'd done this herself. 'I'm not as light as I used to be,' she admitted.

The look on his face didn't change. 'But you filled out in all the right places.'

Her teeth gnawed at the inside of her cheek. What had she been thinking to agree to this?

'One, two, three.'

This time she flew to the sky, but he only managed to catch one of her feet. Her right heel slipped out of his hand, and she tilted sharply as she started to fall. Training made her keep her body stiff, and she fell like the second hand on a stopwatch.

'Whoa!' Cody said sharply. The spotters reached for her, but he was the one who caught her.

The air left Brynn's lungs when she found his hand clamped solidly over her left breast.

'Why did you do that?' he barked.

'Do what?' she said as she squirmed in his arms. He set her on her feet and turned her around by her shoulders.

'You fell like a log.'

'That's what I'm supposed to do.' She hurriedly reached for her jog bra. His grabby hands had pulled it out of place, and it was twisted across her body like a boa constrictor. Her face flamed when she saw that her breast had popped out entirely. She quickly clamped a hand over her nakedness. She yanked the Lycra back into place, but her breast still plumped outside the edges.

'Here,' Cody said.

She went shock still when he caught her bra with one hand and slid his other hand underneath it. He cupped her breast and coaxed her yielding flesh back into place. His thumb brushed over her nipple before he pulled back to review his handiwork. 'There.'

Brynn's pulse thundered in her ears. He'd just pawed her in front of nearly fifty people, but her body didn't seem to care. Her nipples were putting the Lycra to the test.

'That's better,' he said. He leaned down to look her in the eye. 'Now, why didn't you try to save yourself?'

'That's your job,' she said breathlessly. He was tall enough to shield her from his players' eyes, but she quickly looked over her shoulder to see if anyone on her squad had noticed what he'd just done.

The look in Hannah's eyes told the truth soon enough.

Brynn glanced down quickly. Her bra was grey. She couldn't see the colour of her nipples, but she could clearly see the outline of their shape. She closed her eyes in embarrassment. Oh God, not again! 'My job is to stay tense,' she said through clenched teeth. 'It makes it easier for you and the spotters to catch me if I fall.'

He let out a gust of air. 'So what did I do wrong?'

Other than practically rip her clothes off of her? Other than feel her up in front of both their teams? She brushed another loose strand of hair out of her eyes. She wanted to hit him, but all she could do was act like it never happened. 'You need to turn your palms upward so I can land on them.'

'OK,' he said, full of determination. 'Let's do this.'

Brynn didn't know if she could. Her knees felt like spaghetti, and her nipples felt like hard little buttons. Still, she'd challenged him. She couldn't be the one to back down. She turned and cupped her hands over his wrists.

'One, two, three.'

It took three more tries before they accomplished the skill. By that time, Brynn's body was in an uproar. Every time she'd fallen, Cody had managed to catch her in the most inappropriate ways. His hands had grabbed her ass and her breasts more times than she could count, and the last time, he'd even managed to slip one hand between her legs and catch her right where it disturbed her the most.

Through it all, though, she'd had to put on a professional face and *teach*!

'Now what?' he grunted when he finally caught her feet, and she was standing on his hands at shoulder level.

Brynn's lungs worked hard as she stared over her squad's heads. She kept her body stiff as he worked to get a better grip on her feet. She had to admit that she trusted him with her safety more than she'd expected. With his strength, good hands, and quickness, she wasn't afraid of him making a mistake that would get her injured. She was more worried that she'd lose her concentration. She'd never done a lift while she was so aroused. It was like trying to do the hundred-yard dash after stopping in the middle of masturbating.

'This is it, the half-elevator.'

'Oh, come on. I know I'm supposed to lift you.'

'Fine. Push me straight up into a full elevator,' she said as she kept her body rigid. She was glad it was on autopilot, because her brain was too scrambled to think.

'Like this?' he asked.

A little thrill shot through her stomach when he lifted her more easily than Mike ever had. His strength made her feel tiny, feminine and vulnerable. He was holding her at least eight feet in the air. She lifted her arms in a high vee and held the position. 'Go Trojans!' she cheered out of habit with a smile on her face.

Both the cheer squad and the football team broke out in applause.

'You stud, Jones.'

'Way to go, Coach Montgomery.'

'Now what?' Cody grunted.

Oh, thank goodness. It was almost over. He'd been too close for too long. One more touch from those hands and she might do something she'd regret. 'I'll pop down.'

'What?'

'Boost me, and I'll hop down. You'll need to catch me about the waist to break my fall. Just give me another three count when you're ready.'

'That might be a while.'

There was something about his tone of voice. Brynn looked down at him sharply and found that he was looking straight up at her crotch. With her legs spread and him holding her feet, there was nowhere to hide. Her shorts blocked his view of anything personal, but her pussy lips clenched just the same.

From her point of view, she could tell that he wasn't unaffected, either. The front of his shorts was tented around his swelling cock. Her balance rocked, but he moved with her until she stuck it again.

Brynn couldn't take it; she called an end to the stunt on her own. 'One, two, three.'

He tossed her a few inches upwards and caught her firmly about the waist when she came down. He pulled her close and his hips rocked against her backside. 'Ever do that naked?' he whispered.

Her body squirmed against his. She could see him standing like a Greek Adonis with a full-on erection, holding her naked over him with her legs spread wide.

'Want to try?'

God, did she.

'Way to go, Coach,' Hannah said as she hurried over.

Cody's hands tightened on her waist. 'Hide me for a minute, Brynnie.'

The words whispered along her skin, and she instinctively planted herself in front of him to shield the innocent little cheerleader from what could be an embarrassing moment.

'We got it all on tape!' Hannah said excitedly.

Brynn's jaw dropped. 'What?' She gasped when she saw the red light blinking on the camcorder she'd set up to tape the squad's practice. 'Oh, no!'

She slapped at Cody's hands and lurched away from him. Let him deal with his embarrassing erection on his own. She hurried over to the camcorder and hit the stop button. Good Lord, how much of that had been caught?

Cody followed her unabashedly and planted his hands on his hips. The stance drew even more attention to his surging cock. 'That's one for the archives.'

'Shush!' She tried to shut the camera off, but not before other people crowded around for a look. Before she could slap the hands away, fingers reached out and hit the rewind and play buttons. Soon, she and Cody were on the tiny screen engaging in what could only be called athletic foreplay.

Brynn's breath caught. She hadn't realised how good they looked together. He was a head taller than she and his arms were about as big around as her legs. He was in incredible shape – a former professional athlete who hadn't let himself go, and she was still strong and lean. Her blonde hair matched the highlights in his brown hair. She blushed. The erotic chemistry between them practically leapt off the videotape. From her naked breast to his intimate clenches, it was all caught for posterity.

'Oh my God!' She hit the off button, and the sound of Cody's harsh breathing rattled her ears.

'Mind if I keep that?' he asked in a low voice.

'Yes, I mind,' she said sharply. She hit the eject button and grabbed the tape. 'This is mine.'

Her face turned white when everyone around them started to laugh.

Cody held up his hands. 'If you want it that bad, it's all yours, baby.'

'I meant that I'm going to destroy it.' Brynn marched away from the crowd to her gym bag, and her hands shook as she put the tape into its box.

'Right,' Cody said with another chuckle.

He interlocked his fingers and stretched his arms out in front of him. It was a stretch she saw his players do all the time, but with him, it was different. She could see the muscles that had just tossed her around like a beanbag. His barbed wire tattoo flexed, and her spine went ramrod straight. She'd let him get way too close. Again. 'Don't you have coaching of your own to do, Cody?'

His smile didn't fade, but he did glance at his wristwatch. 'Football practice is over, but you make a good point. I've got to go review tapes of Midwestern Texas's defense.'

She turned around to face him. The weekend's away game seemed like a much safer topic. 'Fine. You go do that.'

'Will I see you at tomorrow's luncheon?'

The luncheon. Damn, was she ever going to get away from him? 'I have to go ask for donations for new uniforms.'

'It's not fun, but you'll get used to it.' He reached out and brazenly tweaked her nipple again. 'Prostituting ourselves for donor support is the price we have to pay to keep jobs that let us play for a living.'

Brynn jerked back from his shocking touch. Her gaze flew to her team, but most of them were already practising their own lifts. She glared at Cody, and hoped he didn't know that her toes were curling inside her shoes.

She crossed her arms defensively over her chest, but his attention focused on the tape she still held in her hand.

'Loan it to me?' he asked. 'Defence tapes can get pretty boring.'

'No.'

'Please?' He stepped forward, invading her space again, and his hands went to her waist.

Awareness made the hair on the back of her neck stand on end. 'Here,' she said, reaching into her bag for another tape. 'Try this.'

'Is it of you?'

'It's of the squad's practice yesterday.'

'That's not the same.'

'It will have to do.'

'Are you in it?'

He caught the tape, but let his thumb rub across the back of hers.

She cleared her throat. 'I come into the picture every now and then.'

'Good enough,' he said, snatching it out of her hand. He took advantage of her surprise by leaning in and whispering into her ear. 'You still move like sin, Brynnie.'

Brynn closed her eyes as he turned and followed his team across the field to the locker rooms. How could she have let that happen? Why did she always weaken whenever he was near?

She turned and slammed the R-rated videotape into her bag. 'Damn you, Cody Jones,' she hissed.

The man was trouble. Big trouble.

4

Brynn glanced up from the quiz she was grading when she heard a knock on her office door. 'Come in,' she called.

The door swung open, and Dean Hawthorn leaned inside. 'Are you ready to go?'

A quick look at her watch told her it was time to head over to the Student Union for the donors' luncheon. She sighed. She'd have to take the quizzes home to finish grading them. Her schedule was too jam-packed today. She wished she could skip the lunch, but she dropped her red pen and stood. 'I'm as ready as I'll ever be. I hope you're not expecting much of me, because I didn't know how to prepare.'

'You'll do fine. All you need to do is say a few words about the squad, your goals, and your fundraising efforts,' he said as he walked to her desk. 'A short question and answer session usually follows.'

He flicked a piece of lint off the sleeve of his jacket, and Brynn suddenly found herself tongue-tied. Oh boy, did he look good today. Not that many men knew style or how to wear it. To Hawthorn, it came naturally. The dark, tailored suit brought out the silver in his hair, giving him a dashing, elegant look.

She tore her gaze away and reached for her purse, only to come up short when he subjected her to the same once-over she'd just given him. For some reason, she sensed she didn't come up to par.

'What?' she said. She looked down at herself and

smoothed her hands over the red suit she'd chosen. 'Is this not appropriate?'

'You look lovely as always, dear.'

The unsaid 'but' nearly echoed off the walls of the room, and Brynn got that queasy feeling a woman usually got when she showed up at a black tie event in a flowered sundress. 'Is it the red? Is it too bright? I thought it would be nice to wear a school colour.'

She'd gone back and forth between her red and blue suits for that very reason. The red had just seemed cheerier. 'Tell me,' she said shortly. 'I'd rather know now before I step into the banquet room.'

Hawthorn rubbed his chin and one eyebrow lifted. 'I didn't mean to upset you. I just assumed that you'd wear something reflecting your position as cheerleading coach.'

Brynn blinked. 'I don't understand.'

'I'm sorry, I'm not explaining myself well.' He absently waved his hand in mid-air. 'Coach Jones will undoubtedly show up in a warm-up suit of some sort. He's yet to wear anything resembling a tie, and it's not expected. Our donors don't want a businessman running our football programme. They want . . . Well, how can I put this? A jock.'

Brynn's fingers wrapped around the bottom of her jacket and tugged at it uncomfortably. 'Do you think I should change into my warm-up clothes?'

'No, no. That's not necessary, but maybe . . . No, you're fine. Let's just go as you are.'

'Maybe what?' Her heels dug in. She wasn't moving until he told her what she should do. She wasn't good at this sort of thing, and she wanted to fit in as well as she could.

'I hesitate to even suggest it. I wouldn't want to offend you.'

65

'Just say it. Please!'

'Would you consider taking off your blouse?'

'My what?' she said, her voice going high. Her hand automatically went to the collar of her starched white button-up shirt.

'It was just an idea. You'd still look classy, but without that thing buttoned up to your neck, it would be easier to see you as the coach of the cheer squad. Right now you look like a librarian.'

'But I'm a professor.'

He rubbed his chin again. 'That won't get us any donations.'

Her stomach sank. 'I don't know, Dean. I wouldn't feel comfortable going half-dressed.'

'Your jacket should still cover you. Why don't you just try it and see how it looks?' Presumptively, he reached out and closed the door.

The room suddenly pressed in on her. Did he want her to strip in front of him? 'Maybe next time,' she said.

He shook his head, this time more determinedly. 'If I've learned one thing about fundraising, it's that a good first impression is everything. Make money today, and you'll have less to do in the future.'

Her heart started to stutter-step. This was just surreal.

'Take it off, and we'll give her a look,' he said, his voice becoming more and more chipper.

He stood there looking at her expectantly, and Brynn felt trapped. She looked down at the red suit. The jacket hadn't been cut to allow her to go bare underneath it. It buttoned below her breastbone, and she was busty enough that the gaping material would leave her in a precarious position.

'Here, let me be of assistance.'

She took a smooth step back. Her backside banged against her chair and spun it around on its base. It seemed like a good idea, so she spun with it and gave Hawthorn her back. The very idea of letting him assist her made the muscles of her lower belly quiver. 'I've got it.'

Her hands shook as she undid her jacket and shrugged it off her shoulders. She draped it over the chair and looked down at herself. She couldn't believe she was doing this, but Hawthorn sounded like he knew what he was talking about. She'd never raised money for anything before.

'It's an unfortunate fact, but sex sells, Ms Montgomery.'

The quiet words made her heart skip a beat. Feeling deliciously naughty, she reached for the top button at her throat and undid it. Taking the plunge, she quickly undid the rest and the crisp white material gaped open. She pulled the shirt out of her skirt and the swell of her breasts forced it to drape wider, exposing her to the waist. A shiver wracked her body, and her nipples tightened.

She heard Hawthorn's breaths behind her. He'd moved closer, and she froze with her hands at her sides. Her palms became sweaty when she saw his hand reach out in her peripheral vision and pick up her jacket.

'Here you go,' he said.

He wasn't making this easy on her. Like a robot, her hands lifted, and she pulled her shirt off her shoulders. For a long moment, she stood there facing the wall in only her short skirt, her red high heels, and her snow-white lace bra.

She felt rather than heard Hawthorn take a step closer. He draped her jacket over her shoulders, but she could feel him looming over her and looking down at her cleavage. Her breasts swelled inside the cups of her bra, and her breaths went short.

'Yes, this should work very nicely,' he said close to her ear as he took the blouse away and helped her slip her arms into the red sleeves.

Her stomach clenched when his arms circled her from behind and his hands dealt with the buttons. His fingers brushed intimately against the underside of her breasts, and she swayed back towards him. The cut of the jacket didn't leave much to the imagination, and riotous feelings crashed inside her belly.

'Let's take a look-see.'

His hands settled on her shoulders, and he turned her slowly around.

'Oh yesssss,' he said when he saw her. The heat of his stare made colour rise up Brynn's neck. He swallowed hard, but tapped her politely on the shoulders. 'That's lovely.'

'Lovely' wasn't quite the appropriate description in her opinion. Decadent was more like it. 'I can't go out there like this,' she finally blurted. 'I'm not decent.'

'It is rather bold, but you are covered.'

His finger traced the line of her lapel, and she pressed her thighs tightly together as her long-ago crush roiled up in her pussy. Talk about hot for teacher. He looked like every schoolgirl's dream in that fancy suit, and he was acting like he could just eat her up.

She was more than tempted to let him.

She forced her short breaths to deepen and looked down at herself. She wished she had a mirror so she could see how she looked to others. From her point of view, all she could see were breasts everywhere.

'Are you sure the short skirt isn't enough to bring in donations?'

His dark, hot gaze swept down her body, and she almost wished she hadn't brought up the subject. The skirt was insanely short. Funny now to think she'd been nervous about wearing it. Her hands clutched the lapels, trying to bring the jacket together, but it wouldn't close over her bust line.

'Let go of it,' he said, his voice like gravel.

She blinked in surprise.

'I told you I would keep control over this programme, and I meant it. We're here to raise money today, and you need to do what I tell you.' His dark gaze bored into hers. 'Now, let go of it.'

'It wasn't made to be worn this way.'

He reached out and prised her hands off the material and held them away from her body. The material fell into its natural position, gaping wide across her chest. 'But it will do,' he said.

'My bra is showing,' she said with embarrassment. Colour stained her cheekbones. She couldn't believe she was having this discussion with him of all people.

'Yes.' He let go of one hand to trace the lace of the cups and the bow between them. 'It's sexy.'

Oh God. He thought she was sexy. All of a sudden, Brynn didn't want to go to the stupid luncheon. She wanted him to lower her to the floor and do all the naughty things a guy did to a girl dressed this way.

'However, if you'd prefer to go without it, I wouldn't stop you.'

Her jaw dropped.

'If not, let's be moving along,' he said. His English accent was becoming more pronounced every second.

Brynn tried walking, but stopped when her breasts jiggled. 'I can't.'

'You can, and you will.'

She went still when he reached out and centred the necklace she was wearing. It hung deep between her breasts and made her even more aware of how exposed she was. The back of his hand brushed against her, and her stomach plunged. 'Please, Dean. My reputation.'

He lifted one eyebrow. 'I thought you wanted to raise money for your cheerleaders' new uniforms.'

She swallowed hard. 'I do.'

Her stomach turned over when he reached out and cupped her breasts. He pushed them upwards, emphasising her cleavage even more. Her knees wobbled, and she knew she'd do whatever he told her to do.

'A little T&A can go a long way, Ms Montgomery. You want money? This is what will get it for you.' He fondled her until she reached up and caught his forearms. The teasing was nearly tortuous. He chuckled under his breath and took a step back. The distinguished veneer was firmly back in place when he picked up her purse and handed it to her. 'Let's go make thousands.'

He offered her his arm, and Brynn took it to steady herself. She was aroused and breathless, and she knew she had to look that way. She also knew the kinds of stares she'd receive if she walked out that door half-dressed.

Still, she went.

She was on the arm of one of the most powerful men on campus. Nobody would dare say anything to her while she was with him, and maybe she didn't look as scandalous as she thought she did.

That hopeful thought was doused the moment she set foot outside her office door. A group of football players was walking down the hallway, and each of them stopped dead in his tracks when he saw her. Brynn bit the inside of her lip when she recognised Scott Jetson.

'Gentlemen,' Hawthorn said with a nod of his head.

They mumbled a hello, but she doubted they even realised to whom they were speaking. She self-consciously rolled her shoulder and pulled her jacket together to try to cover more of herself.

'Stand up straight,' Hawthorn said under his breath as they walked out the door of the Clausen building into the sunshine. 'It only gapes open when you slouch like that.'

Brynn pulled her shoulders back, which did tighten the fit of the jacket. The only problem was that it thrust her breasts even more to the forefront. The glaring sunshine felt like a spotlight, and her footsteps hastened towards the Student Union.

Hawthorn slowed her down by tightening the grip on the hand she still had wrapped around his arm. 'Patience, Ms Montgomery. We'll be there soon enough.'

Brynn wished she had at least worn flats. The high heels forced her gait into a short, crisp motion that made her breasts bounce with each step.

Out of nervous habit, she reached for her necklace. It hung heavily between her breasts, making its home deep in her cleavage. Whenever it tapped the side of one of the bouncing globes, her nipples would itch for attention.

'Coach Montgomery? Coach!'

Brynn closed her eyes when she recognised the voice. She wanted to ignore it, but the dean stopped to look behind them.

'Coach,' Hannah Stiles said as she hurried towards them. 'I wanted to let you know that I've made arrangements for the car ... wash.'

Brynn knew the precise moment that her cheerleader saw what she was wearing, because her eyes practically bugged out of her head. Two perfect circles of colour graced the girl's cheeks, and she quickly looked away. Brynn looked down anxiously to make sure she wasn't spilling out any more than she thought she was.

'That's wonderful, Hannah,' she said, trying to act as normal as possible. 'When and where?'

'Albertsons' grocery store on Saturday.' The cheerleader took time straightening the books she carried. 'I know it's short notice, but almost everyone has said they can make it.'

'That is fast, but your timing is perfect,' Brynn said. Her fingers curled around her necklace. 'I'll announce it at the luncheon Dean Hawthorn and I are attending.'

'You're going to see the donors?' Hannah asked as she stole another quick look.

Brynn could practically hear the words 'dressed like that?'. Automatically, she tugged at the hem of her jacket. She knew she was shocking the poor young thing, but she nearly laughed aloud when she thought of how she might have reacted to finding Mrs Vestry, her old coach, spilling out of her clothes. It wouldn't have been a pretty sight.

'We really need to be going,' Hawthorn said. 'We wouldn't want to be late.'

Brynn reached out and squeezed her cheerleader's shoulder. 'I really appreciate you taking over practice for me this afternoon so I can attend that symposium. Be sure to watch everyone's hand positions. I'm seeing blades when there should be buckets and vice versa.'

The cheerleader nodded again and reached up to smooth her hair. 'I'll see you tomorrow. You, uh, look *great*, by the way.'

'Thank you, Hannah.'

The cheerleader spun around and hurried away. Brynn watched her go with a pleased, but sinking feeling creeping into her stomach. If Hannah said she looked great, then maybe Hawthorn was right. Maybe she had achieved the right balance of sexy sophistication. Still, she knew how it felt to lose people's respect. She hoped this little stunt wasn't going to have repercussions she wasn't expecting.

'Oh, don't worry about her,' Hawthorn said with a pat to her hand. 'She's just a shy little innocent.'

Brynn started walking again, but she'd learned to keep her back straight. She looked down at her jiggling breasts, barely kept under control by her bra. 'I just don't want her to get the wrong impression.'

He chuckled. 'Anything cut below the neck is shocking to Ms Stiles. Why, she's just like you at that age, so naïve and repressed. It would take a crowbar to pry open those thighs of hers. Believe me, I've thought about trying.'

Brynn's head snapped back to him so quickly, she nearly gave herself whiplash. Her mouth was still hanging agog when he opened the door to the Student Union for her. He chuckled when he saw her reaction and tapped her chin.

'Now, remember,' he said as they walked into the full banquet room. 'Shoulders back, breasts up, and smile.'

Cody was listening to old Windbag Clausen prattle on about the shotgun formation when he sensed a change come over the room. People seemed to be gathering around the entrance to the banquet hall. Shifting slightly, he peered over the man's shoulder. It looked as if Dean Hawthorn had arrived. The guy knew how to make an entrance; that was for sure.

'You really should be passing more,' Clausen said. 'That JJ Stone is a rocket.'

Cody nodded. Whatever. What was all the hubbub at the door about?

He caught a glimpse of shiny blonde hair, and his radar went on the alert. Brynn. Nothing like a blonde bombshell to get the old timers' blood rushing. Or his blood rushing.

'I'll take your suggestions into consideration, Mr Clausen,' he said. He shook the man's hand absently, and left him standing mid-comment.

Cody started across the room, but his footsteps slowed when the sea of people parted. What the hell? He squinted to make sure he was seeing clearly. By God, what was she wearing? Or to be more blunt, what the hell was she not wearing? She was practically bursting out of that suit jacket, and that skirt . . . If she bent over, half the crowd was going to hyperventilate.

His feet got back on track, and he nearly stomped across the room.

'Oh, there you are, Coach Jones,' Hawthorn said. 'It looks like we've got a good turnout today.'

'Yeah.' He didn't even look at the guy. Instead, he reached out and caught Brynn by the arm. 'Coach Montgomery, could I have a word with you?'

'Cody!' She tried to break away from his grip. Her jacket bunched up, giving him an unrestricted view of her bra.

'Now.'

He guided her across the room, leaving Hawthorn floundering.

'But Coach Jones,' the dean called. 'The luncheon.'

'We'll be back.'

Hawthorn hurried across the room with a plastic smile affixed to his face, but took the time to nod at a well-moneyed widow as he passed her. 'We're on a tight time schedule,' he hissed. 'The team bus leaves in an hour for Midwestern Texas.'

'I know.'

'Ms Montgomery also has an appointment.'

'She'll be there,' Cody bit out. He straight-armed a door at the side of the room, and it hit the wall as it sprang open. He pulled Brynn inside and swung it shut in Hawthorn's face.

'What is wrong with you?' Brynn said as she pulled her arm out of his grip.

'What's wrong with me? Honey, in case you didn't look in the mirror this morning, you forgot to finish getting dressed.' He jabbed a finger at her cleavage. 'I wasn't serious about prostituting ourselves to the donors.'

Pink spots coloured her cheekbones. She folded her arms over her chest, but it only served to plump up her firm breasts. 'Sex sells,' she said uneasily. 'And I need to raise money for new uniforms.'

'Is that right? Well, sex also gives eighty-year-old men coronaries.' The door bumped open, and he shoved it closed with the palm of his hand. He turned the lock and stared at her. What the hell was he going to do with her? He didn't mind seeing her half-dressed, but he'd be damned if he'd let her walk back out into that crowd looking that way.

'OK, here,' he said as he shrugged out of his wind-breaker. He reached for the back of the T-shirt he was wearing and yanked it over his head. He pulled his arms out of the shirt and raked his fingers through his hair. 'You can wear this.'

He held the white T-shirt out to her, but she seemed frozen in place. Her eyes were big as saucers as her gaze glued itself to his chest.

Cody felt a jolt in his groin. There was desire in that look.

He stood still as her eyes practically ate him up. A heavy silence filled the room as awareness overtook them both. His stomach tightened as she looked at his six-pack, and a sizzle ran down his spine. Those long hours in the gym had been worth it.

He took a cautious step towards her. He didn't want anything to break this spell, but God, he wanted to touch her. She couldn't look at him that way and expect him not to do anything.

His movement snapped her out of her reverie. She looked at the T-shirt in his hand, and her eyes lit up. She reached for it, but he held it out of her reach.

'You want it?' he asked.

She licked her lips, and her gaze was pulled like a magnet back to his chest.

Oh yeah, she wanted it all right.

He moved closer. *Keep it slow, Jones.* He didn't want to spook her.

'How about a trade, Brynnie?' He held up the T-shirt like a prize. 'I'll give you the shirt if you give me something.'

Her tongue ran nervously over her dry lips. 'What do you want?'

Slow, he reminded himself.

'How about a good luck charm?' He eased up to her. 'A kiss for tomorrow's game.'

He watched the expressions on her face closely. She wasn't bolting; she must want that T-shirt badly. Gently, he reached up and caught the nape of her neck. Keeping his eyes open, he brushed his mouth across hers.

He heard her breath hitch. 'One good luck kiss, and the T-shirt is yours,' he coaxed.

He brushed his lips back and forth across hers until her lips parted.

'Damn you,' she said. Slowly, her arms came up around him, and he slid his tongue into her mouth. Her tongue met it timidly.

His cock reared towards her, wanting her, but he kept

his body under rigid control. Taking care not to startle her, he undid the two buttons that were barely holding her suit jacket together. Before she had time to realise what he'd done, he slid his hand around the smooth skin at her waist to catch her close. His cock ached when it touched her flat belly, and he had to rub it against her or go a little mad.

'Mmm,' she murmured in surprise. Her hands flattened on his chest.

He tightened his hold on her before she could pull back. 'They're a really good team,' he whispered against her lips.

'You said one kiss.'

'That was half a kiss – a quarter at best.' He rubbed her lower back. 'Come on, Brynnie.'

He caught her mouth again. His tongue swept deep, searching for hers. The heat nearly singed his brain when he found it. Their tongues tangled, and he felt his leg give out.

'Damn knee,' he muttered.

Turning, he pulled her with him to a nearby table. The room he'd dragged her into was set up for an afternoon meeting. He had no idea when people would start straggling in, but he didn't rightly care. Brynn was in his arms. He wasn't about to waste an opportunity like this.

He settled his hips against the edge of the table and pulled her to stand between his legs. 'Come here,' he said.

She resisted. 'That's it, Cody. I've lived up to my part of the bargain.'

'But Midwestern Texas has been averaging 35 points a game.'

'Then you'll need more than luck to win.' She snapped her fingers. 'The T-shirt.'

He held it out of her reach. 'Seems like I'm coming up with the short end of the stick. You'll get the shirt and I'll be naked.'

'You have a jacket.'

'So do you.'

'But yours zips up to the neck.'

'Maybe you should have thought of that.'

'Fine,' she declared. She backed away and, for the first time, noticed that he'd undone her suit. With a huff, she quickly put herself in order.

He could see she wasn't entirely comfortable with her appearance, and it made him even more curious. He just didn't get it. She'd always been a looker, but she'd never flaunted herself. And with her history at Southern Trinity, he figured she'd guard her reputation like a bulldog. 'What's up with the tart look, Goody?' he asked. 'It's not like you.'

An embarrassed look crossed her face. 'Never mind. Keep the T-shirt. I've got to get back to the luncheon.'

He quickly caught her wrist. 'Hawthorn can handle it.'

'We need to go. Your team will be waiting for you on the bus.'

'They can wait. The bus won't go anywhere without me.'

She pulled her arm away and tugged at her lapels. It just didn't help. Her breasts spilled out no matter what she tried. Finally, she gave up and dropped her hands.

'Let's get this finished,' she said. 'I have to get over to Palmer.'

Palmer. Cody felt the muscles at the back of his neck clench, and his sense of humour vaporised. 'Palmer?'

She brushed her hair back into its prim little bun. 'I registered for a symposium they're conducting. I need to be there in two hours.'

'At Palmer College,' he repeated dumbly.

She lifted an eyebrow. 'Is there another?'

Cody felt as if he'd just been doused with a bucket of ice water. He caught the edge of the table and gripped it hard. He looked into her face. Did she know? He doubted it. With her sense of right and wrong, she'd never been a good liar.

No, it was just a coincidence. It had to be. She'd told him she hadn't kept in touch with anyone from their college days. Still, uneasiness built inside him. 'What symposium?' he said in a low, careful voice.

'It's on computer security.' She rubbed her temple as if she was wearying of the conversation. 'If you must know, I've been giving JJ extra credit work to keep him interested. I thought I could pick up some good ideas there.'

Damn. She was trying to help his hardheaded receiver, but why did it have to be at Palmer? 'Don't go,' he blurted.

'Don't go? I have to go. I RSVP'd, and I have a meeting scheduled afterwards.'

His jaw went hard. 'With who?'

'The cheerleading coach,' she snapped. Her hand dropped to her side and curled into a fist. 'What's with the inquisition, Cody?'

He couldn't even begin to explain what was going on inside his head and inside his chest. He just didn't want her going anywhere near that college. He'd keep his reasons to himself. If he came straight with her, she'd only be even more determined to go.

And he didn't want that. Not yet. They hadn't had time to work everything out between them, and he couldn't afford to have things get all tangled up again. She'd just come back into his life, and this time he wanted an honest-to-goodness shot with her.

He pushed himself away from the table. 'You can't go to Palmer College looking like that.'

She took a step back as he came at her and lifted her hands to ward him off. He brushed her objections aside easily and reached for the buttons of her jacket. He undid them and began pushing it off her shoulders.

She clutched at the material like a security blanket. 'What are you doing?'

'Giving you the damn shirt.' He let out a gust of air. He wasn't angry with her. He was angry with fate.

He worked the jacket off her arms and tossed it onto the table. He turned back towards her with the T-shirt in hand, but went still when he saw the picture in front of him. The innocent eroticism caught him unexpectedly. She stood there wearing red high-heeled shoes, a tiny red skirt, and a pretty, snow-white bra.

'Damn,' he breathed.

She became uneasy under his stare and lifted her hands to cover herself. He caught them gently and lowered them to her sides. Her soft breaths brushed against his chest as he moved closer. His hand lifted of its own volition and cupped her breast almost reverently. Her breaths hitched as his thumb traced the lace edging, and he slowly backed her up against the door.

He bent his head next to hers. 'New deal,' he whispered into her ear. 'Your bra for the T-shirt.'

She reached up and caught his forearm. 'I gave you a kiss.'

'I can't put a kiss in my pocket.' He rubbed his cheek against hers. 'I want you with me at that game tomorrow, and I want to be with you at Palmer this afternoon.'

He let his thumb brush over her nipple before he slowly reached around to the clasp at her back. It let go under his coaxing, and her head dipped. Her forehead rested against his chest as he traced the strap up her shoulder blade. 'I want my shirt touching your skin, your nipples, your belly.'

The strap slid down her arm, and her stomach trembled as his hand brushed against it. 'I want it to surround you. I want you to feel as if I'm holding you all afternoon.'

He brushed a kiss across her temple. 'I want you to think of me even when I'm not there.'

Her breaths shuddered as his hand finally palmed her naked skin. He took the weight of her breast gently and strummed his thumb across her pink nipple. It was growing stiff and tight.

'Deal?' he whispered.

She bit her lower lip. At last, she nodded.

'You're so beautiful,' he murmured.

He kissed her gently as he worked the bra down her arms. They both watched as he folded it carefully and slid it into the pocket of his sweatpants close to his cock.

Brynn's head fell back against the door. Her face was flushed and her eyes were glassy. He knew if he slid his hand up under that short skirt, he'd find her wet.

It was tempting, but he stopped himself from following through on the inclination. She'd think about him more if he left her right on the edge.

A guy only had so much willpower, though. He braced his hands on either side of her head and leaned towards her. Their naked chests came together, and she moaned. He rubbed against her, and he had to grit his teeth at the feel of her stiff little nipples raking across his skin.

He kissed her one last time. 'Think of me,' he said softly.

He pulled away and her arms lifted as if to catch him. He avoided her touch, though, and picked up the T-shirt from where it had fallen onto a chair. She looked at him in confusion. He'd left her half-naked and wanting.

On purpose.

'Here you go,' he said. He gathered up the material of the T-shirt and pushed it over her head. Her thinking was still clouded. He took full advantage of her weakness and lifted her arms one at a time as he dressed her. The T-shirt came down to nearly mid-thigh, but that was fine with him.

'You wear this to Palmer College and remember who gave it to you and *how*,' he crooned.

He unzipped her skirt. He tucked in the T-shirt, but the sight of her rosy nipples shining through the white material nearly snapped his resolve. Swearing, he reached for the jacket that had been his and nearly a whole crowd of men's undoing. He put the garment on her, securing it in the front.

He took a step back. 'Can you feel me?'

Her palms opened wide across her stomach. 'Yes,' she breathed.

It was getting harder every second to stay away from her. His cock ached at his self-imposed denial, but he made himself put on his windbreaker. He zipped it up over his bare chest. Better him than her.

Her forehead was lined with confusion, but he couldn't explain. Instead he moved in to kiss her one last time. He kept it light and seductive. He needed to leave her wanting more.

He pressed her open palm against his pocket. He could feel the under wire of her bra against his hip. 'Thanks for the extra luck, Goody. There's no way we'll lose now.'

'Cody,' she groaned.

He leaned his forehead against hers. 'Just remember who makes you fly, Brynnie.'

Without another word, he turned and headed back to the luncheon. He couldn't stop her from going to Palmer College, but he'd done the next best thing. He was going with her.

5

'Have you considered moving her to the end?'

'Hm?' Brynn said, momentarily snapping back to attention.

'Hannah,' Julie said, pointing at the television screen. 'If you move her away from front-and-centre, she might not stand out so much.'

'Oh.' Brynn looked at the videotape and tried to focus. It was difficult. Things had been one big blur since ... well, since what had happened in the meeting room with Cody.

She brushed her hand across her cheek and hoped that it wasn't as red as it felt. She'd been warm all afternoon, and she didn't discount that wearing his shirt was contributing to the problem.

'Are you OK?'

'I'm fine. It's just a little warm in here.'

'Really?' Julie said as she walked over to the television to turn down the volume. 'That auditorium is usually like ice.'

The symposium. That was a blur to Brynn, too, although somehow she'd managed to take notes. She hoped she'd be able to decipher them well enough to give JJ something to do. She ran a hand through her hair and tried to concentrate. 'I've thought about moving Hannah, but she deserves to be in the captain's position. She'd be crushed if I tried to hide her.'

Julie wrapped her arms about her waist and tapped

her fingers against her elbow. 'What about sending the whole squad to a training camp?'

'It's mid-semester, and we don't have the money.'

'It's too bad you don't have at least one more like her. Then you could balance them off of each other.'

'I've been looking, believe me.'

Julie leaned back against a desk, her brow furrowed in thought. 'Maybe a weekend retreat would help. Take an away-game weekend, since you have those off anyway, and just spend two solid days working with them.'

Brynn sighed. 'That might be a possibility if I wasn't a full-time professor. I'd –'

Her words came to an abrupt halt when someone suddenly burst into the office without knocking.

'Goddammit, Julie!'

Brynn flinched and swiftly turned to see who was accosting her friend.

'How many times do I have to tell you to stop monopolising the trainer's time?' the man barked. He waved a piece of paper in the air. 'I've got a cornerback with a sprained ankle, but he's having to schedule his physical therapy sessions around your glamour girls.'

Brynn took an unsteady step backwards and bumped against a chair. Reaching down, she caught it to steady herself.

Oh ... dear ... Lord! This couldn't be happening again!

'Glamour girls?' The look on Julie's face turned dark. 'One of those glamour girls has a torn ACL and the other broke her wrist. My athletes have just as much right to that trainer as your big crybabies do.'

Brynn absently noted that he must be the football coach. The thought barely penetrated her brain due to lack of oxygen.

'Crybabies? Why you little –'

Feeling light-headed, she let herself sink down onto

the chair. The man saw the movement out of the corner of his eye, and his head swivelled towards her. Brynn's fingers curled around the armrests of the chair as she looked at him in astonishment.

'Rex!' she said on a long exhale.

The look in his blue eyes hardened. First disbelief, then anger appeared. Only it wasn't anger like the irritation he'd shown Julie. No, this was a deep-seeded, long-nurtured fury that seeped up from someplace deep inside.

'Well, isn't this just fucking perfect?' he snapped. 'The queen bitch has returned.'

The paper he carried in his hand went flying across the room and fluttered uselessly to the ground. Brynn never saw it. She couldn't stop staring in disbelief.

He was older. Ten years older, to be precise. His face had filled out, but those blue eyes were the same. His hair had thinned a little, while his waistline had thickened, but it was him, Rex Stanton, her college boyfriend.

His gaze darted from her to Julie to the television. 'Would someone like to tell me what in *the fuck* is going on here?'

Julie was clueless. She lifted her palms upward and looked to Brynn for help.

Brynn couldn't get any words out. There was so much to say; she didn't know where to begin. 'Rex,' she repeated dumbly.

'Yes! It's me. Or do you forget the men you leave in your wake?'

The words were like a slap in the face. Brynn recoiled, but quickly came to her feet. 'Rex, please. I'm just surprised to see you.'

'Not as surprised as me.' He let out a cynical laugh that grated on her nerve endings. He looked her up and down with loathing and shook his head. 'You fucking cunt.'

Her face went white as she watched him turn and walk out the door. It slammed behind him, and the booming sound made her flinch.

'What was that about?' Julie said carefully.

Brynn didn't have time to explain. The shock of seeing him again was wearing off, and she knew she had to move. She had to talk to him. She'd never gotten a chance to right things with him, and she'd regretted it. Her feet began shuffling before she decided what she should say. All she knew was that she had to catch him before it was too late.

'Rex!' she called as she pushed open the door. She looked around quickly and saw him halfway down the hallway. 'Rex, wait!'

His steps didn't slow, and she broke out into a run. 'We need to talk.'

She caught up with him as he rounded the corner near the restrooms. 'Let me at least apologise,' she begged as she reached out to him. 'I never got a chance before.'

'Apologise?' he said as he yanked his arm out of her grip. 'That should be a neat trick. Just how does one apologise for screwing the wrong man?'

Brynn looked around quickly to see if Julie had heard. It was late, but there were still other people in the building. 'Let's go to your office,' she said, trying to calm him.

'No, if you want to talk, let's do it right here. At least it will be out in the open that way – not behind my back like everything else apparently was.' His shoulders went up and down as he fought to catch his breath.

He was still upset with her; Brynn was just surprised

by how much. Time had passed, but his fury was just as raw as it had been on that infamous night. Obviously, her betrayal had cut deep. She watched anxiously as he raked a hand through his blond hair.

'Why Cody, Brynn?' he asked in a flat tone. 'You knew how much we hated each other. We were at each other's throats from the day the university assigned us as roommates. Is that why you picked him – because you knew how much it would hurt me?'

'I didn't pick him.' Her hands clenched together until her fingers turned white. How could she explain? 'It was all a big misunderstanding. I thought he was you!'

His eyes narrowed. 'Say what?'

'I thought he was you,' she repeated more softly. 'I've wanted to tell you that for years. The whole, ugly incident never should have happened.'

He looked at her incredulously. 'And just how did you make that mistake?'

She knew how it sounded, but it was the truth. She swallowed hard and focused on his face. She only had one chance at this. If he didn't listen to her now, he never would. 'I went to your dorm room to see you after the Chisholm game,' she said carefully. 'It was late when Cody answered and the lights in the room were off.'

'So?'

'So I assumed it was you. He let me in, and . . . I swear to God, Rex. My eyes didn't adjust to the darkness.'

His blue eyes bored into hers. 'That's your excuse? It was dark?'

He caught her chin when she began to shy away. 'We dated for a year, and you never once opened those sleek thighs for me. Why that night? Why did you spread like a wishbone for him?'

She blanched. 'I was excited about winning such a close game. I thought you were excited, too.' She met his piercing blue gaze timidly. 'I was ready to make love to you.'

'"Make love"?' He took a sudden step forward until his nose nearly brushed against hers. 'Stop sugarcoating it. That wasn't lovemaking I walked in on. It was down and dirty screwing.'

She shifted uncomfortably, and her eyes dropped. It was true. Cody had come on so fast and strong, she'd had no defences against him. He'd tapped something deep inside her, something strong and impatient. Things had quickly gotten out of hand.

She stepped back. With a shaky hand, she reached up and rubbed her aching forehead. 'I didn't knowingly cheat on you. I just wanted you to know that.'

His gaze raked over her. 'You think that makes it all OK?'

'No. I know it doesn't. I'm just trying to explain what happened. We never got a chance to talk that night.' She wrapped her necklace around her forefinger. 'I'm so shocked to see you. I know this is coming at you from out of the blue.'

He let out a long breath of air. 'So let me see if I've got this straight. It was dark. Cody made a move, and you couldn't tell the difference between him and me.'

Brynn shifted uneasily. She'd never thought about it, but she had felt a difference. The touches had been different, the kisses more intense.

'He got you down on that floor, and you let him do whatever he wanted to you.'

She couldn't say anything. Couldn't justify a thing. She held her hands palm-upward and looked at him beseechingly. 'Because I thought –'

'Because you thought that he was me,' Rex said, drawing each word out.

'Yes,' she said, nodding emphatically.

'Well, if that's true, then there's only one way for you to apologise.'

She'd do anything to make things better with him.

'You owe me a fuck.'

She froze.

'Don't give me that look. You heard me.'

Shock nearly stole her breath. She looked down the hallway, horrified that someone might have heard. He couldn't have meant that; he was just striking out at her. She went still when she looked at him again. He was dead serious.

Surprisingly, she felt a tingle of anticipation in her belly. His bold order shocked her sensibilities, but at the same time, it excited her.

He was still a handsome man – blond and chic in that GQ sort of way. People had accused them of being Barbie and Ken dolls when they'd been dating. She hadn't minded the comparison, because she'd always thought he was the perfect guy for her.

And he still could be if she fixed things with him.

After a long, excruciating moment, he jerked his chin at her. 'Let's go somewhere private.'

She followed uncertainly as he led her down the hall. He turned into a room at the far end, and she found herself in the trainer's room. Gauze, tape, and hydrogen peroxide sat on a tray beside a massage table. A hot tub took up a good portion of the room, while hand weights, flex bands, and an exercise ball were neatly aligned along the wall.

He walked across the room to the trainer's desk and leaned back against it. 'OK. So get on with it.'

Brynn looked uncomfortably around the room. He wanted to do it *here*? *Now*?

His stare was hard and unforgiving. 'If you want to apologise properly, you're going to have to get naked.'

Her belly clenched. Nervously, she glanced over her shoulder towards the door.

'A locked door didn't save you last time,' he growled.

She couldn't believe she was even considering it. She couldn't do this. She shouldn't do this.

Suddenly, Brynn didn't care anymore. She could do it, and she'd worried about the 'should and shouldn'ts' enough to last her a lifetime. Look where it had gotten her. She'd done her best to follow the rules in college, and she'd still been run out of town by a sex scandal.

It was true; she owed him. More importantly, she owed herself.

She shrugged out of her jacket and draped it across a nearby chair. His interest piqued, even though he tried not to let it show. She could feel it in the way he looked at her. Her fingers caught the zipper at the back of her skirt and slid it downwards. She looked at him shyly as she let it drop and stepped out of it.

'Is that a man's T-shirt?'

Her hesitant smile faltered. Looking down, she saw Cody's white T-shirt clinging to her curves. How could she have forgotten? Her fingers wrapped around the material at her thighs and started gathering it upwards.

'Stop.' Rex pushed himself away from the desk and crossed the room. His fingers pushed hers away, and he caught the soft cotton material in his fist. 'Cheating on someone again, Brynn? I'm beginning to see a trend.'

Cheating? The concept nearly made her gag. There was nothing going on between her and Cody Jones.

Except what had gone on between them in that conference room just this afternoon.

'There's no one,' she said firmly.

'This is an odd combination for a fashion plate like you.'

'I spilled something earlier. A friend lent it to me.'

'A male friend, I see.' The back of his fist rubbed intimately against her upper thigh. 'Apparently, that spill went right through to your bra, because you aren't wearing one of those either.'

Her nipples perked up. She couldn't tell him where her bra was.

'What exactly is your line of work these days, honey?'

Brynn's eyes widened, and she couldn't help but let out a laugh. He thought she was some kind of call girl! She glanced down at herself. She could see where he might get the wrong impression. The shirt hugged every curve. Her nipples were stiff from the cool air in the room, and down lower, she still wore her high-heeled red shoes.

She smiled. 'I haven't changed that much, Rex. I've taken a new university job as a computer science professor – and part-time cheerleading coach. That's why I was here talking to Julie. We were looking at tapes of my squad's practice sessions.'

'University job? Here at Palmer?'

'No, I'm back home.'

His head snapped up. 'Southern Trinity?'

'Yes.'

The T-shirt pulled tight over her back and buttocks as he yanked her to him. The material lifted, exposing her underwear, her belly button, and even the bottom curves of her naked breasts. He looked at the offending white material, and he knew. Brynn didn't know how, but he knew.

'Jones,' he spat out. 'I should have known. You're with him.'

'No! I didn't even know that he worked there. I needed a job, and Dean Hawthorn hired me.'

'You just told me you're the cheerleading coach. Do

you think I'm an idiot? Cody's the frickin' football coach!'

'I swear, Rex. I didn't know that I'd be working with him.'

'*Working* with him? God, you are a liar. You're wearing his clothes.'

He dropped the shirt like a hot potato. His gaze raked down her body, his eyes flashing with something not quite anger, but more like determination. 'Finish.'

'Finish?' she asked in confusion.

'I thought we were going to fuck.'

Brynn shivered. His voice was cold and authoritative, but it made her toes curl. Obediently, she reached for the shirt.

'Leave that.'

Her eyes widened. Leave it? He knew it was Cody's.

Something clicked inside her head. *He knew it was Cody's.*

'The shoes are hot, but they'll have to go along with the nylons and the panties. I want everything off of you except that shirt. I like how it makes your tits look.'

Oh, God. He was going to fuck her while she wore Cody's clothes. The statement was subtle, but effective. Her nipples tightened under his intense stare, and little tremors coursed through her abdomen. He was playing a dangerous game.

Her knees felt weak, but she balanced herself as she stepped out of the high heels. She lowered her eyes as she reached under the T-shirt for the waistband of her nylons.

'Turn around,' he said in a low voice.

She obeyed. She realised his intent when she had to bend over to work the clinging nylons down her legs and off her feet. The position thrust her backside at him and pulled the T-shirt high on her thighs.

From his position, he had to be able to see the crotch of her underwear.

The muscles in her legs quivered, and she slowly stood upright.

'Now the panties,' he whispered. 'And Brynn? Make it slow.'

Her breaths went shallow as she reached under the T-shirt again. The soft material felt slippery under her fingertips, but she caught the thin strips at the sides of her hips and tugged downward. The elastic waistband popped over the curve of her buttocks and goose bumps went up her spine as the cool air hit her. She paused briefly with her panties pulled tight across her thighs.

'That's right, real slow,' he said from behind her. Her belly clenched when he ran a finger down her spine. 'Bend over nice and slow and let the football coach see your pretty pink pussy.'

Her breaths heaved in her lungs when she momentarily saw Coach Hendricks from ten years ago. She could only imagine what would have happened if she'd put herself on display for that caveman.

But was it really so different now? She knew the outcome was going to be the same.

She swallowed hard and gradually bent over to push her panties to her knees. They became loose there, and she let them drop. A hand against the small of her back stopped her from standing upright too quickly.

'Down,' Rex ordered. 'Grab your ankles, slut.'

The harsh name blindsided her, but it made her pussy clench just the same.

'Oh, that was nice.'

He'd seen.

She felt him move and, suddenly, she wasn't even partially covered. He flipped the back of the T-shirt over her buttocks and let it rest around her waist. She didn't know why, but her sudden nakedness surprised her, and her breath caught in her lungs.

It lodged there when he stroked her.

'I told you to grab your ankles,' he said, this time with steel in his voice. 'And spread those legs wider. I want to get a good look at my prize.'

Her entire body shook as she stretched downwards. Her fingers wrapped around the slim bones of her ankles, and she felt the blood rush to her head. Gravity made the T-shirt slip and it caught around her breasts in an added caress.

'Very pretty,' he said as his finger became bolder. He determinedly traced every line and crevice of her pussy, this time with a stronger, more invasive touch. 'Too bad you weren't this obliging in college. Imagine all the fun we could have had.'

She let out a cry when he jammed his thumb into her. He spread his fingers over her ass, and one brushed intimately against her anus. He clamped his hand together, and she whined at the lifting pressure in her pussy.

'Tight as a vice,' he murmured.

Cody's face flashed in front of her eyes. He'd said the same thing. Embarrassingly, she felt her juices gush.

'And eager.'

His thumb circled inside of her until she was rocking up and down on her toes. The hardness was pulled out of her, and she bolted up straight when he suddenly smacked her on the ass.

'Get into the hot tub.'

Her bottom stung, and her pussy throbbed. Not waiting for another love tap, she hurried to the tub. She reached for the T-shirt as she climbed up the short set of steps.

'I want it on.'

She glanced over her shoulder. Rex was pulling at his clothes. His sweatshirt was already off, and he was reaching for his belt. She hesitated at the lip of the tub. His chest was heavily muscled, and his arms were thick.

She could only imagine what his cock must be like.

Her pussy tingled. His mood made her nervous, but she wanted this. Call it guilt or call it debt, she wanted to pay the price.

Moist heat seeped into her muscles as she stepped into the hot tub. The water came up to her hips, and the white T-shirt went nearly transparent. The blonde curls between her legs were wet, tangled, and clearly visible. Her eyelids drooped with arousal, and she sat down on the seat that rimmed the tank.

'Oh!' she said in surprise when she sat directly on a water jet. She started to move, but Rex's voice stopped her.

'Right there. Let it tickle you, because I won't be getting there for a while.'

Brynn glanced up when she heard a splash. She was met with the vision of a cock coming right at her face. Her eyes widened, but she didn't have time to react as he walked up to her and pressed the bulging tip against her lips.

'Suck it. Suck it, lick it, and swallow it.'

She hesitated. She wasn't very good at oral sex, and she didn't particularly like it.

'You owe me, bitch.'

She squirmed on the jet of water. His cock butted up against her lips again, and she closed her eyes. Timidly, she opened her mouth. He wasn't shy about pressing himself inside. Her hands clamped down on his tree-trunk thighs, and she fought to stay calm.

'Oh yeah. Sweet,' he grunted. 'Give me some tongue.'

His hands slid into her hair to hold her head. The wet

ends brushed against her shoulders, and the T-shirt stuck to her body. Brynn inhaled sharply through her nose and let her tongue rub the underside of his pulsing dick.

He was thick. She had to open wide to take him, but surprisingly, he was very short. She wasn't disappointed by that. His stubbiness relaxed her. She wouldn't have to worry about gagging like she had the other time she'd tried this. She sealed her lips around him and sucked experimentally.

'Shit!' he hissed.

'Mmmph!'

A momentary fear grabbed her when he began to pump. Her eyes snapped open, and she saw the tangle of his pubic hair coming towards her. His size forced his thrusts to be short, and soon he was retreating again. She relaxed and adjusted to his tempo. Water splashed around them as he thrust, and her uneasiness fled.

She liked it.

She liked the feel of his cock in her mouth. She liked the texture, and she liked the taste. Most of all, she liked the way it made her feel so naughty. She'd never let herself be naughty before. Never.

'I always knew you'd give a good blow job,' he grunted through harsh breaths.

Brynn felt wonderfully debauched. Her hands finally left his thighs. She wanted to touch him. He bucked harder when she lightly caressed his balls. Soon, she tasted saltiness. He was almost ready to come, and her mouth became greedy.

'No you don't,' he panted. 'You're not keeping that prime pussy from me – not after Cody Jones has had his share.'

He'd pulled out of her mouth and left it gaping in surprise.

'He never – Ah! Rex!' She didn't even have time to lick her lips as he grabbed her, spun around, and switched positions. He sat on the bench and pulled her down to him.

The T-shirt hindered his first thrust. 'Goddamn Jones! Let me at her.'

He yanked the wet shirt out of the way, nearly ripping it, as his hips swung upward. He penetrated her and went as deep as he could. Brynn let out a long groan. His thickness was uncomfortable, but she pushed down, trying to take him deeper to where she needed him.

He pulled back, and soon she was bouncing on his lap. His thrusts were jagged and harsh. He began pumping faster and each ram caught her right against her clit. Her fingers dug into his broad shoulders as her head fell back.

'Ride me,' he barked. Her hair drifted in the water, and he caught it in his fists. 'Harder.'

She slammed down as he reared up, and water thrashed around them. She needed his roughness. She deserved it after what she'd done to him.

His mouth came down on her breast. He took her nipple, T-shirt and all, and began sucking voraciously. The pull was met by a corresponding tug in her belly, and she felt herself spiralling upwards.

'Oh Rex. That feels so good.'

She caught his shoulders and looked down. Her nipple ached even more as she watched his cheeks puff in and out with every suckle. She looked so depraved in the see-through shirt.

The vision blurred. The pounding of his cock inside of her, the pull of his mouth, the clinging of the T-shirt. It was almost as if Cody were holding her tightly as Rex screwed the daylights out of her.

The combination was too much. When he thrust upwards one more time, she snapped. Tremors wracked her body, and her pussy milked his thick prick. He pounded into her endlessly until the tight grip of her cunt pushed him over the edge. At last, his fingers bit into her ass, and he spurted into her.

'Oh Rex,' Brynn sighed. She sagged against his solid chest and held on to his shoulders so she wouldn't go under. She kissed the side of his neck and snuggled against him.

He wasn't in the mood for cuddling. Her breath caught when he lifted her abruptly, pulled his limp cock out of her, and set her to the side. 'Well, as apologies go, that's a start,' he said flatly.

Her mouth gaped open as she watched him slosh through the water to the steps. He climbed out, grabbed a towel, and began to dry himself. He didn't even look at her as he rubbed the terrycloth over his crotch.

Suddenly cold, Brynn didn't know what to do. By the time she made it to the steps, he already had his pants on. He finally spared her a look as he pulled his sweat-shirt over his head.

'You can tell Jones he's got a pretty damned good slut.'

He tossed a towel at her, and her head snapped back. She caught it and held it against her chest as the T-shirt hung heavily on her body. It dripped onto the floor and a puddle formed around her feet.

With an unreadable look, Rex turned and walked out the door. She watched numbly as it slammed shut.

'Oh Rex,' she said with a catch in her throat.

She ran a hand across her forehead. He'd done it on purpose. He'd fucked her in that cold, impartial way to try to get back at her, but her reaction had probably made him even angrier. Instead of being debased, she'd been a willing participant. Even now, her body wanted more.

She pressed a hand low on her belly and felt the arousal still coursing through her system. Her nipples looked like big ripe strawberries as they strained against the wet fabric. Lower, her pussy was pink and swollen. Nothing was hidden by the weighty, clinging tee.

The tee!

'Oh no!' Brynn was rocked with a realisation. It had been the shirt! No wonder he'd reacted so strongly. She might as well have waved a red flag in front of a bull.

'Damn you, Cody!'

He'd given the T-shirt to her because he'd known there was a chance she'd run into Rex. 'Think of me,' he said over and over again. He might as well have put his brand on her.

The cling of the material became suffocating. Clenching it with both hands, she wrestled it over her head.

'I hate you!'

Every time she and Rex started to get close, Cody found a way between them.

Infuriated, she looked around for her clothes. She needed to get dressed, but there was no way she was putting that thing back on. She gathered her belongings and headed to the bathroom. She had to get herself into some kind of order. Julie would come looking for her soon.

With stiff movements, she dried off with the towel Rex had thrown at her. The hand dryer in the restroom got the rest of the dampness out of her hair. She put her wrinkled clothes back on, but scowled when she pulled her jacket over her shoulders.

She was right back where she'd started this horrid day. If she went back to Julie's office looking this way, the woman was going to notice her boobs hanging out. She didn't even have her bra to hide her.

'Men!' Brynn hissed. Between Dean Hawthorn, Cody, and Rex, they'd all managed to put her in this embarrassing position.

She spotted a laundry basket in the training room and pawed through it until she found another white T-shirt. It was crumpled and smelly, but she had no choice. Her nose curled and she cringed as she pulled it over her head, but she forced herself to wear it. When she buttoned the suit jacket over it, it wasn't so noticeable.

'All you need to do is get home,' she told herself. Then she could take the gross thing off, burn it, and treat herself to a shower. Preferably, a nice long hot one.

Cody's T-shirt was still a problem. 'Stupid thing,' she muttered as she wrung it out in the sink.

She couldn't leave it behind. For one thing, it would be like rubbing it in Rex's face. For another, Cody would ask her about it. She balled the material up in her hand and headed to the door. She didn't know how she was going to explain it if Julie asked. She'd just have to improvise.

Her footsteps sounded loud as she walked down the empty hallway, and the T-shirt left a trail of water behind her.

'Brynn, is that you?'

She clattered to a quick stop. 'Yeah. I'll be there in a minute,' she called as she looked around frantically for a place to ditch the evidence.

'Are you all right?' Julie asked.

She heard the woman moving around in her office, and a tingle of anxiety hit her between the shoulder blades. She knew she was overreacting; Julie wouldn't have a clue what the wet T-shirt signified. Still, she couldn't bear the idea of being caught. Suddenly, she found herself winding up like a quarterback. She let the T-shirt fly and it whizzed down the hallway past Julie's office. She grimaced when it landed with a splat.

Julie didn't react.

A bemused smile settled onto Brynn's lips. She couldn't believe she'd done that! The sex must have affected her brain. She shook her head and wiped her wet hands on her skirt.

'Sorry I took so long,' she said as she walked into her friend's office. 'I hope I haven't kept you from anything.'

A look of concern crossed Julie's face. 'What in the world was that all about? How do you know Rex?'

Brynn shook her head and lifted her hands in a hopeless gesture. Just how did one explain the tangled web she found herself caught in? 'We dated in college. It ended . . . badly.'

One of Julie's eyebrows lifted. 'I'd say.'

She hit the eject button on the VCR and put the tape she'd been watching in its box. 'I can't blame you for dumping that asshole.'

Brynn chewed the side of her cheek. 'Actually, it was the other way around. I behaved poorly. I think his feelings are still hurt.'

Julie rolled her eyes. 'Oh, please. Rex Stanton is a spoiled little rich boy. You shouldn't feel bad no matter what happened.'

Brynn caught her necklace. She doubted her friend would say that if she knew the whole story. 'I'm sorry to bring you into the middle of it.'

'It's all right. I spent the time you were away reviewing your tapes,' Julie said as she passed her the stack. 'I don't think you have all that far to go. Confidence is your squad's biggest problem. Whip that into shape, and they'll be fine.'

Brynn's mind went back to the reason she'd come here, and she was pleasantly surprised. 'Are you sure? Sometimes I get so close, I can't see the forest for the trees.'

'You're on the right track.'

'Thanks, Julie. I owe you one.'

Brynn pushed her tapes into her clutch. She really needed to get going. The borrowed T-shirt she was wearing smelled to high heaven, and her pussy was beginning to ache. Rex had used her hard, but he'd awakened something inside her. She hadn't had sex for a long time. Now that she had, she wanted more. It was embarrassing.

She picked up her bag to go, but her eyebrows lowered. It felt lighter than it should. She opened it and looked inside. 'Weren't there six tapes?'

'I think that's it.' Julie looked around her office. 'Wait, I went to the bathroom. I might have carried one in there with me. I always seem to do that with my remote. Hold on.'

'It's all right,' Brynn called, but it was too late. The woman was already out the door.

Brynn sighed, but then her eyes widened. The T-shirt. She scrambled to the hallway and looked around furtively. The coast was clear. She scurried towards the lump on the floor and nearly fell on her butt when she slipped on a puddle of water.

Muttering awful things about Cody Jones under her breath, she squatted down beside the sopping rag and scooped it up. She felt ridiculous acting this way about a stupid shirt, but she couldn't help herself. She quickly hid it in another compartment of her bag and hurried back to the spot where Julie had left her.

'It's not there,' Julie said as she turned into the room.

Brynn let out a soft breath of relief. She'd barely made it in the nick of time.

'I must have counted wrong,' she said as she shifted her load in her arms. 'My head is all screwed up today.'

No thanks to two hardheaded football coaches – and one nimble-fingered dean.

'No problem. Good luck with your squad.'

'Thanks. Good luck with yours, too,' Brynn said as she turned on her heel. 'See you in a couple of weeks.'

Julie leaned against the doorframe as she watched her leave. 'Isn't that Southern Trinity's Homecoming game?'

Brynn winked. 'We'll be waiting for you.'

Julie laughed. 'Drive safely.'

Brynn waved before hurrying down the hall. She hit the front door of the building and pushed it open to make her escape. The night air hit her in the face, and she shivered. She hunched her shoulders against the chill as she made her way to her car. With each step across the parking lot, she became more and more aware of two opposing things: the heat in her pussy and the coldness of the water seeping through the bag and onto her hip.

Rex and Cody.

She felt as if she'd entered some kind of time warp. It was ten years later. Things had changed. Her life had changed.

So why was it that she found herself caught again between the same two men?

6

By the next morning, Brynn was bright and chipper again. She'd admit that she'd had a rough night. Between guilt over Rex and anger with Cody, she hadn't been able to get much sleep. She'd tossed and turned until she'd finally made herself roll out of bed. Amazingly, doing her laundry had helped.

She'd only done one load: her whites. Cody's T-shirt had been the first thing she'd thrown in. She wanted it gone. She'd washed it, dried it, folded it, and put it in an internal mailing envelope for work. It was going in his mail slot first thing Monday morning. The symbolic gesture alone eased her mind.

She was washing her hands of both of them. They could act like teenage studs for all she cared. She wasn't getting into it this time.

Once that decision was made, her outlook brightened. After all, the day was sunny and clear – perfect for a car wash. Her squad was smiling and energetic when she arrived at the grocery store, and their enthusiasm was contagious. Brynn set herself up as the cashier with a little folding table and chair, a box of change, and a milk crate for her feet. Sunglasses and a bottle of lemonade kept her cool and relaxed as her squad slaved away.

Today was about cheerleading. It was the one area of her life where she felt confident, and she was going to enjoy it.

'Here's your change,' she said as she passed a five-dollar bill to a cute little old man who'd stopped. 'Thank you for supporting Southern Trinity's Cheer Squad.'

'Could you make sure they get the whitewalls clean?' he asked.

'Of course,' Brynn said with a smile. 'Jimmy! Take extra care with the tyres on that Chevy.'

Jimmy nodded and aimed the hose at the old timer's wheels. Somehow, he'd gotten control of the water. Brynn chuckled under her breath. She didn't know if that was such a good thing. He'd already zapped Karen in the butt twice.

'Hey, Coach,' Hannah said as she came over to the table. She dropped her sudsy sponge in a bucket and wiped her hands on her shorts. 'How are we doing?'

Brynn thumbed through the money in her collection box and quickly calculated in her head. 'All right. Traffic is a bit slower than I expected.'

'Me, too.' Hannah wiped her forehead with the back of her hand. 'I wish more cars would stop.'

Brynn looked around. They were in a prime spot, and grocery stores were always busy on Saturday mornings. People were strolling in right by them and coming out pushing carts full of food. 'We are around the corner. Go check our sign; maybe it's blown down.'

'Good idea. I'll be right back.'

A familiar silver Cadillac pulled into an open space in the car wash line as Hannah rounded the building, and Brynn smiled. Every car they washed was another pom-pon in their equipment locker. OK, maybe every two cars.

'Dean Hawthorn,' she called when he stepped out of the car. 'Thank you for coming.'

'I wouldn't have missed it,' he said as he closed the door behind him. He rubbed his hands together as he looked at his pride and joy. 'Do try to keep the spots off the rearview mirrors, would you, dear?'

Karen nodded in understanding and called her teammates over to help her get started. As their benefactor, the dean's car would receive extra special care.

Hawthorn looked around the group, and Brynn felt a warm feeling when he winked at her. As always, he looked spotless in his khaki pants and polo shirt. She didn't think the man owned a pair of jeans.

She drummed her fingers on the fold-up table. He was an attractive, mature man, with 'mature' being the key word. And he was interested. He'd made that point perfectly clear. After the games that Cody and Rex had played with her, the idea of a mature man was appealing.

Another door slammed, penetrating her hazy thoughts, and she snapped back to attention. Her eyes narrowed when she looked at the young woman who'd just stepped out of the dean's car. And who was this?

'What a beautiful day,' Hawthorn commented.

'I was worried after how chilly it got last night, but so far, the weather's cooperating,' Brynn said absently. She was distracted by the way the sultry, dark-haired girl rounded the car and draped herself over her boss's arm.

'Autumn is well on its way.' The dean patted the girl's hand and walked her over to the table. 'Coach, I'd like to introduce you to someone. This is Trini Ramirez.'

'Hello,' Brynn said tonelessly. She didn't know why she was reacting so strongly, but something close to jealousy was sitting like a ten-pound weight on her chest. The girl couldn't be half Hawthorn's age, but she certainly looked as if she knew him well. She was rubbing herself against him like a cat.

Brynn's fingers drummed a little harder against the

table. The man certainly got around. Just yesterday, he'd been feeling *her* up.

Hawthorn looked at the young woman dotingly. 'I think I've finally convinced Ms Ramirez to try out for your cheerleading squad.'

Brynn cocked her head in surprise. 'Oh really?'

She looked at the Latino girl again, this time with a critical eye. Trini stood up a little straighter and accepted the challenge with her own cock of the head. Brynn had to admit the girl looked trim and athletic – and she certainly had a sensual air that nobody could miss. 'Do you have any experience?' she asked.

The girl flipped her long hair over her shoulder and a silky smile curled her lips. 'What would you say, Dean honey? Am I experienced?'

'Now, Trini,' Hawthorn chastised. He patted her hand again. 'She was on the all-state squad as a senior in high school.'

Brynn's eyebrows lifted. That was impressive. She forced her personal feelings aside. Her squad was in need of more talent. She couldn't ignore what might be standing in front of her face. 'Have you performed at the college level?'

Something clouded the girl's lively expression. 'No.' She glanced over her shoulder and a devilish look came into her eye. 'But I'd like to give it a shot.'

Steve dropped his sponge, and Mark tripped over the hose.

Brynn sat back in her chair and folded her arms over her chest. The girl was trouble with a capital T. There was no question about that. The real issue was if she would be worth all the hassle. 'What skills do you have? Can you dance or tumble?'

Trini looked at her and winked. 'I can do whatever you want me to do, honey.'

Brynn shook her head, but couldn't help but smile. The girl had gusto. Although that could cause problems, it was something that her current squad was desperately lacking. 'How advanced are you? Have you done stunting before?'

Trini finally unplastered herself from Hawthorn's side. She put her hands on the table and leaned forward. 'Honey, I can fly like a 747.'

'A flyer.' Brynn immediately became more intrigued, but she tempered her response. She pointedly looked away from the gaping neckline of the girl's tight sweater and met her challenging gaze with one of her own. 'That's nice, but what I really want is someone who can be part of a team. Can you do that, *honey*?'

Some of the bravado disappeared, and Brynn finally saw real wanting in the girl's expressive eyes. 'Yes, ma'am. I can.'

'Are your grades high enough?'

Hawthorn stepped forward. 'She maintains a respectable grade average. Personally, I think she could do better, but she has to split her time between work and school.'

'Where do you work?'

'I waitress at The Pit.' Trini pushed herself away from the table and planted her hands on her trim hips. 'I make great tips.'

Brynn didn't doubt that. The Pit was one of the rowdiest bars in Campus Town, but it also served the best pizza within fifty miles. The girl's brazen personality would fit in well there. But with her squad...? 'Listen, I'll be honest with you. The squad is just coming together, and I'm not inclined to add somebody who might rattle things up.'

'Give me a chance. You need me.'

Did they ever. Brynn was careful not to let her excitement show. She wouldn't make up her mind until she saw the girl's skills, but she had a gut feeling Trini was exactly what she'd been looking for. 'We practise every afternoon at four. Could you be there on Monday for a try-out?'

'Where?'

'The sidelines of the football field.'

Trini ran a hand through her lustrous hair and looked at the squad again. Particularly, the male members of the squad. 'I'll be there with bells on.'

Jimmy's hose suddenly started spurting straight up in the air, and Karen yelped when she was drenched. Brynn clicked her tongue against her teeth. Oh, boy. This was going to be an adventure.

'You're welcome to join us today,' she said, diving in. She might as well check the chemistry now. 'If you make it on the squad, you'll have to participate in activities like this anyway.'

'Activities?'

'Fundraising. Community events. That kind of thing.'

'Which is this?'

Brynn blinked. She'd thought that was obvious. 'We're trying to raise money for new uniforms.'

Trini lifted an eyebrow. 'Oh, honey,' she said dolefully.

Leaning forward, she thumbed through the cash. Brynn immediately sat forward to guard their earnings, but felt more defensive when the girl made a tsking sound. 'Mind if I make a suggestion?'

Brynn looked at Hawthorn, but he just shrugged and smiled.

'Depends on what it is,' she said carefully.

Trini's eyes danced, and she reached for the scissors sitting next to Brynn's elbow. 'Can I wear one of those T-shirts?'

Brynn glanced over her shoulder. The squad was wearing matching T-shirts displaying 'Southern Trinity Cheer Squad' on the back, and she'd taped a few up against the side of the grocery store to catch people's attention. 'Well, OK.'

She stood and took one down from the wall. She passed it to the disarming girl, but her eyes widened when Trini began hacking away with the scissors. 'Hey!'

'There,' Trini said as she held up the ragged remains.

The full-sized T-shirt had morphed into a severely cropped tank top. Brynn stood back on her heels, but nearly fell over when Trini turned her back on the crowd, tugged off her tight sweater and bra, and slipped the tiny tank over her head. When she turned around, Brynn was aghast.

She'd looked like that last night; only the tank was blue and tighter fitting. And dry – although that didn't make much of a difference as the material pulled tight over the girl's perky breasts.

Somewhere nearby a bucket of water hit the ground.

'Coach!' someone said in dismay.

Brynn didn't have to look to know who it was. Hannah had returned. She felt the cheerleader come to stand at her side. 'Coach, what is she doing?'

'She's ... uh ... helping.'

'But she's not on the squad. You can't let her do that. It's *degrading*.'

Brynn felt a smile press at her lips when Hannah's voice dropped to a scandalised whisper. Looking at Trini, the girl didn't seem very degraded. In fact, she seemed confident, and she looked incredible.

Brynn saw the challenge that sparked in the depths of the girl's ebony eyes. She stepped closer and cupped her breasts, lifting them higher for Hannah's review.

'You think these are degrading? Honey, these are our meal ticket.'

'Coach!' Hannah hissed.

Dean Hawthorn gently patted the cheerleader on the shoulder. 'Sex sells, Ms Stiles.'

Hannah's head whipped towards the dean as Brynn turned a thousand shades of red. She began fanning herself with a flyer when she saw another devilish look enter Trini's eyes.

Oh Lord, now what?

Brynn stepped back and Hawthorn sidled up to her. 'This should be interesting,' he commented dryly.

The gauntlet had apparently been thrown. Trini walked up to the flustered Hannah until their toes nearly touched. With one eyebrow lifted, she deliberately gave the blonde an intimate and thorough once over. 'You've got some nice tits yourself, Blondie.'

Hannah's mouth gaped open like a grounded fish, but she was no match for the new girl. Trini let out a laugh and suddenly caught Hannah's T-shirt and tugged it out of her shorts. She backed her up against the cement wall of the grocery store while the rest of the squad looked on in total shock. Water spouted from hoses and bubbles dripped down tyre sidewalls, but nobody moved an inch.

Except Trini. Still laughing, she caught the neck of Hannah's T-shirt and pulled it down, stretching it to nearly the girl's breastbone. She looped the bottom of the shirt through the gaping neck hole and tugged down. The shirt cinched together in an impromptu halter-top, and Hannah's breasts plumped out of the exposing neckline.

'Stop it!' she cried as she batted at Trini's hands.

'Why? You look fantastic. What are you, a 34C?' To

find out, the dark-haired girl cupped the plump breasts in her hands and weighed them.

Hannah's face turned to a colour close to fuchsia, but Brynn clamped a hand over her mouth when she saw nipples perking up between Trini's fingers.

'Your ass isn't bad, either,' Trini said as she looked down in evaluation. 'Maybe if we rolled up your shorts even higher...'

Hannah caught her tormentor's hands as she reached for her thighs. 'Leave me alone.'

Trini pulled back. 'Had enough, Blondie?'

Hannah held up one hand to ward off her new foe and reached for the tie at her breasts with the other. 'There's no way you're joining our squad. I won't let it happen.'

'You've got nothing to say about it, sweet cakes. I can cheer circles around you. I've seen you.'

Hannah's chin came up. What had been horror swiftly changed to anger. She was a Texas cheerleader and captain of her squad. She was a nice girl, but nobody talked to her that way – not about her cheering. 'That's tough talk for someone from a high school squad.'

Trini's eyes narrowed, and Brynn felt trouble brewing. The line had been drawn in the sand, but she didn't know what to do. If Trini really was as good as she expected, they needed her. On the other hand, if she couldn't get along with the squad captain, it could make the season a living hell.

'Do you want to raise money for your squad, or do you want to stand there and whine?'

Hannah's eyes smouldered.

Trini edged closer. Hannah's hand whipped up, but the dark-haired girl caught it before it could slap her face. She moved like a cobra striking and the squad and all their customers gasped when she pushed Hannah back against the wall and took her mouth in a full French kiss.

Hannah stumbled back and her hands swatted at Trini's shoulders, but the girl didn't stop. She caught her by the waist to hold her still and tilted her head. Their mouths sealed in a hot, bold kiss. A tormented moan sprang from Hannah's throat, and Brynn took a step forward. Hawthorn stopped her with a hand on her shoulder.

'Let them work it out,' he said.

After a while, it became apparent that Hannah wasn't fighting anymore. She let out another weak moan as her shoulders sagged against the wall. Trini laughed and lifted her hands to fondle Hannah's breasts again. She pulled back and the look that passed between the two of them was hot and combative. Refusing to break the stare, Trini ran her tongue over Hannah's lips.

Brynn was shocked when the cheerleader's mouth parted to let it back in.

Satisfied that she'd won, Trini suddenly pulled back and slapped her palms against the wall by Hannah's head. 'Now, let's go flaunt ourselves to the public. We need to get cars in here. I want a cute little skirt for my new uniform.'

She grabbed Hannah's wrist and looked at Brynn. 'We're going out to the street to wave cars in.'

She tugged the cheerleader along with her, but stopped when she saw the rest of the motionless squad. 'Come on, you guys. Strip!'

A catcall suddenly whipped through the air. Brynn let out a laugh of disbelief when a bunch of wolf whistles joined it. T-shirts went flying off half her team, and she couldn't help but look on in appreciation. That should bring in the housewives with their dirty cars. There were some rock hard bodies in the group.

One by one, the female cheerleaders got in line for the scissors. T-shirts that had once been proud and chaste soon became proud and skimpy as they were cut left and right. Karen skipped the scissors entirely and went straight to the bikini top she'd worn underneath. Horns suddenly began tooting, and Brynn's mouth dropped when she saw the number of cars in line.

It was working!

She glanced at the street and saw Trini with her arm around Hannah's waist. They were both waving to passing cars, and she could hear brakes screeching as drivers tried to make the turn.

'What do you say?' Dean Hawthorn said. She looked up and saw him brandishing the scissors. 'If you can't beat 'em, join 'em?'

Brynn looked down at herself. With a shrug, she lifted her arms. He stood close and snipped the T-shirt away, turning her around as he went. The crop he gave her hit her right below the breasts, leaving her stomach bare for the world to see. The wide strip of red fabric hit the ground, and he caught her with a hand flat across her stomach as he stood behind her. 'I seem to be stripping you a lot these days.'

His hand felt hot and possessive. 'Sex sells.'

'And you're making a lot of money.' He pulled away and set the scissors back on the table. Primly, he folded his hands behind his back and turned towards the busy car wash area. 'So what do you think?'

'Of what?' Brynn lifted her hair off the back of her neck. It had suddenly gotten warm.

'Of Trini. I thought she might be the answer to your Hannah problem.' He cleared his throat. 'Although at the time, I didn't realise exactly what Hannah's problem was.'

Brynn levelled a look at her boss. 'She was just shocked. I don't think she knew how to defend herself. I certainly wouldn't have.'

'Wouldn't you?' he said, looking down at her. His gaze dropped to her barely covered breasts. 'I'll have to remember that.'

Brynn found herself standing up straighter, pushing them out for him to see. The green monster hadn't let her out of its teeth yet. 'Where did you find this secret weapon?' she asked cattily.

He chuckled. 'One doesn't find a woman like Trini. She finds you.'

He looked at her paternally, and wrapped his arm around her shoulders. Brynn went still. She didn't want him to look at her paternally. She wanted him to look at her like he looked at his new slinky girlfriend.

'Trini had a full-ride scholarship to cheer at Texas A&M, but she lost it when she got kicked off her high school squad,' Hawthorn said. He squeezed her shoulders. 'I know your high standards, but I wouldn't have introduced her to you if I didn't think she could help your team. When it comes to cheering, she's as strong or stronger than Hannah. I'll admit she's a spitfire, but I think you could benefit from having her on the squad.'

Brynn wasn't quite so sure. 'What did she do to get thrown off her high school squad?'

'The coach, if I remember correctly.'

Her eyes nearly bugged out of her head. She gestured to the wall where Trini had just accosted Hannah. 'She did that to her coach?'

'Mm, I believe it was more salacious than that, but he didn't seem to mind. Unfortunately, the school board did.'

'He?' Brynn looked again at the wall. Trini had seemed rather comfortable kissing another woman. Beyond comfortable, she'd seemed rather adept at it.

'Trini's not particular,' Hawthorn said with another squeeze to her shoulders. 'She's a loving girl.'

Brynn let out a snort.

His thumb ran gently up and down her arm. 'Is that shocking to you, Ms Montgomery?'

'Well, yes!' She looked up at him, but was suddenly taken aback. 'Shouldn't it be?'

He turned slowly and cupped her chin. Her lips trembled as he traced them with his thumb. 'Ah, little Brynn, Trini's just comfortable with herself. You could learn from her.'

He moved, and her breath caught when she felt the front of his khakis brush against her bare stomach. He was hard. Nervously, she glanced at her cheerleaders. They were consumed in each other. Young, fit bodies. Water. Suds. They weren't even noticing her boss coming on to her.

'There's no need for you to be jealous of her,' he said softly. 'Our time will come. You know that I'll be there for you whenever you need me – and however you need me.'

His thumb brushed against the dark circles she knew were under her eyes. 'You look tired, my dear.'

'I . . .' She didn't really want to talk with him about last night. 'I had trouble sleeping last night.'

'You need to learn how to relax.' He slid his hand through her hair and followed it down her spine. The muscles of her lower back clenched when he began rubbing his palm in circles over her bare skin. 'I could help you with that.'

She felt her body start to melt against his, but giggles from the car wash made her pull back. 'I just had a long day. Between the luncheon and the symposium, I over-scheduled myself.'

'I thought the luncheon went rather well.' He gave her an intimate smile. 'Even though Coach Jones leant you his shirt.'

Brynn blushed. 'He thought I was underdressed.'

'You looked beautiful.' Hawthorn stepped forward, closing the distance she'd tried to put between them. His hand tightened, bringing her back into contact with his straining cock. 'And this symposium. What was it about?'

'Computer security.' Her hands came up and hesitantly caught his arms. They were nearly in an embrace and a tiny thrill shot through her system. 'The drive to Palmer was longer than I expected.'

'Palmer College?' His hand stilled on the base of her spine. 'Oh, my dear. I see now why you're so stressed.'

There was something about the tone of his voice. She looked up into his blue eyes. 'You know?'

He shrugged one elegant shoulder. 'If you'd told me you were going there, I would have warned you.'

He remembered. Brynn closed her eyes at her naïvety. Of course he remembered. How could he forget a scandal like that? The man's mind was like a steel trap, and she was beginning to understand that he used it as one, too. No wonder he thought he could come on to her, and she would respond.

She flattened her hands against his chest and tried to push him away. Nobody had noticed him rubbing his cock against her belly, but they would if she let him continue.

'Now don't be that way,' he said as his hand dropped lower to her ass. 'Tell me what happened. Did you run into Mr Stanton?'

She hesitated, but finally nodded.

'The two of you had a difficult break-up, if I recall.'

His hand moved to the back of her thigh and began slowly sliding up under her shorts. He knew exactly what he was doing, combining the mental probing with the physical.

Brynn bit her lower lip as a shiver ran up her leg and her buttocks clenched. She and Rex hadn't just broken up, they'd imploded. 'It was probably best that we did run into each other. It gave us a chance to talk through things,' she said, fudging the truth.

'Talk?'

'Yes, talk,' she said firmly. She wasn't about to tell her boss that she'd tried to suck her old boyfriend's cock off. Not when his fingers were rubbing against the elastic leg band of her panties. He already had too many ideas.

'So that's what they're calling it these days,' he said with a chuckle. His hand slid right under the barrier and wrapped around her bare butt. It was shocking, but he rubbed her ass in a soothing way. 'The truth, Brynn. You're right back in the middle of those two men, aren't you?'

She stared at him for a long moment. She didn't know if he was the right person to confide in. 'I don't know what to do about it,' she admitted.

He clicked his tongue and pulled her close so her head rested against his shoulder. Brynn let out a sigh and allowed his arms to wrap around her. His fingers massaged her neck as his thumb caressed her bottom, and she felt comforted. 'Would you accept some advice?'

'I'm going to stay away from both of them.'

'I don't think that would be wise. You might consider not keeping yourself so repressed this time. Try enjoying the attention.'

She was enjoying his hand up her shorts. 'Attention from you?' she said boldly.

'Of course, but I was thinking more globally.' He

looked down into her eyes and their lips nearly touched. 'You need to take a good long look at yourself, dear. If you do, you'll see that most of your problems have come from stifling your natural desires. You're a sexual woman. Instead of fighting those impulses, you might find it rewarding to go with them. Be it Mr Jones, Mr Stanton, myself, or all three of us – you need to explore your sexuality.'

Brynn felt her cheeks go pink. His remarks hit close to home but, like Cody said, she'd always been a Goody Two Shoes. 'Won't that just bring on more trouble?'

'Opening your legs might open your options.'

His dark gaze became piercing, and her stomach clenched when his hand became more intimate. She bit down hard on her lip when his fingers worked into the crevice of her ass and brushed intimately against her anus.

'Think about it,' he said quietly.

Brynn's throat tightened. The idea excited her, but it also made her uneasy. She'd returned to Southern Trinity to clear her reputation. What he was proposing would have the exact opposite effect.

'Don't look so anxious,' he said with a laugh. He dropped a tender kiss on her temple and finally pulled his hands away from her. Stepping back, he tapped her shoulders in a friendly manner. The tap stayed, though, and turned into a caress. 'I'm sure things will work out fine.'

He nodded to the sidewalk, and she saw Trini still holding Hannah's hand to keep her from running away. Their nubile bodies jiggled provocatively as they enticed cars to the car wash. The line of cars had become so long, it curled around the corner and out of sight.

'See?' he said, gesturing at them. 'Problems have a tendency to solve themselves. That is, if you let them.'

7

The car wash ran an hour-and-a-half longer than scheduled. Brynn didn't know if it was the jiggling cheerleaders on the street or the wet hard bodies in the parking lot, but the cars just kept coming and coming. Such a large turnout was exciting, but it was also exhausting. Between counting out change, hosing down vehicles, and refereeing the bicker matches between Hannah and Trini, she was pooped. And hungry. By the time the last shiny car pulled away, she could have eaten the entire load of groceries in the woman's back seat.

'What do you say we all grab some lunch?' she asked as she folded up her table and chair.

'Let's go to The Pit,' Trini said as she and Hannah approached from the street. 'It's not very busy on Saturday afternoons.'

'Yeah,' Karen said.

'I'm there,' Mark agreed.

Brynn balanced the moneybox on her hip and tried to pick up the table and chair at the same time. Pit pizza and a cold lemonade. She was salivating already. 'Sounds good. I'll meet you there. I want to deposit our earnings in the bank before it closes.'

'How much did we make?' Hannah asked.

Brynn grinned. 'How do warm-ups sound?'

'Really? We have enough for new uniforms and warm-ups?'

'Between today's take and the donations from the boosters, I think we'll make it.'

Smiling broadly, Hannah bounced up and down and clapped her hands.

'See, Blondie?' Trini said with a laugh. She shook her shoulders in a shimmy that nearly sent her boobs flying out from under her skimpy tank. 'I told you these were worth something.'

'Oh please,' Hannah said, scrunching up her nose. 'People weren't stopping for those puny things.'

Brynn choked back a laugh. It looked like her captain was starting to hold her own – and that was a good thing. The tension between the two women was still palpable, but she hoped they could find a way to work together. The rest of the squad had taken a liking to Trini. She was loud and outrageous, yes, but she was also a lot of fun.

'Whatever their reasons, I'm happy they stopped,' Brynn said. She hefted the table up to shoulder level, but Hannah quickly caught the chair before it could clatter to the ground.

'Let me help you with that.'

'Thanks,' she said as Trini took the table from her. Together, they walked across the parking lot and stuffed everything into her car. Brynn closed the trunk and walked around to the driver's side. 'I'll see you in about twenty minutes.'

Hannah wiped her hands as she stepped back. 'I think I'm going to skip it.'

Trini's head swivelled towards her.

'Oh come on,' Brynn said. 'Everyone else will be there. It will be a good way to celebrate our newfound fortune.'

Hannah shrugged. It wasn't like her to skip a squad function, but the glares she was throwing at Trini out of the corner of her eye told the real problem. 'I need to get home. I've got a lot of homework to do.'

'Oh God. You need to get out more,' Trini said. Before Hannah knew what she was doing, she stuck her hand in the girl's shorts. Hannah jumped with a shriek, but Trini searched around in her pocket until she found her car keys. With a laugh, she pulled them out and held them over her head. 'She'll be there, Coach. I need a ride anyway since Hawthorn ditched me.'

'Give me those!' Hannah growled as she swiped for her keys.

Brynn shook her head as she opened her car door. They'd both be at lunch; Trini had won this match. 'Order without me. I'll be there as fast as I can.'

Trini was still playing keep-away with Hannah's keys as she drove away. All Brynn could do was roll her eyes. Things were going to get very interesting if the Latino girl made it on the squad. Just keeping those two from pulling out each other's hair might take more time and energy than she had.

But if Trini was what the squad needed, she'd deal with it.

The trip to the bank didn't take as long as Brynn expected, although she received a few wide-eyed stares when she walked into the lobby wearing her water-splattered cropped top. For once, she didn't really care what people thought. She was having a great day, and the deposit slip she tucked into her purse proved it.

She drove to campus town, but finding a parking spot proved to be more time-consuming. By the time she walked into The Pit, her entire squad was sitting down to cold beers. She did a quick mental sweep to make sure everyone was of age before squeezing her way around the table to the chair they'd saved for her.

'Here you go, Coach,' Jimmy said as he lifted the pitcher to pour her a glass.

'Oh, none for me. Thanks.' She sat down across from

Hannah and noticed the girl's lemonade. 'I'll have one of those,' she told the waiter.

'Ah,' she said contentedly as he set the glass down in front of her. She picked up the frosty mug and took a long drink. It felt so good going down her parched throat. Feeling refreshed, Brynn took a look around the bar. 'Do you know that I've never been in here before?'

'You're kidding,' Jimmy said.

'Me, either,' Hannah said. She did look somewhat uncomfortable in the new surroundings.

'It's colourful; I'll give it that.' Brynn kicked away the peanut shells under her feet. 'Well, what the place lacks in class, it makes up for in the pizza department. I used to have their delivery number on speed dial.'

'Did I hear someone say pizza?'

Trini swivelled her hips around the bar as she came out of the kitchen with two big pizza pies in her hands. She set one down in front of Karen and Mark at one end of the table and found room for the other in front of Hannah. 'Scoot over,' she said as she took the seat beside the blonde.

'Oh, that looks delicious,' Brynn said as she scooped up a slice. The cheese stretched out for nearly a foot before she twisted it around her forefinger and snapped it off.

'It's deep dish supreme,' Trini said. 'It's killer.'

Hannah daintily picked up a piece and nibbled at the corner end. 'Mmm, it is good.'

'Told ya.' Trini grabbed a shaker and liberally applied hot pepper to her slice.

Brynn had forgotten how good a greasy loaded pizza could be – and how much college students could eat. The pizza was half-demolished before anyone spoke.

'Hey,' Mark said as he looked at his watch. 'We forgot

about the game. It's nearly over. Someone turn on the radio.'

'Hal!' Trini yelled. 'Put on the game.'

The raucous rock-and-roll that had been rattling the walls disappeared and myriad sounds filled the bar as the radio dial was turned. Finally, Hal landed on the Southern Trinity/Midwestern Texas game.

'Southern Trinity's been driving down the field,' the announcer said in a scratchy voice. Hal adjusted the tuning and the voice cleared. 'But now they've got a third and long.'

'They'll make the first down,' Jimmy said with certainty. He reached past Hannah for another slice of pizza. 'Midwestern's been hot, but Coach Jones will have something up his sleeve.'

Brynn rolled her eyes. She should have known it would be impossible to avoid anything connected with Cody Jones today. It was a game day.

'Isn't he something?' Karen said from the other end of the table. 'I was worried after we lost so many players to graduation, but I think we've got a shot to repeat as Division III champs.'

The guy was something, all right. Brynn bit her tongue to keep quiet. After the stunt he'd pulled on her – giving her his shirt because he'd known she'd run into Rex. She felt her happy day start to disintegrate, and she reached out and grabbed Trini's beer. The Latino girl's eyebrows rose when she took a long swallow.

'JJ Stone is going deep,' the announcer said excitedly. 'There's the pass . . . and it's caught! He's at the twenty, the fifteen . . . Bremer makes a last ditch dive. Touchdown! Touchdown, Southern Trinity.'

The bar exploded into cheers.

'Yes!' Hannah screeched.

Brynn couldn't help but smile. You could take the girl off the sidelines, but you couldn't take the cheerleader out of the girl.

'That was a great call by Jones,' the announcer declared. 'He caught Midwestern sitting back on their heels.'

Jones this, Jones that. Brynn took another drink of Trini's beer, and the girl finally poured herself a fresh glass.

'Didn't I tell you?' Jimmy bragged. He nodded at her conspiratorially. 'Your boyfriend's a keeper.'

Brynn paused with her beer lifted halfway. 'My what?'

'Your boyfriend,' Hannah said. 'Coach Jones.'

Brynn stared at her blankly. 'He's not my boyfriend!'

'Oh.' Hannah looked quickly at Jimmy. 'We thought he was.'

Brynn noticed other looks being passed among her squad. She set down her mug slowly. 'You thought that we were involved?'

Karen shrugged. 'We've seen the way he looks at you.'

'And the way you look at him,' Jimmy added.

'I don't look at him.'

'Yes, you do,' Hannah said. 'We have it on tape.'

Brynn glared at her captain from across the table. There would be no talk about that infamous tape. It was sitting on her kitchen table right now, but soon, it wouldn't even exist.

'What tape?' Trini said, her natural inquisitiveness asserting herself. 'What is it, a sex video?'

Brynn's beer went down the wrong way, and she began coughing. 'No! No sex ... *hack* ... video.'

'But I'm on the right track. I can tell.' Trini looked around the table. 'What's on the tape? Some hanky panky? A little hoochy coochy? Come on, someone tell me.'

Brynn set down her mug as Jimmy pounded her on the back. Still wheezing, she patted her lips with her napkin. 'It was nothing.'

Hannah leaned toward Trini conspiratorially. 'It was something.'

'Hannah,' Brynn warned.

Her captain ignored her. 'We were practising stunts the other day, and Coach Jones came over to lift Coach Montgomery. It was one of the sexiest, most romantic things I ever saw.'

'Romantic?' Brynn squawked.

Hannah's hand went to her heart. 'He told her that if anyone was going to make her fly, it would be him.'

Trini's mouth rounded, and they both took dramatic deep breaths of air. 'Ohhh,' they sighed dreamily.

'That clumsy ox nearly dropped me,' Brynn insisted.

It was too late to stop Hannah; she was in full gossip mode. She put her head close to Trini's and began talking so fast, she almost didn't stop to breathe. 'He was so strong. I mean, my knees went weak just watching him. His technique is rough, but we all knew he'd never let her fall. Every time she teetered, he was right there to catch her. Oh! And you should have seen the way the muscles in his arms worked every time he caught her to his chest.'

'Would you stop?' Brynn knocked her heavy mug of beer against the table, but nobody heard her over the laughter.

Hannah's voice dropped to a stage whisper. 'There were definitely some moments when grabby hands caught places they shouldn't – at least not in front of other people.'

'Hannah!'

'Oooo,' Trini said. 'Sounds like fun.'

'When he finally did get the hang of it, there was no stopping him. He pushed her up into the full elevator like he was lifting a feather.' Hannah's shoulders relaxed, and her eyes went moony. 'He's such a hunk.'

'God, isn't he?' Trini said. She lifted her hands, palms upward. 'Have you ever noticed the way his shorts cup his cute tight ass? It makes my fingers itch.'

'Hey!' Brynn said.

'What? Can't a girl look?' Trini said innocently. 'I thought there was nothing going on between you two.'

'There's not,' Brynn said huffily. She looked around at her squad and found them all staring at her. She raked a hand through her hair. 'If you must know, Coach Jones and I went to school together.'

'Did you date?' Jimmy asked.

'No.'

'Why not?' Trini asked boldly.

'Because I was dating someone else.'

'Why?' Hannah said, showing uncharacteristic forwardness.

Brynn's eyes narrowed. Maybe having Trini around wasn't such a good thing.

'Because ... Well, just because I was. Cody and I have always rubbed each other the wrong way.'

'We saw the rubbing,' Jimmy said. He wiggled his eyebrows. 'Looked like a lot of sparks to me.'

'Ugh,' Brynn growled. Frustrated, she reached up to rub her temples. She couldn't deny that Cody knew how to draw a response out of her. He'd always been able to do that. She forced the hot memories from her mind. 'This really is none of your business.'

'Shhhh!' Karen said. 'Listen! There's only eighteen seconds left.'

'There's the snap,' the announcer said. 'Jones has

called a full-out blitz! Here comes Southern Trinity. The quarterback is scrambling. He's out of the pocket. And there's Jetson. He takes him down, and there's a fumble!'

'Fumble!' Karen yelled.

Hannah slapped her hands on the table. 'Get it. Get it!'

'Jetson recovers. It's Southern Trinity's ball on the thirty-five yard line.'

'Yes!' High fives were exchanged all around. Brynn was just happy the attention had been diverted from her. She took another drink as everyone went silent to listen.

'This is a major turn in momentum, folks,' the announcer said. 'We've got four seconds left before the game goes into overtime. There's just time for Southern Trinity to try to kick a field goal. It will be a long one.'

'Who's the kicker?' Hannah asked, looking around at everyone.

'Pattagowski,' Karen said with a quieting wave of her hand.

'Pattagowski. That's it. Come on, Patty.'

Even though she'd told herself she wouldn't get caught up in the game, Brynn found herself reaching for her necklace.

'There's the snap. It's clean. The ball is up ... And it's good! Field goal. Southern Trinity wins!'

The bar exploded with yells of triumph. Hannah even hugged Trini when the girl threw her arms around her.

'What an amazing game, folks. That blitz call at the end was key,' the announcer said. 'Jones won it right there. It was a risky play, but it paid off. Midwestern Texas falls to Southern Trinity by a score of 31 to 28.'

Brynn listened with half an ear as the announcer recapped the statistics of the game. That was enough for her. The pizza was gone, and she'd drunk more beer than she'd had in the past two years. It would be best to leave now before she had to answer any more insinuating questions.

'Coach Jones,' the announcer said. 'Great game.'

'Thanks, Phil.'

She hesitated as she reached for her purse. Cody's voice sounded even lower coming across the airwaves.

'What can you tell us about that blitz call? What made you think Midwestern was vulnerable?'

'Hey, it's the coach!' Hannah said excitedly.

Brynn opened her purse and pulled out money to cover her share of lunch. Vulnerabilities? Give her a break. The man could scope out vulnerabilities like a vulture.

'It just made sense,' Cody said, raising his voice to make it audible over the rumble of the crowd. 'Jets had been beating his man the entire game, so I told him he just had to get by him one more time. He was hungry for a sack, and he got one.'

Brynn pushed her chair back and waved goodbye to her squad.

'Did you have any doubts that you'd come away with a victory today?'

'None.'

His tone was so confident, everyone in the bar snickered except Brynn. She'd had more than one brush with the Jones ego. She stood to go.

'What made you so sure?'

'A friend gave me a good luck charm yesterday. I couldn't lose.'

She froze before she could walk away. He couldn't be talking about her! That was private, and this was public radio. Hastily, she looked around the room. There were people listening.

'Must have been some kind of charm,' the announcer said with a laugh.

'Believe me, it was.'

She sat back down hard. Trini noticed the look on her face and elbowed Hannah. The blonde glanced over her shoulder, and her eyebrows lowered. Brynn tried to make herself stand and leave, but her legs suddenly wouldn't work. Heat pooled between them, and she pressed her thighs together hard.

Don't do this, Cody. Don't you dare!

'Well, congratulations on another win, Coach.'

'Thanks, Phil.'

She let out a breath of relief. Damn that man!

'And Brynnie?'

She jolted when she heard her name.

'Thank you.'

Trini and Hannah exchanged a glance, and Brynn suddenly found herself surrounded by cheerleaders. She let out a groan and lowered her face into her hands.

'Nothing going on?' Jimmy said.

'I don't think so,' Hannah said smugly.

Trini leaned closer, and Brynn felt smothered.

'One thing's for sure,' the new girl said. 'If there isn't, there certainly should be.'

Brynn opened one eye cautiously.

Trini sighed and patted her gently on the head. 'And, honey, you know it.'

Cody sat in a seat at the front of the bus and looked out the window at the darkness. Behind him, he could hear the team still reliving the game. Plays were being recalled, and the heroics just kept getting bigger and bigger. Normally, he would have sat there laughing at his players and relaxing from a long week.

Not tonight.

Tonight, his concentration was elsewhere – and it wasn't on the broken white line going down the middle of the long, Texas interstate.

Brynn had gone to Palmer College yesterday. Palmer, Goddammit it.

His fingers resting near the window curled into a fist. The only way he'd gotten through the past day was by concentrating on the game. Now that it was over, though, his attention was right back where it had been riveted before.

On Brynn.

He rubbed his knuckles against the window and watched the condensation roll down the pane. Why did she always fight him so hard? Didn't she understand how good they could be together?

He closed his eyes and saw again the languor that had crossed her face when he'd taken her bra and fondled her breast. Her eyelids had been heavy, her lips had been parted, and her expression . . . She'd looked stunned, but hungry for him. Passion that strong was rare.

He wanted to put that look on her face over and over and over again.

And he would – if that son-of-a-bitch Stanton hadn't already gotten in the way.

'Rich bastard,' he growled, tapping hard against the window.

'You say something, Coach?' Jetson asked from the seat behind him.

'Nah, nothing,' Cody said, shifting in his seat. 'You got an extra Coke back there?'

A cold can of soda was passed up from several aisles back. Cody popped the top and wiped his hand on the empty seat next to him when it fizzed over the top. Sitting back, he took a long drink.

Rex Stanton. The asshole still knew how to push his buttons.

And he knew how to push Brynn's, too. That was what had Cody worried. She claimed she hadn't seen the guy in the past ten years, but he had. The preppy mama's boy hadn't changed one bit. If anything, he was even more spoiled and self-centred now than he had been back in school.

Cody ran a hand through his hair. He was going to drive himself nuts if he kept thinking about this, but damn it, what had happened yesterday? Had she seen the guy? Had they spoken?

Had Rex pulled his mind games on her again?

'Damn it.' Of course he had. That had been the basis of their entire relationship, although Brynn had never been able to see it. Rex had used her like a trophy. He'd wanted a pretty blonde cheerleader on his arm, and he'd gotten her.

But he hadn't *had* her.

'Brynnie,' Cody whispered as he rubbed his tired eyes.

Maybe he was worrying about nothing. It had been a computer symposium; Rex would have had no business there. The chances of the two of them running into each other were small, practically infinitesimal.

And that was why his gut was screaming – because every time he thought his chances with her were good, Rex's were better.

'Goddamn son-of-a-bitch. This time, you're not getting her.'

The sound of constant pounding woke Brynn from a dead sleep. Groaning, she rolled over on the bed and covered her ears.

What was that?

The sound refused to go away. Irritated, she sat up in

bed and pushed her hair back from her face. Her tired mind finally figured out that some idiot was knocking on her neighbour's door.

'Oh, come on!' she said as she pressed her fingers against her temples. How inconsiderate could a person be?

Her patience snapped. She pushed her feet over the edge of the bed and grabbed her robe. She slipped it over her shoulders as she stomped to the living room. Somebody was going to get a piece of her mind.

'Drunken fool,' she muttered.

Her bare feet padded across the carpeting as her mind worked up various forms of verbal attack. She came up short, though, when the pounding became louder the closer she got to her door.

No, it couldn't be.

The drunken fool was at her door!

Uneasiness shot down her spine, and she unconsciously took a step back. Her hand went to her chest as she looked around the room. Should she call the police? Was it the police?

She lowered her hand from her pounding heart and snatched up a brass candlestick from her coffee table. Steeling herself, she quickly crossed the room to the door just off the kitchen. She had to take three deep breaths before she could summon the nerve to look out the peephole.

A large figure was on the other side. Her heart slammed into her throat and she pulled away so fast, she didn't take time to see if she recognised the person. Gritting her teeth, she inched towards the door again.

She went up on her tiptoes and stole another glance. 'Cody?' she said, stunned.

Hurriedly, she reached for the door handle. Her neighbours were already bound to complain in the morning.

She didn't want to hear from them now. She left the chain on as she pulled the door open a few slight inches. 'Cody?' she hissed.

'It's about time you answered. My knuckles are raw.'

The tension swept out of her body, and Brynn sagged against the door. She pushed it shut to take off the chain, but then whipped it open. 'What are you doing here?' she snapped as she reached out, grabbed him by the arm, and pulled him inside.

She looked up and down the brightly lit hallway and was relieved to find it empty. She slapped the switch to turn on the lights inside her apartment and shut the door securely behind her. 'Do you know what time it is?'

'It's around 1.30,' he said over his shoulder as he walked into her apartment and made himself at home. He tossed something onto her breakfast bar and reached up to rub the back of his neck. 'The team bus just got back.'

Brynn's brain wasn't functioning at high speed yet. She looked at the breakfast bar and then back to him. A double take finally brought recognition to the sack on the counter. 'You came here at 1.30 in the morning to bring me Kettle Korn?'

He turned and shrugged. 'It's still your favourite, isn't it?'

'Well, yes.'

'I tasted it when I kissed you after last week's game.' His weary gaze dropped to her mouth. 'Salty and sweet. It's an irresistible combination.'

'Are you out of your mind?' She saw the candlestick in her hand and slammed it down onto the table. 'Why are you here? Really.'

He just stared at her.

She waited for a long moment, but still he said

nothing. Brynn pulled the tie on her robe a little tighter. He was starting to make her nervous. Something was bothering him, that much she could tell. Tension radiated off him in waves.

'Cody?' she said quietly.

His dark gaze suddenly pinned her. 'What happened at Palmer?'

Her stomach dropped. Oh, God. He couldn't know. How could he know? 'The symposium was good,' she said carefully. 'I brought back a lot of things for JJ.'

'Damn it, Brynn!'

His whole body went taut, and her weight went to the balls of her feet. He turned away from her and laced his fingers together at the back of his neck. She could see the breaths working in and out of his lungs.

'You know what I'm talking about,' he said in an eerily quiet voice. It sounded louder than his outburst. 'Did you see him?'

The word 'who' was on the tip of her tongue, but she held it back. They both knew who. 'Yes,' she said.

Her fingers cinched her robe tighter when he slowly turned around to face her. His face was filled with anger, but there was something else there, something she couldn't quite place. It was almost as if his face had lost colour.

'What did he do?' he asked.

Her throat went dry. She couldn't have this conversation. 'It's none of your business.'

There was a reason Cody had been known for his speed in the pros. He was suddenly in front of her before she could draw another breath. 'Say that again, but this time, look me in the eye.'

Her gaze stuck to the middle of his chest. She tried to swallow past the dryness in her throat, but her saliva had suddenly gone dry. She shivered as she forced her gaze up to meet his. His stare was so hot and intense, it went right through her.

'You knew he'd be there,' she said raspily. 'Why didn't you warn me?'

His Adam's apple bobbed. 'What did he do?'

'Nothing,' she snapped. 'He was just upset to see me. Can you blame him?'

'Blame him?' Cody said with a sudden expulsion of air. He leaned forward and braced his hands on the breakfast bar behind her. His dark stare bored into her. 'I should have known. That son-of-a-bitch turned it all back on you, didn't he? That fucking manipulator.'

Her jaw dropped. 'Manipulator? You're one to talk. What do you call what you did to me yesterday in that meeting room?'

He went still, and Brynn hesitated. Why in God's name had she brought that up?

His blue eyes twinkled with dangerously. 'Do you need a word for it? I stroked you, baby. I kissed you. I stripped you.'

'Stop it.'

He leaned in closer. 'What did Rex say to you? Damn it, I think I have a right to know.'

She turned and tried to push his arm out of her way. 'Leave. I want you to go.'

He caught her about the waist, but didn't move any further than that. When she risked a glance at him, she saw a muscle ticking in his jaw.

'Please,' he said.

She stopped fighting. There had been sincerity in his voice.

He took a deep breath. 'Let me guess,' he said tiredly. 'He acted like the betrayed party. He pissed and moaned about how bad you made him feel oh so long ago, and you fell for it.'

'He was the betrayed party!'

That dangerous look re-entered Cody's eyes, but the hand on her waist was gentle. 'Just don't tell me he made you cry,' he said in a voice that cut like steel. 'Because I swear if he did, I'm driving over there right now to kick his preppy ass.'

The muscles in his forearm flexed. Brynn didn't doubt him at his word. 'It wasn't like that,' she said quietly.

She had to look away from his intense gaze. It hadn't been like that at all, but if he ever found out ... She stared at a picture on the wall and toyed with the ends of her robe sash. His edgy mood was making her nervous. He and Rex had gone at it before over her, and it hadn't been pretty.

His fingers moved against her waist. 'He dragged you through the mud again. I can see it.'

She shifted her weight uncomfortably. 'We talked about ... what happened.'

'And he twisted everything around to make you feel like trash.'

The words were clipped, and Brynn flinched with every one of them. They were true, but that didn't mean she hadn't deserved it. 'He was right about everything. What happened between you and me was unforgivable. I had to apologise.'

'You apologised?' Cody said, his voice going dangerously low. 'For what we did?'

'Of course.'

The silence was nearly deafening.

'Just what do you remember about that night, Brynn?' he finally asked.

'You know what I remember.'

'No,' he said slowly. 'I don't think I do. Why don't you tell me?'

Brynn's dry throat worked. It had been bad enough

to go through it with Rex; she wasn't going to do it again with Cody. 'No,' she said. 'You can't barge in here in the middle of the night and badger me like this. Get out.'

She gasped when his hands tightened on her waist. She pushed at his forearms, but she was met with rock hard muscles that wouldn't yield. He picked her up off of her feet, turned, and dropped her unceremoniously on the couch. Before she could bounce up and scurry away, he lowered himself onto the coffee table in front of her. His legs brushed the outside of hers as he settled his elbows on his knees.

She wasn't going anywhere.

'Tell me,' he repeated. 'Tell me everything you remember about that night – every sound, every touch, every taste. And don't even think about leaving out anything, because remember, Brynnie, I was there.'

8

Ten years earlier

There was a spring in Brynn's step as she walked down the hallway of the dorm. Her pompons swished as she swung her arms, and the sound made her smile. The Trojans had won! She could still hardly believe it. Her voice was nearly gone from screaming so loudly. She couldn't remember the last game that had been so exciting – and Rex had been the hero!

Well, technically he and Cody had shared in the big passing play that had won the game. It was enough to make her shake her head. She didn't understand how the two of them could play a stupid game together so well when they could hardly stand each other as roommates.

It didn't matter, she supposed. All the fighting and tension would be over soon, and they'd just have to deal with each other on the field. Rex had decided to move out at the end of the month. It would be best for everyone, because things had really gotten out of control.

She'd tried to act as a buffer between the two of them, but she'd ended up feeling she was part of the problem rather than the solution. She didn't know why, but Cody Jones put her on edge. There was just some-thing about the way he looked at her. He was always there – watching and waiting. Her nerves always went on high alert whenever he was around, and she didn't like the hot and jittery feelings he caused. It would be a relief when Rex got his own apartment. Until then, though, it was the dorm for everyone.

Her steps quickened along the fifth floor hallway. It was quiet for a Saturday night; everyone must be out partying after the big win. She hoped that Rex was home. She didn't know where else to look for him. She'd wanted to be the first to congratulate him after the game, but she'd missed him at the field.

She knocked on the door without much hope and was pleasantly surprised when it swung open. 'You're home,' she said as she stepped inside.

The room was pitch black. Automatically, she reached out for the desk so she wouldn't run into the corner. Clouds had even doused the moonlight. She couldn't see an inch in front of her face.

'What are you doing sitting in the dark?' she teased.

'Waiting for you.'

Brynn flinched and laughed at herself. He was closer than she thought, and his voice was even hoarser than hers. No wonder. He'd had to make all those calls over the roar of the crowd. She giggled when he closed the door behind her and caught her by the waist.

'Congratulations on the game. You were great.'

A tiny spark of excitement lit her belly when she put her hands on his chest and found it bare. His fingers spread wide across her back, and she could feel his heat as he loomed over her. She went up on tiptoe to kiss him. Their lips met with uncanny accuracy, and her heart did a crazy little dip.

Oh my! That was ... *Wow*. She didn't know if it was the adrenaline or the darkness, but his kiss was different. It made her feel all melty inside. He nudged her backwards, and her feet stumbled over each other until the door pressed at her back. He slowly broke off the kiss, but his weight kept her firmly trapped.

'Whew,' she said.

'Like that?'

Was he kidding?

'You know I did.'

'Want more?'

Her lips curled upwards. She'd never known Rex to ask. 'Yes, please,' she laughed.

Her giggle was cut short when his mouth settled hard over hers. Brynn's heart exploded into double time when his tongue pressed at the seam of her lips. She was so stunned, she did nothing to stop him when it pried her mouth open and sought entrance.

A low moan gurgled up from her throat, and her pompons whooshed to the floor. She'd always gotten nervous when he'd come on this strong before, but tonight ... tonight, the temptation was stronger than her uneasiness.

'Mm,' she sighed. She reached for him and found hard muscles and bare skin. Oh, he felt so good. She wrapped her arms around him as he ate at her mouth, and let her hands run up and down his back. His muscles clenched and released under her touch, and the sensitive pads of her fingers felt raw.

Breathing hard, Brynn turned her head away from his kiss. She'd let Rex do things before, but this was on an entirely different plane. The dark, seductive pull of it scared her.

'Whoa,' she panted. 'Maybe we should slow down.'

His agile tongue dipped into her ear, and her shoulders clenched at the hot shivers that coursed down her neck.

'Maybe we shouldn't,' he whispered into her ear.

He suddenly pulled her away from the door, and she clutched at his shoulders for balance. It was so dark.

Their legs tangled as he walked backwards to the couch. Like all dorm rooms, there wasn't much space. It only took a few steps before they were there.

The sofa was one of those cheap foam foldout varieties. Still nibbling on the lobe of her ear, he reached out blindly and caught the seat cushion. She heard it unfold and plop to the floor, and her palms went damp.

'Relax, Brynnie,' he whispered as he kissed the side of her neck.

She went with him when he lowered himself to the flat mattress. She had to. Her legs suddenly didn't feel so steady.

He rolled, and suddenly she found herself flat on her back. Her heart beat hard against her ribcage and nearly broke through when his hand found its way underneath the sweater of her cheerleading uniform.

Brynn couldn't see a thing, but she could feel – and the feelings were sinful. She felt the brush of his calloused fingers against her naked belly. She felt the hot puffs of his breaths against her neck.

She felt the darkness tugging at her.

She reached for him, but instead of pushing him away, her fingers threaded through his hair. They clenched tight when both his hands burrowed underneath the hem of her sweater.

'Oh!' she gasped.

He'd slid them right under the cups of her bra! The straps pulled hard against her shoulders, and the hooks dug into the middle of her spine. Her back bowed. His hands!

She caught at him, and her fingers wrapped around his muscled forearms. He moved, and she felt dominated as he straddled her and settled back onto his haunches. Scared with how fast things were moving, she turned her head away. There wasn't even a moon outside the window. The darkness was gaining strength. It tugged at her, making her feel things she shouldn't.

'Do you feel it, Brynnie? The want, the *need*?'

'Yes,' she whispered.

His hands began to squeeze. They didn't caress or tease. Instead, they went right to the heavy petting. His fingers moulded and shaped her and became even more insistent when they plucked hard at her tender nipples. Her fingernails bit into his forearms. It was too much.

'Ahhhh,' she cried. His grip on her tightened to the point where it was almost painful. Her neck arched in pleasure, and her legs worked helplessly.

'Harder?' he whispered close to her ear as he leaned over to her.

No! She couldn't stand it.

'Yes,' she begged.

'What do you need?'

'I . . . Oh God. I don't know!' She'd never let him get this far before.

His teeth raked softly over her earlobe. 'I've got some ideas.'

He suddenly let go of her. Her breasts ached at the loss, and she reached for him. He crooned soft, scandalous words to her as he caught her sweater and pulled it over her head. He tossed it away, and something clunked as it was knocked over.

Her bra hung limply by the stretched-out straps, and Brynn reached to cover herself. She didn't know why she was suddenly so shy. It was dark, and her bra certainly hadn't offered any resistance to him up till now. Still, her teeth caught her lip when he reached underneath her.

He undid the hooks, and her bra went flying into the dark recesses of the room. She started to say something

– anything to slow him down – but the words lodged in her throat when his mouth was suddenly upon her. An open-mouthed kiss pressed against the side of her breast, and she felt the scratch of teeth.

Desire hit hard in her belly and swirled outwards. Her nipple tightened in anticipation, but he circled around it, kissing, licking, and sucking until she thought she'd go crazy.

'So soft,' he murmured.

She didn't know where to put her hands. One found its way to the hard muscles of his back. The other wove uncertainly through the hair at the back of his head. Need coursed through her, sharp and intense.

'Please,' she said.

His hot tongue licked firmly across her stiff nipple, and she cried out. He did it again, and her hand fisted in his hair. She pulled him to her, and he latched on. His mouth opened wide, taking her nipple deep, and began to tug hard.

Brynn whimpered and squirmed underneath him. The pleasure was fiercer than anything she'd ever known. He moved to her other breast, and she lifted her shoulder to offer it up to him eagerly. He sought it in the darkness, and she lifted her hand to guide herself to him.

'Fuck!' he groaned when he finally came up for air.

The world suddenly spun, and Brynn gasped. 'What's wrong?'

He'd rolled her onto her stomach. Anxiously, she propped herself up onto her elbows. It was unnerving to feel his imposing presence behind her in the darkness.

'Nothing's wrong. For once, everything's right.'

She went still when he flipped up the back of her skirt.

With that small movement, things became much more personal and revealing than she'd ever dreamed.

They were rushing rapidly towards sex, but this wasn't how she'd imagined her first time. There were no sheets to hide under. The room wasn't lit with glowing candles and soft music wasn't filling the air. Instead, she was half-naked on a bare mattress in a pitch-black room. A heavy metal band screeched from speakers somewhere one floor up, and the air felt hot and cloying. Their harsh breaths echoed off the closed-in walls, and her skin felt damp with perspiration.

Darkness seeped around her and into her, frightening her – yet thrilling her at the same time. She couldn't see him, but she could feel his weight pressing hard against her thighs as he straddled her. Not knowing where he was going to touch, how, or when . . . It was terrifying.

And provocative.

She went a little crazy when his fingers wrapped around the waistband of her underwear and began tugging downwards.

'No, you can't!' she gasped. Frantically, she reached back and caught his wrist. Things were moving into unknown territory much too quickly for her.

'I've got to get at you,' he said in a strained voice. His hand settled on the small of her back and pressed her down to the mattress. 'Relax, Brynnie. It will be good.'

She closed her eyes and pressed her forehead against the back of her hand. She felt . . . *slutty*. Her breasts were flattened against the bare pullout mattress. There was no bedding to even give this encounter the hint of a seduction. Worse, her nipples felt raw against the coarse fabric. She squirmed helplessly as he caught her cheaters more firmly.

'Lift.'

She closed her eyelids tightly, but pressed her knees down and lifted her hips.

'Two pairs of panties?' he said as his hands explored her silk bikinis. 'You are virtuous.'

Calling her attention to her inexperience wasn't helping to ease her nerves. 'They're cheaters,' she said shakily. 'It's part of the cheerleading uniform.'

'Oh, I get it,' he chuckled as he pulled the stretchy blue fabric down her legs and over her tennis shoes. 'In case your skirt flies up.'

Her cheeks went hot. Her skirt was up now.

Her fingers clenched into fists when he caught the remaining barrier that separated them. Her panties slowly began sliding down over her curves. The air hitting her bare buttocks made her shiver, even though it was hot. Everything in the room was hot. The air, her cheeks, his hands . . .

'Oh God.' She ground her forehead more tightly against the back of her hand. 'Oh, God!'

'Come on now, lift for me and let me get them off.'

She cut off a cry at the back of her throat.

'That's a good girl. Come on, Goody.'

Her panties clung to her ankles, and he nearly had to rip them to get them over her shoes. She didn't know why he didn't take those off, too, but he left them in place. She was so happy she couldn't see herself. She could only imagine how lurid she looked with her skirt around her waist, but her preppy white ankle socks and shoes firmly in place.

She nearly stopped breathing when he caught her ankles and spread her legs wide.

'I can't. I can't,' she moaned.

But she wanted to.

'You can, and you're going to,' he whispered.

He settled between her legs, and her hips rocked convulsively when his big rough hands settled over her bare ass. He began squeezing and shaping her, and her shrill short cries bounced off the walls of the room.

He scooted up closer, and his knees nudged her legs open even wider. The denim of his jeans felt rough against the inside of her thighs. Brynn sputtered a protest, but the words came out sounding more like encouragement.

She'd never dreamed of anything so wicked, and she clung to the darkness for protection. This position – it was lascivious. She was on her belly with her legs spread wide. The hot air was brushing against parts of her that rarely saw air. Her pussy clenched and released as if it had been starved for the oxygen.

'How do you want it, Goody?' he asked in a low voice. 'Slow and easy or hard and rough?'

Her throat clenched. How should she know? Slow and easy sounded better, although that would take longer. He'd drag it out, and she didn't know if her heart could stand it. It might be better to get it over quickly, but could her pussy stand hard and rough?

Her face flushed, and she concentrated on simply breathing. She'd never had such naughty thoughts in her life.

'Any way you can get it, huh?' he said.

His hands were still having their way with her ass, but she reared up and twisted around when his thumbs slipped into the crevice. 'Oh, please,' she begged. 'Don't –'

Her protest was cut off when he caught her by the back of the neck. His mouth covered hers in the darkness and held her in the contorted position as his thumb continued its explorations.

'Don't?' he asked.

Her entire body quivered when he boldly rubbed her anus.

'Maybe I should take you here,' he said as he ate at her lips.

'No,' she almost sobbed. 'Not there. Not for my first time.'

The pad of his thumb stilled on top of the pursed bud, and his lips pulled back a millimetre from hers. 'First time?'

Brynn wanted to just die. 'You know I've never done this before.'

'Never?' The grip at the back of her neck tightened.

The twisted position was beginning to become uncomfortable, but he held her put. Brynn squirmed helplessly as that inappropriately placed hand finally moved. The pressure against her anus was relieved, but her thigh muscles clenched when his touch dipped lower. There was no hiding from that seeking hand.

'A virgin,' he said with wonder as his finger gently stroked and probed the contours of her pussy.

Brynn forgot to keep breathing, and her ribcage expanded with pressure. He rimmed her opening and the air exploded out of her lungs when he determinedly pushed a finger inside. 'Ah,' she panted. 'Ah, ah!'

The hand at the back of her neck gentled. 'Lay down, Goody,' he whispered. 'Open up and relax.'

Relax? His finger was jammed up inside her!

Her morals surged inside of her. Sex wasn't something someone should go into so lightly. The decision should be preceded by long thought and deliberation. She shouldn't let this happen.

Gravity, though, pulled her back to the mattress. She was quickly finding that sex had nothing to do with thought and everything to do with animal desire. She clutched at the edge of the mattress as his finger became bolder. It circled inside her, exploring the wet tightness and probing ever deeper.

'I'll be damned,' he whispered. His finger stilled, lodged deeply inside of her.

Brynn's heart was beating way too fast, and she couldn't get enough oxygen. He leaned up over her, and his hot chest pressed heavily against her naked back. She moaned when he buried his face against her neck.

'You're mine, Brynn Montgomery. *Mine.*'

He pulled back, and her body quaked. He was only touching her in that one, secret place, but that one place was enough. His finger swirled, and her back bowed. 'Mine,' he repeated.

He slowly pulled out of her, and her pussy fluttered. Even after he was gone, it clutched for him. Brynn pressed her eyes together so tightly colours began to dance behind her eyelids. The feelings ricocheting inside her were powerful.

She wanted to be his – in every sense of the word.

'Mmmff,' she cried on a burst of air when his hands suddenly slid under her. He took the weight at her hipbones and began lifting her into the air. 'What ... What are you doing? Oh, my God. Oh, my God!'

Her legs swung recklessly as they left the mattress. The only resting place for them was on his shoulders. She cried out sharply when that placed his face directly against her crotch. Blood rushed to her head as her weight was transferred up to her shoulders. 'No,' she said impulsively. 'Not like this. Can't we start with something ... something *normal*?'

His breath bathed her pussy in heat. 'Let's start with something memorable.'

She braced herself on her forearms and let out another cry when he gave her an intimate kiss.

What he was doing was unimaginable – at least to her. He'd contorted her into a position where she couldn't avoid his touch. Or his tongue. Waves of reaction buffeted her when he began to lick her. Is this what people did in the privacy of their own bedrooms? It felt absolutely depraved.

She couldn't believe that he was doing it. That she was letting him do it.

And that she liked it.

Her fingers raked across the bare mattress, looking for a handhold. 'Like' was such a tame, unemotional word. It didn't come close to the emotions roiling inside her chest.

'Mmm,' he murmured when her thighs clenched at his ears.

His grip adjusted her hips, and Brynn clenched her teeth when her breasts bounced. They were swinging freely with their nipples turgid and waiting. She nearly reached down to ease their distress, but with the way her weight was balanced on her elbows, it was nearly impossible.

Smacking sounds came from between her legs. He was practically eating at her now. He tugged her skirt so it covered his head, and his mouth became more voracious. He licked, kissed and sucked in the most shameful, greedy way. 'You taste like honey,' he growled as he nipped at her.

Brynn's world was quickly spinning out of control. Her pussy had hardly ever been bared before. She could hardly stand the duress it was under now. She was swelling down there; she could feel it. Her pussy lips were so sensitive; the bristle of the whiskers on his face was making her squirm. Her juices were pouring from her, making everything sticky. She gasped for air as her body surged and swayed.

He took a soft bite of her ass. 'You're hungry for it,' he growled. 'You're hungry for *me*.'

He let his shoulders take her weight as his hands

reached forward to catch her breasts. The moment his hands cupped her, Brynn knew it was over for her. She couldn't fight him anymore. She couldn't fight herself anymore.

She wasn't prepared, but she wanted this – and he wasn't going to let her get away without taking it.

Her toes curled inside her shoes, and her legs bent at the knees when his tongue began toying with that sensitive little bud at the apex of her pussy.

'Like that?' he growled, his voice a husky rasp.

'Yes,' she whined. 'Yes!'

His mouth closed over her clit, and her entire body went rigid as he began to suckle. His fingers clamped down on her nipples, and stars danced behind her eyes.

'Come for me, Brynnie. I want to feel you explode against my mouth.'

'Oh, oh, oh,' she panted in rhythm with his tugs. Her body was careening upwards with a force that scared her.

'So sweet,' he said with a suggestive lick. 'So fucking sweet.'

She was there. Shivers racked her body. Her hips lifted up to his mouth as his hands ground her breasts in tight circles. 'Oh, oh my! Ahhhh. Help me!'

'You can do it. Come on, Goody. Come for me.'

She blanked her mind and felt herself spiral up that last peak.

The sound of keys clinking outside the door had her skidding sharply backwards.

'No!' he said more harshly between her legs.

His tongue pressed deeply, spreading her tight pussy, and her back arched. Her head snapped to the side, though, when a key slid into the lock.

'No! He can't see us like this,' she gasped in horror.

Cody was about to walk in on something incredibly private. She couldn't bear to let him find her like this. Not him!

Her muscles clenched as the tumblers of the lock clicked into place. There was nowhere to run, nowhere to hide. She couldn't even move from the position Rex had manoeuvred her into.

'No!' she called out when the door swung open. Light spilled into the room. 'Go away, Co–'

The name caught in her throat, because it wasn't his name!

Her mind froze. It wasn't Cody standing in the open doorway with two of his teammates. It was Rex.

The world tilted crazily on its axis. If Rex was standing there . . .

Brynn nearly had an aneurysm. Oh, dear God!!!

Bracing herself on one forearm, she reached back and pulled up her skirt to see who was sucking on her pussy.

Over the curve of her buttocks, she discovered brown eyes levelled on her face – and the look in them was determined. The suction of his mouth increased to an insufferable pressure, and his tongue batted her clit.

He wasn't going to stop!

'No!' she gasped. 'Cody!'

It was too late, and she was too close. There, in front of Rex and two of their teammates, he sucked her off. She watched the men in the doorway helplessly until they became a blur. She was horrified to be caught out in the open at such an intimate time, but there was nothing she could do about it. She moaned in regret, but her breasts quivered and her tennis shoes pointed to the sky.

The moan slid into an excited cry as she came, and came hard.

'You fucking son-of-a-bitch!' Rex roared. He'd been stunned momentarily into paralysis, but with her cry, he burst into the room.

Cody lifted a forearm to protect himself as Rex came at him swinging. Brynn dropped to the mattress and her ass jiggled when she bounced. She lay there frozen with her legs spread wide and her skirt around her waist as the two men scuffled hardly a foot from her feet.

She couldn't move. Couldn't even think. The erogenous zones of her body still pulsed, and the world was fuzzy.

Cody Jones had just screwed the daylights out of her.

Cody Jones! And with his mouth!

The sound of fists crashing against flesh made her cringe. Gingerly, she pushed herself up onto her elbows and looked over her shoulder. Rex and Cody were beating each other to bloody pulps and, although Cody had been caught unprepared, he seemed to be getting the better of the draw.

A sound at the doorway reminded her that they weren't alone. Scrambling upward on the couch, she clamped her arm over her dangling breasts and yanked her skirt down over her wet, blonde curls. When she looked at the door, to her horror, there weren't just two men. The entire dorm floor was crammed into the tiny hallway, struggling to get a look at her and the fight.

'You motherfucker!' Rex roared.

Cody blocked the right cross and buried his fist in his roommate's belly. 'Get it right, asshole. I'm a cheerleader fucker.'

Rex fought for air, but instead of buckling over, he rushed forward. He tackled Cody, and a chair went flying as they both crashed to the ground.

Brynn was mortified. How much had everyone seen? How much could they see now?

And Rex! Tears pressed at her eyes. How was she ever going to explain this to him?

The two men rolled around on the floor, fighting to get the dominant position. Cody cursed when his head banged into a desk leg.

Brynn didn't know what to do. She wanted the fight to stop. She wanted to get out of the room and run away. She wanted the men at the door to stop ogling her.

She wanted to change what she'd just done with Cody!

For God's sake, she'd just given him her innocence. She was still technically a virgin, but did it matter?

Her teeth bit into her lip so hard, she nearly drew blood. How had she not known it was him?

'Rex, I'm sorry,' she sobbed.

'Sorry?' he yelled. He tried to slam his knee against Cody's privates. 'You fucking cunt! How long have you been doing this creep behind my back?'

Her face went white. 'I haven't,' she swore.

Laughter came from the doorway, and her head snapped to the side. It was one of the football players who'd seen her at her most vulnerable.

'Looked like you were pretty experienced to me,' he laughed. 'Hell, my girlfriend won't do half of that.'

Brynn's pulse began pounding so hard at her temples, she felt faint. 'No,' she murmured.

'All I heard was "yes, yes, yes",' another man snorted.

She scrambled to her knees. This couldn't be happening. She was a good girl. She'd never done anything like this before. Ever. Yet, here she was, half-naked for an entire dorm floor to see. She'd performed for them like an X-rated actress, and she could see in their hungry eyes that they wanted more.

She looked around the room for her clothes, but they

were scattered everywhere. Her sweater was on the other side of the room behind the grunting Rex and Cody. There was no way to get to it.

'Need this?'

The guy with the shy girlfriend began swinging her bra around his finger like a windmill. Another stooped down, and she was horrified to see him pick up her panties. Not her cheaters, but her panties. She came to her feet with a cry when he lifted them to his nose and took a deep whiff.

'Let me out,' she said as she hurried to the door. 'Let me out, or I'll scream.'

'Your screaming is what brought us down here in the first place.'

'Get out of my way!' she screeched.

She squeezed her way between the men to get out of the room. Behind her, she heard Cody yell her name.

She kept on going.

Hands pawed under her skirt. She slapped at one that caught her wet pussy and squeezed. Another slipped under her forearm to catch her breast. Brynn didn't care anymore. She screamed. She screamed and screamed and screamed until she hit the stairwell.

Her feet beat down the steps at a frantic pace and her breasts bounced uncomfortably. She passed three women from the fourth floor, and she wanted to die when she saw the looks on their faces.

They knew. By tomorrow, the entire school would know.

'And they did,' Brynn said as she came out of the memory. She glared at Cody as he sat on the coffee table in front of her. 'I endured sly comments, pinching fingers, and disgusted looks until I couldn't take it anymore. You want to know what I remember? That's it. I remember you tricking me, using me, and making sure the whole world knew.'

There it was, the truth in black and white. Putting the memories into words brought back all the faded emotions, and Brynn felt raw on the inside. The second hand on the clock above her head clicked slowly but steadily as she waited for his response.

'That's bullshit,' he finally said in a low, scathing voice.

Her head snapped back.

'Utter and *total* bullshit.'

Cody stood up and began to pace the room. The injustice of it all seared the inside of his chest. He stalked across the room, but came back to look at her. He couldn't believe half of what he'd heard. He planted his hands on his hips as he glared down at her.

'At least you got the sex part right,' he barked.

She flinched, and he let out a rough curse.

'We did do the nasty, Brynn,' he said, 'But you were right there with me every step of the way. You let me stick my face in your pussy, and you liked it. You liked it so much, you came like a fucking volcano.'

She looked away. 'I would have stopped you if I'd known it was you.'

He wasn't having any part of that. Leaning down, he caught her chin and made her look at him. 'You knew it was me.'

Her eyes widened. 'I did not!'

'It was dark, but you couldn't have made that big of a mistake.'

'I did.'

'Bullshit. I'm at least five inches taller than Rex, Brynn, and we're not built the same. You knew!'

'No.' She shook her head and ripped her chin out of his hand.

Cody felt frustration building inside his gut. 'From what I could tell, you never let him get by second base. Yet, that night, you were hot to go all the way. What changed? Why then?'

She shrugged uncomfortably. 'I don't know. The game had been exciting. Maybe my adrenaline got the best of me.'

He laughed, but the sound held no humour. 'You'd been to hundreds of games and you never spread for him. Why? What was different?'

'*It* was different!' she blurted.

He eased up on her, and she clamped her hand over her mouth when she realised what she'd admitted. Finally, they were getting somewhere.

'Of course *it* was different,' he said. 'God help me if it wasn't. The touches were different. The kisses were different. Your reactions were different, because you were with a different guy. *You were with me!*'

'I didn't know,' she swore. She pushed herself off the couch and went to the breakfast bar. Her fingers were white as she clutched at it for support. 'I didn't know until I looked . . . under my skirt.'

He wasn't going to let her stick her head in the sand. So help him, she was going to face this. He walked over to her, but kept a good distance between them. He could prove it to her if he touched her, but she had to come to the conclusion on her own. 'I talked to you the entire time. You should have recognised my voice.'

She shook her head. 'It was hoarse, like mine.'

She twirled away from him and raked her hands through her hair. 'You did everything you could to hide your identity from me. You left the lights off. You turned me on my stomach so I couldn't look at you. You hid under my skirt!'

He turned her back around to face him. 'You might

not have known up here,' he said, tapping her on the forehead, 'but you knew down here.'

He'd told himself not to touch her, but his willpower was nonexistent. Reaching out quickly, he caught her between the legs. She gasped and tried to bat his hand away, but the robe and whatever she was wearing beneath it did nothing to hide her heat. 'You were raring to go, Goody. I didn't trick you into doing anything. I just gave you what you wanted.'

Her cheeks turned pink when he squeezed his hand for emphasis.

'I gave you what you needed,' he hissed.

She lurched away from him, but her eyes were full of challenge. 'And you made sure you did it in front of everybody.'

Cody ground his teeth together. She was poking at old wounds that hadn't healed. 'I didn't know Rex was coming down that hallway any more than you did. If I'd had my way, we would have spent the whole night rolling around on that mattress like two horny minks. It was nobody's business but ours.'

She looked at him in disbelief. 'If it wasn't anybody's business, why did you run my cheaters up the flagpole the next morning? Out of everything that happened, that hurt the most, Cody! You dragged my name through the mud. I might have been able to stay at the university and deny the rumours if the evidence hadn't been flapping around in the breeze.'

'Goddammit, Brynn. I didn't do that! And I'm sick and tired of hearing how I'm the bad guy and you're the innocent victim. I'm the one who was in that room nursing aching ribs before you bounced into the place swinging your pompons and wearing that too-short skirt.'

'I –'

'Shut up,' he barked. He ran a hand through his hair. It was nearing three o'clock in the morning. He hadn't slept for two days and, for once, he was going to tell his side of the story. 'You kissed me. The whole thing started when you kissed me.'

'It doesn't matter. You knew it was me. You knew I was with Rex. You should have stopped things.'

'Should have, maybe. Could have, no way. I'd lusted after you forever. I wasn't going to pass up an opportunity like that, especially when you were throwing yourself at me.'

'You should have known things would get ugly. I got hurt, Cody.'

'I know,' he said, pulling himself in. 'I regretted that, but you weren't the only one that walked away wounded. Remember those bruised ribs? They ended up broken. I got a nice black eye and a bloody nose to go along with them, courtesy of your buddy Rex.'

She paled. 'I'm sorry, but you can't blame him for what he did. He walked in to find his roommate screwing his girlfriend.'

Cody let out a harsh laugh. 'You really think that hurt him? Hell, the only thing hurt was his pride.'

'He was the true victim in all of this! If you'd seen him yesterday, you would know that.'

Cody took a step forward and caught her by the lapels. The idea of her anywhere near that guy made him see red. She struggled, but he pulled her close until their noses brushed.

'I wasn't finished,' he growled. 'You know what the worst part was? That night, I ended up with a hard, aching cock. You came, Brynnie, but I walked away in worse shape than I'd ever been, because I came *this close* to having you.'

He wrapped an arm around her and pulled her tight

against his hardening cock. She had to go up on her tiptoes, but he looked her straight in the eye. 'You need to understand that things are going to be different this time. You and I are going to finish what we started and nobody, including Rex Stanton, is going to get in our way.'

He caught her mouth in a hard, blistering kiss. She pushed at his shoulders, but he worked his tongue deep into her mouth. She fought him, but he knew her better than she knew herself. He let his fingers squeeze the sweet curve of her ass, and she finally let out a groan. Her fists relaxed against his shoulders, and she started to melt against him.

It cost him, but he pulled back. 'I'll give you the fucking of your life, Brynn,' he rasped. 'Only this time, both your legs and your eyes will be open wide.'

Determinedly, he turned and walked out the door. He only had one chance to make his point, and this was it.

9

'See that? I told you that you needed to step back. You're out of line.'

'Me? You need to step up. Look at the rest of the squad.'

Brynn glared at Trini and Hannah. The two had been bickering ever since they'd started watching the tape of yesterday's practice, but she really didn't know what to do anymore. Much to Hannah's chagrin, Trini had not only made the squad, she'd been voted co-captain by her new teammates. While their cheering styles complemented each other on the field, their personalities still collided head-on like two Mack trucks. 'You're both fine,' Brynn insisted. 'Stop nitpicking.'

'It's not nitpicking,' Hannah said. 'If our squad is going to improve, she needs to stay in line!'

Trini let out a harrumph and plopped down in a chair in front of the television screen. 'So maybe I am a little out of line; I'm still catching up pretty damn fast. There! Look at you. What was that, Hannah? A blade hand? It's buckets. Buckets!'

Hannah grabbed the remote and rewound the tape. 'My hand position is fine. I'm . . . Oh.'

Brynn ran a hand through her hair and tried to concentrate on the paper she was correcting. She was so far behind. This homework had been turned in three days ago, but she hadn't found the time to get to it. Her eyes blurred as she looked through the code Scott Jetson had written.

'That pyramid looks weak. I should be the apex,' Trini said grumpily.

'You need to be the base,' Hannah argued. 'You're stronger than I am.'

'Who says?'

'I say. Look at the way you bullied me.' Hannah's cheeks flushed and her head whipped back to the TV.

'At the car wash?' Trini laughed. 'Yeah, I guess I did girl-handle you pretty easily.'

'You two!' Brynn snapped. She didn't have time for this. Between lecturing her class and preparing the squad for this weekend's homecoming game, her patience had worn thin. Combine that with the fact that she hadn't slept well since Cody had stormed out of her apartment the other night, and she was at the end of her rope.

She rubbed her throbbing temple. She couldn't let herself think about him; it would only wind her up more. He'd confused her – twisted everything around until she didn't know what was right and what was wrong. Damn the man!

'You're in a snit,' Trini said as she came over and perched her hip against the desk. 'What's wrong, honey?'

Brynn closed her eyes. She'd given up on trying to stop the girl from calling her that. To Trini, everyone was 'honey'. 'It's nothing,' she sighed. 'I've just got a bad headache.'

Hannah immediately scooped up her purse. 'I have some aspirin.'

'Thanks, but I don't think it will help.'

Trini's eyebrows lowered. She glanced at the late paperwork and the half-eaten king-sized bag of M&Ms sitting on the desk, and enlightenment lit her eyes. 'You've got man problems.'

Brynn's head dipped. The girl was too intuitive for

her own good. 'It's nothing. Go back to the tape. I need to finish correcting these papers.'

'Nothing, my ass.' Trini's dark hair slipped over her shoulder as she reached out and slapped her palm across Jets' homework. 'You're eating chocolate.'

Hannah quietly came to stand by Brynn's side. 'That doesn't mean anything,' she said defensively.

Trini lifted one of those expressive eyebrows. 'Since when did you become the sexpert, Blondie?'

Brynn put down her pen and sat back. Good grief. Was she that transparent?

She raked a hand through her hair. She really needed to talk to somebody, but these were her cheerleaders. She shouldn't get them involved in her personal life. She was supposed to set a good example for them.

'Come on. There's nobody here but us. Tell us what happened.'

Her shoulders sagged. She hadn't been able to figure out how to handle things on her own, and she felt like she was about to burst. Would it really hurt to get an unbiased opinion? Trini might be young, but she obviously knew more about men than anyone else in the room. 'Have you ever made a mistake that you just can't seem to fix?'

'Hello! Remember who you're talking to.'

Brynn glanced at Hannah, but the cheerleader just shrugged. Of course, she'd never made a mistake big enough to regret. Oh, to be so innocent again.

'I made a mistake ten years ago, and I'm still paying for it,' Brynn finally admitted. 'It's like time has stood still, and I don't know how to move on.'

Hannah gently placed a hand on her shoulder. 'Does this have anything to do with Coach Jones?'

Brynn looked at her sharply. 'Why would you say that?'

'You said that you went to school together. I just assumed . . .'

'That he was the problem?' Brynn started to deny it, but immediately felt a pang in her chest. She couldn't lie to Hannah, and Trini would catch her if she did. Reflexively, she reached for the M&Ms. 'He's part of it,' she mumbled.

'Honey, Coach Jones is not a problem!' Trini leaned forward and snatched the bag of M&Ms away. 'Look at him. He's the definition of an opportunity. That is one prime hunk of manhood, and he wants you.'

'It's not that simple,' Brynn said. She reached for her candy, but Trini held it out of reach and began searching through the bag herself.

'Of course it is,' she said with a roll of her eyes. She found two green M&Ms and suggestively popped them into her mouth. 'Stop fighting yourself and take him to bed. That will solve everything.'

Brynn stood abruptly. She grabbed her candy and held it to her chest. She never should have gotten into it with these two. Looking around for an escape, she saw her clutch on the floor. She picked it up and set it on the desk. Trini's fingers began sneaking towards her unguarded M&Ms, and Brynn quickly switched them to her other hand. Using her free one, she opened her bag. The first thing she saw was a thick manila envelope with Cody's name written in bold marker. Hastily, she flipped past it. 'Here,' she said as she pulled out a magazine. 'Try looking at this for a while. I've got work to do.'

Hannah's eyebrows lifted. 'It's a uniform catalogue.'

Trini's eyes smouldered. 'I don't understand you. If I had a chance with a guy like that, I'd latch onto him and refuse to let go.'

Brynn's jaw tightened. 'Trini, I'm not you. There are a

lot of ... *issues* ... between Cody and me. And even if there weren't, we don't get along.'

'You don't get along because you've both got an itch you can't scratch! At least give the guy a shot. You'll kick yourself if you don't.' Trini looked over Hannah's shoulder and immediately became distracted. 'Ooo, that's cute.'

Brynn clicked her clutch shut. Please, please, let them fall for the diversion. 'Hawthorn gave me the go-ahead today. We just need to pick out the style of uniform we want.'

'We're ready to order?' Hannah said excitedly.

'You'll let us pick?' Trini asked, talking right over the top of her.

'You're the captains, but I've got the last say,' Brynn said as she sat back down. 'Actually Hawthorn does. He's already told me that he wants red cheaters.'

'He would,' Trini said, rolling her eyes. 'Let me see that!'

The two cheerleaders fought over the catalogue as they moved to another table, but their heads bent together as they flipped through the pages. Brynn watched them thoughtfully. For all that they bickered, they did work well together when pressed. If the two of them ever joined forces, there would be no stopping them. She just hoped she could stay out of their way if they ever decided to focus their attention on her personal life again.

With a deep breath, she turned back to her desk and picked up her red pen. She knew she only had a few minutes before the fighting would start anew. There wasn't a chance that those two would agree on the same style of uniform.

'OK, Jetson. You've got my attention,' she said as she looked again at the computer code he'd written. Her pen swept down the paper as she followed his logic, and she was pleasantly surprised to see that he'd done well.

He might actually be paying attention in class. She knew he watched everything she did in class, but more often than not, she'd suspected he was only studying her hem length.

'Oh, there you go,' she sighed. The nested loop was wrong. The programme would get stuck endlessly without an exit. She marked up the corrections, and put a B at the top of the page.

She set the homework aside and was reaching for the next in the pile when she heard a knock at her door. Irritated by the interruption, she glanced up with a scowl on her face, but froze when she saw who was standing in the doorway. The pen dropped out of her hand.

'Rex!' she exclaimed. He was here – at Southern Trinity – where Cody could walk in at any moment. She stood so suddenly, her chair skidded a good foot before it screeched to a stop. 'What are you doing here?'

'I came to see you.' He leaned against the doorframe and let his gaze run up and down her figure. 'I've been thinking a lot about the other night.'

Brynn's mouth went dry. She'd thought about it a lot, too, but this wasn't the time or place to discuss it.

'And who is this?' Trini said silkily. She moved like a cat and, before Brynn could blink, she was at Rex's side. The girl's hand slid down his arm, and she practically cooed when she felt the muscles underneath his sports jacket.

'It's Palmer's coach,' Hannah said uneasily. Like a loyal soldier, she came to stand by Brynn's side.

Trini, however, was intrigued.

'Palmer?' She ran her finger over the muscle of his bicep. A thought occurred to her, and one dark eyebrow lifted. 'This doesn't happen to one of those *issues* you mentioned, does it, Coach?'

Brynn's air hiccupped in her lungs. She'd never been good at lying.

'It is!' Trini said, her mouth dropping. She looked at Rex more closely, and he returned her evaluation without blinking. 'Why, Coach Montgomery! I never would have suspected it out of you.'

Hannah stood there dumbfounded. 'What? You and him? But what about Coach Jo–'

Trini hurried over and clamped a hand over her fellow cheerleader's mouth. 'Come on, Blondie. We'll go look at the catalogue someplace else.'

'But –' Hannah stumbled along as Trini pulled her out of the room.

'I'll explain it to you later.'

'Cheerleaders?' Rex asked as he closed the door behind them. He eased his hip onto the edge of her desk where Trini had just been, but he was much larger and imposing than the sleek Latino girl.

'My co-captains.'

'The dark one's a handful, but that blonde ... Now, she reminds me of you.'

Brynn nervously straightened her papers. She'd heard the comparison enough times. 'Innocent?'

She went still when he reached out and twirled a strand of her hair around his finger. 'On the surface.'

She pulled back. His touch sent a thrill through her, but his actions were so contrary to the other night, it made her uneasy. 'Why are you here, Rex? Really?'

He smiled. 'Isn't it obvious? I'm here to see my girl – or did I misinterpret our encounter in the hot tub? We are back together, aren't we?'

Brynn looked at him blankly. Back together? He'd been so cold and distant when he'd walked out of that trainer's room, she'd thought it was a one-time thing. Her lips tingled at the memory of what they'd done, and she pressed them together tightly. Their 'encounter' had left her feeling rather used. 'I don't know, Rex. Do you want to be a couple again?'

'Hell, yeah. I'll couple with you anytime, sweetheart,' he said, wiggling his eyebrows.

She looked quickly to the door. It was closed, but she knew how little protection a closed door provided. She and her cheerleaders had commandeered the dance hall in off-hours, but the weight room was just two doors down. She never knew when she'd find Cody in there. If he heard Rex ... Oh, she didn't even want to think about it. 'Can we go somewhere and talk?'

A small smile pulled at Rex's lips. 'Worried he'll find me here?'

'No. Yes.' She rubbed her pounding forehead. She didn't want to get into the Cody Jones issue. 'I really want to talk with you. I just want to do it in private.'

Rex shrugged as if he didn't care, and his gaze drifted past her to focus on the television. 'Still trying to get your pompons synchronised?'

Brynn walked over to the VCR and quickly punched the stop button. It had been an outdoor practice and Cody and his team were in the background. Rex acted as if it didn't bother him, but she knew it did. She didn't need to flaunt that she worked side by side with his worst enemy every day.

'Let's go get some lunch,' she said.

He looked at her again, but his eyes were unreadable. Brynn felt perspiration dampen her palms.

'OK,' he finally agreed.

'Good,' she said with relief. She wouldn't be able to think until she got him out of here, and she definitely needed her wits about her. She'd wanted to patch things up with him for a long time, but he was already jumping to the conclusion that they were an item again. She didn't even know if she wanted that! 'I'll just run up to my office and grab my jacket. Can you meet me in the parking lot?'

'I need to make a few calls first. Mind if I use your phone?'

He picked up the receiver, and Brynn nearly groaned. What was it going to take to get him to leave? 'Fine. I'll meet you in the parking lot. Five minutes?'

He winked at her. 'I'll be there, sweetheart.'

She nodded and hurried out, closing the door firmly behind her. She hoped that five minutes wouldn't be five minutes too long. Cody liked to lift weights over the lunch hour.

Brynn was nervous as she let Rex into her apartment. Lunch had gone relatively well, although they hadn't really been able to talk about anything. They'd gone to a little Tex-Mex place in Campus Town and all through the meal she'd felt like she had to keep a close watch on the window. The possibility of Cody stumbling upon them was remote, but too dangerous to ignore. Finally, she'd suggested that they come back to her place for some privacy.

'Can I get you something to drink?' she asked as she set her purse down on the breakfast bar.

'I'm fine,' Rex said as he followed her inside.

He openly evaluated her home. Brynn knew it wasn't much. She hadn't had the time nor the money to spruce the place up after the semester had started. Of course, that was something that he would never understand. Stanton money had always been at his disposal.

After a while, he turned to her. 'So how did Cody react?'

Goose bumps popped up at the back of her neck. He'd said Cody's name much too casually. 'React to what?'

'To finding out I'd banged you.'

Her stomach curdled. Was that all it had been? Revenge? 'He doesn't know,' she said tightly.

'Yeah, right.' Rex sauntered across the room and ran his fingers along her jaw line. 'He knows. A man knows when his woman's been screwed.'

Brynn took a step to the side, away from his touch. 'I am not Cody Jones' woman, and I never have been,' she said firmly. 'How many times do I have to tell you that?'

Scepticism put a hard look in Rex's eyes but, after a moment, he let out a low curse. He ran a weary hand over his face, and his vengeful mood gave way to remorse. 'I'm sorry. I shouldn't lash out at you like that. I know now that it wasn't your fault. It's just . . .'

'Just what?'

'I can't get the picture of you two out of my head.' He looked straight at her, pinning her with a hot look. 'Cody took something that was mine, something you meant to give to me. You'll have to forgive me if it still upsets me, sweetheart, because it hurt.'

Brynn went still. They were finally getting to the heart of the matter.

'Finding you back in town . . . Well, it's just stirred everything up again.'

'I know,' she said. 'For me, too.'

'You were my girlfriend, Brynn. That should have been me.'

She cautiously stepped towards him and put her hands on his chest. 'I've regretted for ten years that it wasn't,' she said softly.

The last trace of bitterness left his face. His walls of defence were crumbling, and she just wanted to reach out to him. He was finally allowing her to see behind his anger to the pain she'd known was there. It was a pain she wanted to heal.

His gaze became thoughtful as it slowly strolled down her figure. 'It's too bad we can't get that night back.'

She felt a tug at her heart. 'I've wished that, too, but I've learned that I can't change the past no matter how much I want to. All I can do is to try to move on to my future.'

'Maybe we could do both – change the past and move towards the future if we . . .' His eyes darkened, but then he shook his head. 'No, I couldn't ask you to do that.'

'Do what?'

He looked at her almost sheepishly. 'Role play.'

'Role play? Do you mean you want to pretend?'

He rubbed his forehead and then waved her off. 'It's a bad idea. You've probably had enough nightmares about that night. You wouldn't want to go through it again.'

Brynn looked at him closely. The idea obviously appealed to him, but he didn't want to push her. His concern touched her – and his idea intrigued her. 'Maybe . . . Maybe it would be healing.'

He went still. 'You'd consider it?'

She felt her heart begin to pound in her chest. She'd wished a million times that she could do precisely that – replace Cody with Rex in all her memories. That one little switch would have changed her whole life. She would have been embarrassed for Cody to find her in such a compromising position, but that would have been the end of it. The situation would never have resulted in such a scandal. She could have graduated from Southern Trinity. The rift between her and Rex would never have occurred. They might even be married now for all she knew.

But could she really do it? That first time with Cody had rocked her world in a hundred different ways. And to be honest, not all of them were bad. Did she really want to wipe out that night of passion?

'OK, now I see,' Rex said tightly. 'That time with him did mean something to you – even if you claim you didn't want it.'

'No,' Brynn said quickly. 'Let's try, Rex. Please, I just want us to move past this.'

'Really? You're not just saying that?'

'I think it might help.'

The tension on his face lifted. 'Good,' he said with a broadening smile. 'Then get out of those clothes.'

Brynn smiled back infectiously. He was right. This would do both of them a world of good. They'd replace all the bad memories and start over fresh. Together. She went to stand in the middle of the room. The afternoon sun beat through the windows. Tentatively, she started for them.

'Leave them open.'

'But it was dark.'

'And this time it will be light. I'm not going to copy the bastard move for move.' Rex took a deep breath and held up his hands in apology. 'Sorry. I'm trying.'

'I know,' she said softly.

'I promise you, sweetheart, we'll make everything our own.' He smiled ingenuously. 'After all, we did a pretty damn good job of that the first time.'

Her lips began tingling like a bumblebee.

'Get out of those clothes,' he growled as he winked at her. 'I want you naked on your elbows and knees when I come back.'

Brynn excitedly began to strip, but she hesitated with her jacket halfway down her arms when, without even a glance over his shoulder, he left her.

What in the world?

Her stomach gave a dangerous dip when she heard him clattering around in her bathroom. What was he doing? She didn't know, but her pulse took off. She hurried to get out of her clothes. Naked, she lowered herself into position on the carpet. The low weave bit into her knees. Clumsily, she dropped onto her elbows and forearms. The illicit position thrust her butt up into the air.

Was he going to kiss her back there? Suck her like Cody had?

Blood rushed to her head as she bent over. She couldn't compare the two. She mustn't compare the two.

She heard footsteps as Rex came back into the room, and she glanced over her shoulder. He stopped just behind her.

'Now, isn't that a picture?' he said.

He carried something in his hands. She tried to see what it was, but he quickly hid it behind his back.

'Eyes forward.'

She stared at the floor as he slowly walked around her, evaluating her from every angle. He wasn't touching her, but she could feel his gaze on her plump ass, her dangling breasts, and her exposed pussy. The rug burned against her knees, and she inched them wider.

That made him laugh. 'Always eager to please, aren't you, Brynn? Leave 'em happy. Is that the cheerleaders' code?'

She flinched when he dropped to his knees behind her.

'Easy,' he crooned as he leaned over her. His chest pushed heavily upon her back as he reached in front of her. Her eyes widened when he set a mirror against the entertainment centre in front of her. He'd taken the mirror off her wall! He leaned back and she could see their reflections, her face down low and his up high.

'There, now I can see every response that crosses your face.' He rubbed her ass gently. 'I'll never forget the look that was in your eyes when I walked in that door, Brynn. I want that innocent thrill for us.'

He stood, and she watched his reflection as he got rid of his clothes. With the angle of the mirror, she could only see as high as his waist. It was high enough. When his boxers were unceremoniously pushed down, she could see all she needed to see. His stubby cock was standing straight up.

He walked away from her, but she kept her nose down. Anticipation made her heart beat hard. She flinched again when he came back and dropped something on each side of her. Her pompons. Her shoulders relaxed. They looked pretty splayed out around her, and he wanted his cheerleader. She shifted into a more comfortable position and thrust her butt up into the air. His cheerleader was happy to have him.

His cock swung as he lowered himself into position behind her. His hands settled onto her butt cheeks and squeezed. 'Look at that nice tight ass,' he said softly. 'Shouldn't it be up closer to my face?'

She looked sharply over her shoulder. 'You want me to ...?'

'Don't you want to?'

Cody had lifted her. How was she supposed to climb onto his shoulders? Her face filled with colour. His stern but hopeful gaze met hers in the mirror, and she swallowed hard.

Balancing on her elbows and one knee, she straightened her other leg and lifted it up behind her. Her thigh skimmed along his arm, but he made no move to help her. Her back arched uncomfortably as she kicked high behind her and finally managed to settle her thigh on his broad shoulder.

She stopped to catch her breath, but one look in the mirror told her not to dilly-dally. She bit her lip. This was debasing. He was making her push her pussy into his face.

'Could you help me?' she asked timidly.

'Did he?'

She knew better than to answer that. Her fingers bit into the carpeting. With a deep breath, she bolstered herself. She found her centre of balance and kicked her other leg up and behind her. She teetered uncertainly until he at last had mercy on her and caught her waist. She gratefully accepted his aid and lowered her other leg onto his shoulder. The position brought back vivid memories.

'Look up,' he said. 'I want to see your face.'

Her head lurched up when a strong lick swept over her pussy from her clit all the way back to her anus.

'Is that right?' he asked. 'Is that how you like it?'

Her hips rolled. She liked that just fine.

His mouth began seeking out all her secrets, and she couldn't control her hips as they bucked up and down. The nip of his teeth stung, and his tongue prodded hard. He didn't have Cody's agility, but his attentions brought old reactions to the surface. Her teeth ground together as excitement rolled through her veins.

'Not yet!' he said sharply when he took a breather and looked over the curve of her buttocks into the mirror. 'Don't come yet.'

Her body undulated more wildly when his tongue slid up and poked into the crevice of her ass. Oh God! 'Oh no,' she said without thinking. 'He didn't –'

A sharp smack on her buttocks made her cry out. 'He might not have, but I am.'

Rex's hands circled her hips until his fingers dipped into her butt crack from both sides. Brynn closed her eyes in shock. She let out a soft mew when he spread her buttocks wide to give his tongue access.

'Ooo, Rex!' she gasped when his tongue began teasing her.

He licked and prodded and nipped until she was crying out. Her back arched sharply when he thrust two fingers into her wet pussy. It was dripping with excitement.

'Ow, oh! Yes, right there,' she said as his fingers burrowed into her.

'Is this better than that night, Brynn?'

It wasn't better, but it was too good to ignore.

'Please,' she begged. She needed something – anything to ease the wild unrest in her belly.

She cried out in distress when he lowered her back to her knees. She craned her neck to look over her shoulder as she wiggled her ass at him.

He was reaching for something he'd found in her bathroom. It was a container of petroleum jelly.

'Still the naïve little innocent, I see. There wasn't any real lubricant in your bedside table,' he said as he swirled his finger in the thick goo. He came up with a large dollop. 'We'll just have to use the old stuff, even though it won't make you as slick.'

Brynn came right off her elbows when his thickly coated finger burrowed between her cheeks and slathered her anus. She reached back for his arm, but his finger wiggled against her tight opening. He watched her face in the mirror as it pushed harder and overcame the muscles that denied him entrance.

Her mouth dropped open, and her fingers bit into his arm. 'Ohhhh,' she groaned.

'You do want to do this, don't you, sweetheart?' he asked as his finger worked deeper into her. 'You said you wanted to give me your innocence.'

Brynn's breaths went so short, she wasn't sure if oxygen was reaching her lungs. Wide-eyed, she looked at him in the mirror. She knew what he was asking. Cody had taken her innocence, but he wanted another intimacy from her. He wanted to be her first *back there*.

'Can I, Brynn?'

How could she deny him? He'd be even more hurt if she said 'no'. 'Y-yes,' she said nervously.

His eyes gleamed as he slowly pulled his finger out of her. 'Then spread those cheeks for me, sweetie. You're going to need more lubing.'

Brynn turned her face into the carpet and closed her eyes as she reached back. She didn't know if she wanted this, but she'd do it for him. She owed him this much.

She caught her buttocks with both hands and timidly spread them, but a familiar swishing noise made her eyelids fly open. She saw his big hand close around one of her pompons, and her already palpitating heart kicked into double time.

'This will be perfect – and so poetic,' he said as he fingered the thick handle. It was curved to fit comfortably in a palm, thinner on the ends, but thick in the middle. 'Look in the mirror. I want to see your face as it goes in.'

Brynn's throat tightened. She hadn't said yes to that!

Her entire body began to shake. She watched in fascinated horror as he painted the plastic handle with Vaseline. She knew deep down he wouldn't force her. This was a test. She'd let Cody do something he shouldn't. He was seeing how far she'd let him go. By all rights, it should be further.

She took a deep breath and stayed exactly where she was.

She felt the rope of the handle touch her first. The loop circled around a cheerleader's wrist so she wouldn't accidentally drop her pompon. There were certain things a cheerleader never did. She never lost a hat, she never stopped smiling, and she never dropped a pom. Brynn's eyelids closed tightly. Apparently, this was something that hadn't made that 'don't do' list.

'Open your eyes,' he cooed to her.

She let go of one butt cheek to take the weight off her shoulders. Propping herself up, she was able to watch him better in the mirror. That seemed to satisfy him.

'And in it goes.'

The pressure against her tight opening increased. He'd coated the rope, but it was going to burn. Her body fought the invasion, but he pressed harder and harder until *pop*! Her muscles released, and the tip of the handle slid in an inch.

Brynn let out a sharp cry and panted for air. The plastic was thick, but the rope wasn't smooth. She could feel it rubbing inside her.

He gave her only a second to adjust. 'How's that feel?' he asked.

'It burns.'

'Good. That will make this even hotter.'

His gaze dropped back to his task, and she couldn't watch anymore. She ground her forehead against her arm as the pressure increased. The handle burrowed deeper into her, and the coloured plastic strands brushed against the back of her legs. The scratching was uncomfortable, and she kicked backwards trying to push it away.

'Whoa there, horsey,' he laughed. His hand cupped the back of her thigh and settled her leg into place.

Brynn fought for air. The handle was up to the thickest part now. The invasion felt unholy. Her ass burned, and the pressure was intense. She'd never taken anything back there – not even a finger. This felt wicked and depraved.

Yet her pussy only wept all the more. She could feel the strands of the pompon sticking to her legs.

Rex finally got tired of going slow. He settled his hand against the base of the pompon and gave a firm push. Brynn reared upright with a cry, and he caught her in his arms. The scratchy strands of the pompon caught between them, and she felt his firm cock somewhere in the plume. His hands caught her breasts and pinched her stiff nipples.

'Get on your back,' he panted into her ear. 'I can't wait any longer.'

Brynn squirmed in discomfort. Her ass was impaled and the pompon's strands were driving her crazy. They brushed her everywhere. She reached to get them out of the niches and crannies of her pussy, but Rex wouldn't wait. He caught her shoulders and she found herself on her back, looking at the ceiling. A slant of afternoon sunshine crisscrossed her body as he pressed her knees to her chest.

'Oh!' she gasped.

'The handle?'

'No.' Her face coloured. The problem wasn't the hard piece of plastic shifting inside her; it was the pillow of sharp plastic strands under her butt. 'It's prickly.'

He let out a short laugh. He didn't do anything to

help her, though. Instead, he reached down to guide his cock to her wet opening.

'Ahh!' she cried as he pushed into her deeply. Her shoulders came off the floor, and all she could think of was how happy she was that he wasn't longer. She was already overfilled as it was. The unaccustomed pressure in her anus had already tested her limits. The addition of his thick cock pushed her past them.

'Rex! Oh my God. I can't. I can't.'

'Sure you can, sweetie,' he said as he began to thrust.

Her fingernails bit into his shoulder as her legs worked uncomfortably. Down low or up high, she couldn't find the relief she needed. The pressure between her legs simply built as he plugged and chugged.

'Oh, help me,' she begged.

'Look at me,' he said. He caught her hair in his fist and looked into her eyes.

Brynn could hardly keep them open. The pain, the pressure, the *pleasure* ... They were rolling and broiling inside her. His chest rasped against her nipples, and she raked her fingers down his back. The pompon swished and crinkled with every thrust he made. Her ears focused on the sound until she could hear nothing else.

'That's it, sweetheart,' he said roughly. His breaths were coming as hard as hers. He rolled them onto their sides and, without breaking rhythm, grabbed the base of the handle of the pompon and began pumping it, too.

'Aaaaahh!' she cried. Her hips bucked and swayed as he fucked her from both ends. 'Aaah, aaah, Rex!'

Brynn's neck arched back with a snap when the orgasm hit her. Her legs wrapped around his hips and clung as the waves smashed over her. She forgot to breathe as they hit her, one after the other.

'Oh yeah,' he grunted. 'Oh yeah.'

Another rush hit her when he spurted into her and lodged the pompon deep inside its new home.

'Rexxxxx,' she whined as she squirmed in his arms.

It took a long time before the stars stopped dancing behind her eyelids. When they did, she opened her eyes and saw his face. Sweat beaded his forehead, and a look of supreme satisfaction filled his eyes. The tension left her body, and she sagged onto the floor.

They'd just put the past firmly behind them.

'That was what I wanted,' he said. He brushed her hair out of her face and hooked it behind her ear. 'I wanted to be the one to put that innocent thrill in your eyes.'

She smiled weakly and turned her head to kiss his palm. 'You've always thrilled me, Rex.'

He kissed her, and they were content to just nuzzle each other until her discomfort returned. She couldn't forget the pompon that was still embedded in her ass. The strands pricked her everywhere they touched. 'That was amazing,' she said as she traced the line of his shoulder. 'But I really need to get back to work.'

'Me, too,' he said with regret. He pulled his hips back, and she bit her lip as she gave him up. He held her close and watched her face as he reached around and slowly removed the pompon from its intimate home. She groaned with every inch he made her give up.

'God, you're hot,' he whispered into her ear.

'So are you.'

His lips closed over hers, and the passion began to grow again until he rolled away.

'Go. You take the first shower,' he said as he lay flat on his back staring at the ceiling. 'I need some time to recover.'

10

Homecoming night. Brynn had forgotten how exciting it could be. In awe, she looked around the stadium filled to capacity with students, parents, and alumni who'd returned to Southern Trinity for the big game. All around her, people were going through their routines in preparation. The groundskeeper paced along the sidelines worriedly looking at each blade of grass on the field. Band members noisily tuned their instruments, while the equipment manager polished the game balls with a towel until they gleamed. Homecoming was always a big deal, but with this year's game against archrival Palmer College, the air was electric with anticipation.

'Trini. Hannah. Come over here. I want to talk to you.' Brynn waved her co-captains into the tunnel away from the crowd. She usually wasn't one for pep talks, but tonight was special.

'I'm so excited!' Hannah said breathlessly as she bounded into the tunnel. 'Did you see how many people are in the stands?'

'It's a good turnout.' Brynn reached out and caught the blonde by the shoulders to calm her down. Excitement was good, but too much adrenaline could be a bad thing. 'I just wanted to take the time to tell both of you how proud I am of you. You've worked really hard to get the squad ready for tonight, and it shows.'

Trini wasn't bouncing like Hannah, but tension radiated from her as she paced like a lynx ready to spring out of its cage. Brynn reached out and caught her by the shoulders in an impulsive hug. 'Tonight we show every-one that Southern Trinity Cheerleading is back in town.'

Hannah let out a squeal, and Brynn couldn't help but laugh.

Trini was too anxious to be contained. She pulled back, and her pompons swished noisily as she resumed her pacing. 'I'm worried about the pyramid. Karen is having problems sticking it.'

'She'll be fine,' Brynn assured.

'She's the second layer. Hannah can't get up to the apex if she doesn't stick it.'

'It will be OK,' Hannah said.

'It will be better than OK,' Brynn said. 'It will be fantastic. Just don't think about it too much. You've practised enough now that everything should be auto-matic. I can't wait to see the stunned looks on people's faces when they realise there are more athletes on that field than just football players.'

Hannah stuck out her pompon. 'To cheerleading,' she said proudly.

'To cheerleading,' Brynn agreed as she covered the pompon with her hand.

Trini stopped pacing and added her pompon to the stack. 'To Southern Trinity cheerleading!'

As one, they threw their hands into the air. 'Go, ST!'

Thunder echoed in her ears, and Brynn looked down the tunnel. The Palmer Patriots were leaving their locker room and heading to the field. 'Come on, let's get out of their way.'

She ushered her captains into the stadium, but the band filled the end zone. The only way to their sideline was to cross the Patriots' path onto the field. 'Let's wait here,' she said.

The sound of cleats on cement made her cringe, but a low roar blotted out the sound when Palmer College's fans noticed their team entering the stadium. Half the crowd came to its feet as people whistled and cheered their support.

Rex led the team's way. He looked strong and powerful as he trotted out of the tunnel onto the soft grass, and Brynn felt a delectable shiver run down her spine. She hadn't seen him since the day he'd taken her to lunch. He was the enemy tonight, but she lifted her hand in a tiny wave. It went unnoticed as he concentrated on the job at hand.

Instead of running onto the field, though, he stopped at the sidelines and looked up to examine the crowd. The rivalry between Palmer and Southern Trinity was old and colourful. The crowd was already at a low roar. The pitch would only crescendo when the teams took the field.

But Palmer wasn't moving.

Southern Trinity fans started to boo, but the team stood there like a bunch of high-strung racehorses ready to go into the shoots. Players stretched, hopped up and down, and knocked their helmets together to psyche themselves up. One player, however, remained motionless.

Number 69 had his sites on Hannah. He stared at the blonde with unblinking gold eyes until Brynn took an unconscious step towards her innocent cheerleader. Those eyes were all that could be seen under the player's helmet, but the way they glittered reminded her of a big cat on the prowl. Hannah caught her wrist, and she patted her hand comfortingly. The player wasn't doing anything. He was just looking – and looking hard. He towered over them, six feet tall and two hundred and twenty pounds of pure muscle.

'Hey, 69,' Trini called. 'Can you live up to that promise?'

Hannah's face turned so red, it nearly went purple. 69 grunted, but Trini hardly entered his consciousness.

He wanted Hannah.

'Let's go around the long way,' Brynn suggested. Hannah's tennis shoes bumped into her heels in her eagerness to leave. Brynn came to a stop, though, when another clatter arose inside the tunnel to her left. The Southern Trinity Trojans were coming out of the home team's locker room. Her eyes widened. She glanced back towards Rex, but he looked right past her towards the mouth of the tunnel.

Her stomach tightened. He was stalling on purpose!

'Why aren't they taking the field?' Hannah asked.

'Because he wants to cause trouble,' Trini said.

Rex! Brynn should have known. He and Cody were going to make more out of this than just a game. She backed her cheerleaders out of the way, but escape was impossible. They were going to be caught in crossfire.

Cody's face was stormy when he came out of the tunnel and spotted Rex. It was customary for the visiting team to take the field first. To refuse, especially at a Homecoming game, was an incredible insult. Brynn's heart began to pound in her ears, and the din inside the stadium rose. The bleachers rattled as the crowd came to its feet.

'Stanton,' Cody yelled. 'What in the hell do you think you're doing?'

Rex crossed his arms over his chest. 'I'm just taking it all in – the crowd's anticipation, their excitement. It's a shame we have to crush their hopes so quickly. Your runts won't last the half with us.'

A muscle worked in Cody's jaw. He signalled for his team to stay and began heading across the field.

Brynn's breath caught. This wasn't good.

Rex never had been one to back down from a challenge. Chin first, he stalked across the field, and the two coaches met under the goalpost.

'Oh no,' she breathed.

'Don't even try, Rex,' Cody said loudly enough for her to hear. 'Your mind games won't work on me. I know you too well. Just get your team's collective ass on the field.'

'No.'

'You're the visiting team. Take the field.'

'You go first.'

'Oh my,' Trini said under her breath. 'Would you look at that?'

Brynn couldn't look anywhere else. It was like watching a train wreck.

'They're magnificent!' Hannah whispered.

'What?' Brynn said, snapping out of her reverie. Her neck twisted as she looked at her two cheerleaders.

'Who would you pick?' Trini asked, leaning forward to talk around her.

'Me? Well, Coach Jones is taller.'

'All right, he gets five points for that, but that Palmer guy has arms like pistons. That evens them out.'

They were rating her men! Brynn felt heat rush through her face. OK, Cody had never been her man, but he wanted to be. She looked at the two arguing coaches and tried to see them from her cheerleaders' perspective. Both were good-looking, fine-tuned, male athletes. Twenty-first century warriors, really. Their kind drew women's attention like flies.

And they both wanted her.

'Subtract fifteen points from the Palmer guy for being a jerk and not taking the field,' Hannah said with a disdainful sniff.

'Add ten to Coach Jones for those dark eyes. I love his eyes.'

'And plus twenty for his cute butt!'

Brynn's eyes rounded. 'Hannah!'

'What? You know his butt is adorable.'

'Probably better than any of us,' Trini laughed. She propped her pompons on her hips and cocked her head. 'There's something about that Rex guy, though. He's so sturdy. They say that guys built like fireplugs usually have dicks like –'

'Uh-uh. Minus fifteen,' Brynn said before she could stop herself.

Her cheerleaders looked at her with wide eyes before doubling over with laughter. The humour in the situation got to Brynn, but she clamped her hand over her mouth to hide her grin. There was a fight about to break out less than ten feet away. She'd only make things worse if the boys thought she was laughing at them, but really ... hadn't things gotten to the ridiculous point?

'OK, OK,' Trini said as she fought for air. She huddled closer. 'What about Coach Jones? I've been dying to know.

Brynn bit her lower lip. 'I'm not sure.'

'Arrg!' Trini reached out and pinched her. 'I told you to fix that.'

'I could make a good guess.'

Hannah's cheeks were pink, but she asked, 'Plus or minus?'

'Definitely a plus,' Brynn said with a grin. 'Plus twenty-five.'

Squeals erupted. The three of them bent their heads closer together to try to keep a low profile, but a few band members turned around to see what was so funny.

'What else?' Trini whispered. 'Come on, spill!'

In for a penny, in for a pound. 'Ten points to Rex for creativity,' Brynn offered.

Trini passed the back of her hand over her forehead as if she were about to swoon. 'I loooove creativity! Make that fifteen. Creativity's important.'

'All right, but give Cody fifteen for concentration. He's got the focus of a heat-seeking missile.'

'Oooo,' Hannah sighed. 'What about romance? Any points in that department?'

'Rex doesn't call,' Brynn said grumpily. She'd expected at least an email after he'd left her with a peck on the forehead and a tap on the butt. For all his talk about wanting to get back together, though, she hadn't heard a peep from him.

'Wham. Bam. Thank you, ma'am?' Trini said in distaste.

'Minus twenty-five!' Hannah declared. 'And Coach Jones?'

Brynn watched the two men going toe-to-toe. Her stomach gave a little dip, and she reached for her necklace. For all she'd tried to deny it, he'd scored big in the romance department without even trying. 'He brought me Kettle Korn,' she sighed.

'What?' Trini and Hannah said in unison.

'Kettle Korn.' Brynn shrugged. 'It's my favourite. He showed up at my door in the middle of the night with a bag of it after an away game.'

'Ohhh.'

'That's so sweet.'

Brynn dropped her hands to her side. 'Yeah, but he did something to me in college that was unforgivable.'

Trini's pompons swooshed as she made an out-of-bounds call. 'Nope. Anything before this football season doesn't count.'

'Who says?'

'I say. I made up the game; I can set the rules.'

'And Coach Jones wins by a long shot,' Hannah said

firmly. She wove her arm around Brynn's and, together, they all ogled Cody.

The argument seemed to be escalating. The teams had picked up the tension and were automatically choosing up sides. Instead of facing the field, players were turning on each other. Brynn looked around nervously for a school official, a referee, or anyone who could stop this.

Cody and Rex looked as if they wanted to do serious harm to one another, and she knew from experience that they could. Muscles flexed and chests heaved as oxygen fuelled the fire. She couldn't let the flames get started. This was partly her fault. She started towards them, but her cheerleaders latched onto her and held her back.

'There's a ref,' Hannah said. 'Let him take care of it.'

Brynn spotted a man in a striped shirt walking towards them. Thank God.

'OK, boys,' the man said. 'Let's break it up. Coach Stanton, have your team take the field.'

'No problem, ref,' Rex said as he backed up and put on an innocent look. He waved at his team, and they took off to the roar of the crowd.

He wasn't done, though. Brynn pulled up short when he turned a cocky look on her. For all the attention he'd paid to her up to this point, she hadn't realised he'd known she was even there. She watched uneasily as he stuck his hand in his pocket.

'Thanks for the good luck charm, sweetheart,' he yelled.

She jerked when he waved her panties at her. Cody had said the same thing to her on the radio, and Rex knew it. She recoiled when he blew her a kiss. Cody lunged at him, but the ref and two of the Trojan players held him back.

'That was low,' Trini hissed.

'Minus a hundred points low,' Hannah said with indignation.

Rex laughed and backtracked onto the field. He slapped a hand on the official's shoulder and trotted after his team.

Brynn felt as if she'd just been slammed upside the head by a two-by-four. Cody had warned her. He'd told her that Rex's pride meant more to him than she did. It had all been a game of one-upmanship.

'Are you OK?' Hannah asked.

Brynn felt like she was going to be sick. The things she'd let him do to her ... He hadn't cared about her; he'd just wanted to rub Cody's face in it.

Trini caught her by the shoulders and looked her in the eye. 'I'll drive you home. Don't worry about the squad. Hannah can handle it.'

'No,' Brynn said. She shook her head and stood up straight. Talk about a homecoming. It was the first time that she, Rex, and Cody had been together since she'd left school and, although it had been distasteful, the reunion had opened her eyes to something she'd been fighting not to see. 'I'm staying.'

'Are you sure?' Hannah asked.

Brynn felt anger starting to brew inside her belly. 'Oh yeah. I'm sure. I'm going to stay and watch Cody kick that jerk's ass.'

'Damn straight,' Trini said.

'And he's not the only one. I want to see my cheerleading squad kick those staid old alumni right onto their feet.'

The game turned out to be a disaster. Palmer rolled over Southern Trinity by a score of 35–3. It was the worst loss Trinity had taken all season, and the dejected Homecoming crowd walked away with their shoulders slumped and hot dogs souring their bellies.

Cody stomped out of the locker room and swore viciously. Somebody was going to pay. His footsteps sounded like gunfire as he walked down the tunnel. He couldn't remember the last time he'd been so pissed off. He stopped at the edge of the field and looked around. Cups and napkins littered the stands as the clean-up crew began their work.

'Goddammit, where is she?'

Brynn had some explaining to do.

He'd come to expect this kind of thing out of Rex, the asshole, but Brynn? What had he done to make her so vindictive? What had his team done?

The gleam of blonde hair caught his eye, and he zeroed in. It was her. He turned on a dime and headed under the bleachers. She was putting the cheerleaders' megaphones away in the equipment cabinet. It was as good of a place as any to have it out.

'Hiding, Brynnie?' he growled.

Her hair slid over her shoulder as she glanced up quickly. When she saw it was him, a guarded look settled onto her face. She paused for a moment before turning to pick up another megaphone. 'I'm sorry about tonight, Cody,' she said. 'What Rex did was horrible.'

His fists clenched. 'How could you sink so low?'

She stopped with the megaphone in hand. 'If it means anything, I was just as upset with him tonight as anybody.'

'What were you thinking, Brynn? God, I thought you had more class than that.'

'I do,' she snapped. She tossed the megaphone into the cabinet, and it clattered around before coming to rest. 'I just didn't realise I was the prize in this macho game between you two. I didn't know what he was doing.'

Cody's air heaved in his chest. In three steps, he had her trapped against the steel trusses supporting the bleacher section. 'You had to know. I just don't understand how you could do that to your own alma mater. It was Homecoming, for Christ's sake.'

'Do that to my alma mater? Why, you conceited pig!' She pushed at his chest, but he didn't budge. 'I dated him. That doesn't make me a traitor to the university.'

Cody swore hard. He felt so betrayed and blindsided, he was seeing red. 'Is that how you justified it? By pretending that your personal life and your professional life are separate? I doubt my team would see it that way.'

'What does your team have to do with anything?'

'You sold us out, Brynn.'

She let out a sound close to a growl. 'My personal life –'

He didn't want to hear it. 'What did you do, Goody? Break into my office and get the playbook?'

She went still. 'What are you talking about?'

He leaned closer and used the weight of his body to press her more firmly against the bleacher's support pole. 'The football game. Palmer was ready for everything we threw at them. At first I thought that maybe they were just well-prepared, but damn it, I know Rex. He's too lazy for something like that.'

Her jaw dropped, and red colour slashed across her cheekbones. 'That's what this is all about – a football game? My God, here I am trying not to trample on anyone's feelings, but you're both still in a peeing match.'

'It's a pissing match, Brynn. *Pissing*.' He slapped his

hand on the crossbar and the bleachers rang with the vibration. 'God, how can you be so righteous and still stab us in the back? I know you've got it out for me, but what about JJ? What about Jetson? Those guys deserve a hell of a lot better.'

Her forehead wrinkled. 'What, exactly, are you accusing me of?'

'Rigging the game. You gave Rex information to make sure Palmer would win.'

Her head snapped back, and her mouth rounded in indignation. 'I did not! I would never do something like that, even if I could.'

'Not even if it would help Rex forgive you?'

'What could I tell him, Cody? I don't know anything!'

'You've been around football all your life.'

Her chin came up. 'Just like you've been around cheerleading. You like the skirts, but how much do you really know about the sport?'

Cody thought he was going to burst a blood vessel. 'Don't lie to me. He's fucking you. He made that clear to everyone in the stadium. There's no telling what else your guilt has made you do.'

Her lips pressed together hard. 'That's none of your business.'

He felt a kick in his gut. Picturing the two of them together made him want to tear the bleachers apart with his bare hands. 'Yeah, well, this team is my business. You made sure we didn't even have a chance.'

'You lost the game. It's rough, but it wasn't my fault.'

No, it wasn't her fault. It was Rex's. That son-of-a-bitch. He'd always been able to manipulate her around his little finger.

Why had she always gone for that loser? What was wrong with him? He was a nice enough guy – and a hell of a lot more easy-going than Stanton. Maybe that was the problem. Maybe she got her kicks off of being treated like dirt. 'He used you, Brynn, and you let him. You didn't want him to be hurt or angry with you anymore, so you let him walk all over you.'

Her mouth opened, but quickly snapped shut again. It told Cody that he was right on target, and the last thread of control on his temper broke. He leaned down over her and felt her breasts press hard against his chest. 'Now I'm the one that's hurt and angry. Maybe it's time you made me feel better.'

She wrenched herself out from between him and the girder. 'I can't believe it. It's been ten years and neither of you has grown up. I'm a woman, Cody, not a ping-pong ball.'

She threw her hands up in the air and turned away. 'Forget it. I'm through with the both of you.'

'You and I haven't even gotten started,' he growled. He wrapped his arm around her waist and pulled her deeper under the bleacher seats. She turned on him sharply, but he caught her hands and pressed them against the crossbars above her head. The position put her spread eagle in front of him, and he let his gaze rake down her figure. 'And believe me, I've noticed you're all woman.'

He slipped a leg between hers and cocked his hip. She squirmed, but went still when the move rubbed her mound intimately against his thigh.

'What do you think you're doing?' she hissed.

He wasn't thinking. He'd passed conscious thought somewhere around half-time. His head was on autopilot as anger, frustration, and jealousy roiled in his chest.

He watched her closely as he turned his hips. His cock found a warm home in the nook between her legs, and he pressed hard.

'Cody!' she gasped as she went right up on tiptoe. She

looked up anxiously when she heard footsteps overhead. 'There are people around.'

He looked her dead in the eye. 'I don't care.'

He'd been cheated too many times. Tonight, his torment was going to end. If he had her once, maybe he could get her out of his head. Out of his system.

He pulled back to look at her. God, she was beautiful. Her arms were spread wide in sacrifice, and he laced his fingers through hers. She was breathing hard and wriggling against him. The feel of her soft body made his head spin.

'You'll regret this.'

'I don't think so.'

He let go of one of her hands and reached for the tab of her jeans. Without ceremony, he yanked it down. She tried to step away, but he wrapped his arm around her thighs and clamped down hard. Holding her still, he began tugging at her boots. She tried slapping and even kicking him, but the boots thudded onto the ground anyway. Her socks followed, and her toes curled into the dewy grass.

'It's cold,' she hissed.

'I'll warm you up.'

Her eyes flew open when he caught her jeans and pulled them down. He took her panties with them and, suddenly, she was naked from the waist to the knee. A sound slipped from the back of her throat, and she quickly cupped her hands over the blonde curls he'd uncovered. Her head twisted this way and that, frantically looking for anyone who might see them. 'Cody!'

'Step out of them,' he ordered.

Her legs twisted, knotting the clothes around her, but he didn't let that stop him. He simply stood and lifted her out of the jeans. He kicked them aside and pressed her back against the steel girder.

She looked at him with a mix of horror and fascination on her face. All she wore was a leather jacket and a white sweater. Nothing more. Her nakedness was made all the starker by the glare of the flourescent lighting.

His face muscles felt rigid as he reached for his pants. He dealt with them quickly and pulled out his aching cock. Her furtive looks around the area stopped, and she stared at him with round eyes.

'See something you like, Goody?'

He did. He liked everything he saw in front of him. He just had to remember she was working for the enemy.

His teeth ground together. Damn it. He hadn't wanted Rex to enter into this, but it was unavoidable. The asshole had always stood between the two of them like a ten-foot brick wall.

Tonight, that wall was coming down.

He reached out and caught her by the backs of her thighs. She murmured something, but his pulse was pounding so loudly in his ears, he couldn't hear. He lifted her and pulled her legs around his waist. His body was racked with shudders when the tip of his cock found her warm opening. In the cold night air, it felt like a blast furnace. He wanted in, but he forced himself to hold back.

'Look at me,' he said hoarsely. He waited until she opened her eyes. There wasn't going to be any misunderstandings this time. 'Who am I? Who's fucking you?'

Her eyes flashed fire. 'You cocky son-of-a-bitch.'

He knew he was getting to her if she was cussing.

'I'm cocky, all right,' he said, thrusting an inch into her.

The muscles of her face went limp. 'Oh!' she gasped.

'Who ... am ... I?' he grunted. Holding back was costing him dearly.

'Cody,' she whispered at last. Her hands clenched into fists on his shoulders.

'That's right, Brynnie,' he said as he finally gave in to the need and thrust into her. He groaned when she gloved him. 'It's Cody.'

She was hot and achingly tight. He nearly shot off only halfway into her, but he closed his eyes and fought for air. Adjusting his weight onto the balls of his feet, he repositioned himself. Her legs pulled higher against her chest. He grabbed the crossbar above her head and thrust again. The penetration was slow and inexorable, but he didn't stop until he was fully seated deep inside her.

'Christ,' he said on a short breath.

Little sounds left her throat. Her fingernails dug into the back of his neck, and her legs clamped around his waist. 'Not yet,' she gasped. 'I'm not ready.'

But he was. God, he couldn't wait any longer.

She was dry. Brynn closed her eyes so tightly, red darts raced across the back of her eyelids. He'd pushed into her before her body was ready, and her pussy felt like it was on fire.

'Not yet. I'm not ready,' she breathed anxiously. He was as thick around as Rex, but twice as long. He filled her to the point of discomfort, and her pussy had to stretch to accommodate him.

She clutched at his back and dug her fingernails into his sweatshirt. It wasn't enough. She wrenched the fabric upwards and clawed at his skin.

'This will help,' he grunted. He wedged his hand between their writhing bodies and found her trigger. Her head fell back the moment he brushed against it.

'Oh God!' she panted as her body surged.

He began pistoning in and out of her. A cry formed in her throat, but she choked it off when she heard footsteps right overhead. She looked up.

Hawthorn! She'd recognise those expensive Italian shoes anywhere.

Cody was oblivious. His hands clutched at her hips as he worked her up and down on his big hot cock. Brynn couldn't help the groan that was ripped from her lips. Conversation overhead stopped for a moment, and her heart slammed against her ribcage.

'The dean,' she panted into Cody's ear.

'Fuck the dean.'

He hefted her higher and began stroking more quickly. She was dripping wet now, but the fire in her pussy only intensified. Her back arched and she reached upwards. She caught the overhead crossbar and braced one foot against the truss behind Cody.

He was thrusting hard and fast. He was past the point of sweet words or even rough sex talk. His breaths wheezed in her ear. There wasn't going to be any lingering over the act. He was set on fucking her brains out.

And it was working.

'Aaah!' she cried. Her mind focused on that one, burning, intimate point of contact. She heard a maintenance man nearby, but she didn't care. She'd been caught with Cody before.

Her excitement jumped. She and Cody Jones were fucking like wild animals outside in the grass and dirt. Cold air brushed over her heated body as they hid in the shadows. Anyone might find them. Anyone might hear.

And she didn't care!

She pulled her foot away from the girder and locked her ankles at the small of his back. She was naked from the waist down, but his pants only sagged as far as his thighs. She ran her cold toes along the back of his leg. He bucked, and she cried out when he went even deeper inside her.

Suddenly, the flame inside her pussy went up in a

flashpoint. She used the bleachers for leverage as her hips began churning in time with his thrusts. Her greedy legs clung to him, pulling him closer and deeper.

'Fuck!' he grunted. He rammed into her one more time and then went rigid.

Stickiness coated Brynn's thighs, and a tremor rocked her. The muscles in her arms went limp, and she lost her grip on the crossbar. She sagged around Cody, trusting him to take her weight.

It had ended way too soon.

'No!' she cried when he began pulling out of her. She'd taken that big cock with difficulty, but she gave it up even less willingly. She swung her hips forward to keep him in place, but he caught her about the waist and held her still as he disengaged their bodies.

He set her away from him, and her legs felt unsteady. She leaned against a steel girder for support. It was bitingly cold against her buttocks, but she needed it to stay upright.

Cody's face was shuttered as he zipped up his pants. He scooped up her jeans, but refused to look at her as he gathered her socks and boots.

Brynn slowly became aware of her surroundings. They'd screwed under the football field bleachers just like the cliché. Popcorn bags littered the ground along with peanut shells and cigarette butts. She stepped away from the mess and accidentally kicked over a half-filled cup of soda. The sticky syrup ran between her toes. All around her, she heard people: the cleaning crew, the maintenance man, Hawthorn...

'You deserve better than Rex, Brynnie,' Cody finally said in a low voice. 'And I deserve better than you've given me.'

He shoved her clothes into her arms. He stepped back into the light, and she was caught by the emotion in his eyes. Hurt. Distrust. Lust. They all swirled in the dark depths.

He turned and walked away, leaving her half-naked in the shadows, but she made no attempt to cover herself as she watched him leave. She stood there with her legs weak and her pussy throbbing until a switch was thrown and the stadium went dark.

11

Cody sat on the floor of the hallway outside Brynn's apartment. He rested his arms on his bent knees and let his hands go limp. Waiting for her was driving him mad, but hell, he supposed he deserved a lot worse after the stupid stunt he'd pulled last night.

'Idiot,' he said, berating himself. He banged his head back against the wall for good measure.

That wasn't how he'd wanted their first time to be. Yeah, the pleasure and excitement had nearly blown the top of his head off, but there had been other things to consider. Like Brynn. He knew she'd come. He'd felt the convulsions of her tight pussy around his throbbing cock. It just hadn't been the right time or the right place.

He'd realised that about an hour later when his head had stopped spinning. He'd found himself in his office with no real idea of how he'd gotten there. He thought he remembered talking with his players and assistant coaches, but he'd be hard pressed to prove it. All he could remember vividly was the game and screwing Brynn.

The feel of her, her scent, the heat . . . He'd remember that until the day he died. And he was going to die of mental anguish soon if she didn't show up.

He slumped back against the wall. He'd looked for her everywhere. Finally, he'd decided to park his butt outside her apartment. She had to come home sooner or later – and he wasn't moving an inch until he spoke with her.

Footsteps echoed down the hallway, and he rolled his head against the wall. Her neighbour had taken pity on him and allowed him to use her bathroom. He didn't need to use the facilities again quite yet, but a cup of coffee might be nice.

He went still.

It wasn't a stooped-shouldered, grey-haired lady. It was a shapely blonde bombshell.

His heart kicked into overdrive, but he couldn't move. And that was probably for the best. He didn't want to spook her. He sat there, motionless, watching as she came down the hall.

Where the hell had she been? He focused on the bags she carried. Shopping? He'd been sitting here all night while she'd gone shopping?

At last, she saw him. She looked up, keys in hand, and her steps slowed.

'Hello, Brynn,' he said quietly. He braced himself against the wall and slowly pushed himself to his feet. Her shoulders sagged, and he shoved his hands into his pockets.

'Cody,' she said in resignation.

She looked at him tiredly, but lifted her keys. His body went rigid when she came right next to him to open her door. Her perfume made his toes curl, but he forced himself not to move.

She glanced at him. 'I'm not really up for this.'

'Just let me say something and then I'll leave. I promise.'

She wasn't as calm and cool as she pretended. He could tell by the way the tip of her key bounced around the keyhole. He was reaching to help her when the key chain fell to the floor with a loud jingle.

'I've got it,' he said.

He picked up the keys and took her hand as he stood.

She tensed. The simple touch made his cock jump, but he forced himself to ignore it. He needed to tread carefully here, very carefully.

'I'm sorry, Brynnie,' he said softly.

He threaded his fingers through hers and braced his other hand on the doorframe beside her head. Carefully, he stepped closer. Her plastic bags crinkled, reminding him not to move too fast. 'I'm not sorry about what we did, but the how, when, and where could have been better.'

She pulled her hand away from his and reached for her necklace. She began twisting it around her fingers in a habit he remembered from college. At least she wasn't slapping his face. He considered that a good sign.

'I'll admit; you drove me a little wild. You were so soft and responsive.' He shifted slightly so he could look directly into her face. 'That doesn't change the fact that I was out of line. I know now that you didn't have anything to do with the game. You didn't tell Rex anything. It was just … Damn it, it was that fucking "good luck charm" thing, Brynn. It set me off.'

At last, her tired eyes flashed. 'It made me angry, too, but I didn't go after you, intent on tearing off your clothes. Why, Cody? Why do you insist on stripping me in public? You know how I felt about being caught the last time.'

He dropped his head back and took a deep breath. 'I wasn't thinking. I just acted on instinct. I needed to get inside you, and I didn't even consider where we were.'

She grabbed the key out of his hand and poked it viciously at the lock. 'I guess I'm lucky you left me with my panties this time. At least you didn't run them up the flagpole.'

'Goddammit. I told you that wasn't me!'

The door flew open, and she stepped inside. He

blocked the threshold with his foot to keep her from slamming the door in his face, but he needn't have worried. He was taken aback when she spun around, grabbed his arm, and pulled him into her apartment.

'We are not having this conversation out in the hallway for all my neighbours to hear,' she hissed.

She slammed the door behind him. He watched as she dropped her bags and walked to the centre of the living room. Her hands went to her hips before she slowly turned to face him. 'I'm so tired of you two using me to get back at each other.'

'Do you think that's what last night was about?'

'Wasn't it?'

'Hell, no!' He raked his hand through his hair. 'And stop comparing me with that asshole! I'm not playing any games here, Brynn. You should have felt that in the way I touched you – the way I've always touched you.'

Her hands flew up into the air. 'What do you want from me, Cody?'

His chest constricted. 'You know what I want. *I want you*. The question is, what do you want?'

Brynn's hands fell limply to her sides. She'd been asking herself that question repeatedly. 'I don't know,' she said tiredly.

She turned around and looked out the window. She plucked at her necklace as she stared at the crisp blue sky. The day was bright and sunny, but deceptively chilly. Just like last night.

She was so confused. What they'd done under those bleachers had been animalistic. There hadn't been any kind words or soft touches. It had been raw, fast and primitive.

And it had shaken her to the core.

She'd never come so hard. It had left her head fuzzy and her legs weak. When he'd walked away, she'd stood there half-naked and feeling lost. She'd wanted him back. More to the point, she'd wanted him back between her legs.

She ran a hand through her hair. 'I've spent so much time worrying about what everyone else wants, I haven't thought about myself,' she admitted.

'I've thought about you.'

She hadn't heard him move, but suddenly he was right behind her. She flinched when his arms slipped around her waist, but her muscles relaxed when he pulled her back against his chest. He was so warm, so strong – and she was so tired of fighting him.

He kissed her temple, and the tension in her neck eased. Gently, he turned her in his arms. 'I know what you need, Brynnie. Give me another chance to show you.'

Her eyelids fluttered closed when his mouth brushed ever so softly against hers. He did it again, and the last bit of tension in her muscles relaxed. He kissed her over and over again until her arms came up to wrap around his neck.

'I swear I'll do it right this time,' he murmured when he came up for air.

She turned her face into his palm when he brushed her hair behind her ear. 'I didn't tell Rex your plays Cody.'

'Shh,' he said. 'We're not going to think about him today.'

Her breath hitched when he leaned down and caught her behind the knees. She grabbed for his shoulders when he lifted her to his chest.

'We're not going to think about him tonight either.'

Brynn bit her lip. His dark eyes were serious, and her stomach flipped when he started carrying her to the bedroom.

He had his game face on.

'Today is all about us,' he said quietly.

He set her on the bed and kneeled in front of her. Her socks and shoes were gone so fast, she didn't know what happened to them. He pulled her to her feet again, and she caught his wide shoulders. He started on her jeans.

Today *was* different. Today she was going to have sex with Cody Jones, and she was going to do it willingly and without regret. She was tired of fighting her attraction to him. And why? She had no obligations to Rex. He didn't see her as his girlfriend; he saw her only as a pawn. With Cody, there was no hidden agenda. He'd made his feelings for her perfectly clear, and he had no idea how sexy that was.

His hands slid under her panties, and she kissed the side of his neck. 'I want to see you naked this time,' she whispered.

A shudder coursed through his body.

'Anything you want, Goody,' he promised as he pushed her clothes away. 'Anything.'

He squeezed her bare bottom, and her fingers dove into his hair. She moaned when he tugged her hands away, but held her arms up high when she realised he was taking off her sweater. Her bra followed and, in a flash, she was naked.

And he was still dressed.

She reached for his shirt and pulled it out of his jeans. This time, it was going to be a two-way affair. 'I want to touch you.'

'And I want your hands on me,' he growled.

She gasped when he tossed her onto the bed. She let out a startled laugh as she bounced, but it died quickly on her lips when he reached for the back of his shirt.

It went flying across the room, but her gaze was riveted to his chest. Her mouth began to water just looking at him. He looked liked the pro athlete that he was – strong, lean and virile. She wanted to trace every muscle that crisscrossed that body.

Her tongue pressed hard against the roof of her mouth when he kicked off his shoes and reached for his jeans. The zipper rasped and gaped open. He looked at her as he caught his white briefs.

'Oh!' she said softly when he pushed everything down and his cock jumped free.

She'd known how big he felt inside her, but seeing him was another thing entirely. He was hung. Her legs shifted against the mattress and unconsciously fell open. His heavy cock was engorged and pointing right at her.

'Roll over,' he said, his eyes glittering as he started to crawl over her.

The mattress shifted under his weight, but she had her own ideas. She caught his shoulders and pushed. 'You roll over.'

He was heavy, but he let her spin him onto his back. She straddled him, and the position planted her cunt right against his prick. His eyelids went heavy with desire as he watched her. Deliberately, she rocked against him. Her pussy lips swelled from the friction, and his cock jumped. She reached down to guide him to her, but he caught her hand.

'You're not wet enough, and I'm not going to do that again. At least, not so soon.'

'I liked it, Cody,' she whispered.

'I know you did, but this time I want you relaxed and running like a river.'

Her eyes went wide when his hand slid around her leg and came at her from behind. Two fingers pressed inside her to test her readiness. 'You're not there yet. Be a good girl while I play.'

She moaned. 'I thought you didn't like good girls.'

'I like good girls too much – especially when they're bad.'

She yelped when he pinched her butt cheek, but retaliated by rolling her thumb across the knobby head of his cock. It made him curse, and he went still underneath her.

'God, you're so hard,' she murmured. 'Everywhere.'

She let go of his cock to spread her hands wide on his amazing chest. Brown nipples poked between her fingers, and she teasingly squeezed. He was breathing hard as she trailed her touch down his arms and pressed at his biceps. They had no give to them at all. Nor did his abs – although they did suck in sharply when she scraped her fingernail along a line of his six-pack.

'Where did you go last night?' he asked as he reached up and caught her breasts.

Brynn did some inhaling of her own when he began toying with her sensitive nipples. 'I ended up at a mall somewhere outside Dallas.'

'I was worried about you.'

'Mmm,' she sighed. The NFL had always said he was good with his hands. 'I had a lot of thinking to do. I crashed at a motel and then did some serious damage to my credit card.'

He caught her nipples in a pinch. 'Buy anything I'd like?'

'Ahh, Cody!'

'You did!'

'Later,' she promised as she leaned over him.

She kissed him hard and touched the tip of her tongue to his lips. He opened for her, and they savoured each other's taste and texture.

Urgency suddenly consumed Brynn. She wanted him *now*.

Without breaking the kiss, she let her hand travel downwards. 'Cody, please.'

His cock was smooth and hot to the touch. He was so thick, her fingers couldn't touch as they curled around him. She wanted that thickness stretching her from the inside.

Her toes dug into the duvet and her hips rocked upwards when he reached around her again. She rubbed her breasts against his chest and bit her lip as he probed her. She let out a strangled cry when he applied pressure to her clit.

'All right, but go slow,' he ordered.

She looked into his eyes when the broad head of his cock touched her opening. She was slick. She could feel her stickiness coating both their skins.

Excitement pushed at her, and she began to drop onto him. He rubbed her tight pussy mouth, trying to get it to stretch and relax, but the feeling was more intense than Brynn remembered. Panic nudged at her, and her thigh muscles clenched. It hurt.

'You're swollen,' he said through clenched teeth. He ran his hands up and down her thighs. 'We went at it pretty hard last night. That's why I wanted you good and wet.'

He pushed her knees wider and swivelled his hips upward, slowly adding more pressure. 'Relax and open for me.'

Brynn's air caught. She looked him in the eye. She wanted this. She wanted his big dick plunging into her. 'Fuck me, Cody,' she said softly.

'I am,' he said with a rare smile.

It made her insides melt, and her resisting muscles gave way. He penetrated her to the hilt and her pussy grabbed him hard. His eyes closed and the muscles of his face tightened.

She sat upright, and he shifted deeper into her. Her head dropped back and her hair brushed her waist. She could feel every millimetre of him. He was big, he was hot, and he was horny.

She took a shuddering breath. They were lying on her bed in the middle of the day with sunshine spilling all around them. This time there was no confusion, no anger, and no misinterpretation. She and Cody Jones were truly screwing – and it felt incredible.

'Are you ready?' he asked. His eyes were barely open to slits as he looked at her.

'Are you?'

He thrust carefully and caught her breasts possessively. 'I've been ready forever. Hold on, baby.'

Brynn began rocking on her haunches, and her fingers curled against the muscles of his chest. 'You hold on. I want to fly.'

Much, much later, a noise made Brynn lift her head. The light coming through the window made her squint, and she burrowed her face against Cody's neck. 'What is that?' she groaned.

He shifted on top of her, but made no move to get up. 'I think somebody's trying to break in.'

He was heavy, but she reached up and began massaging the back of his neck. She liked him just where he was. 'Let them,' she sighed.

But the pounding wouldn't stop.

'Go away,' she called.

'They can't hear you.'

Her hands went limp against his bare back. 'I suppose I'd better see who it is.'

'Ah, hell. I'll go,' he said grumpily. 'I'm on top.'

He caught her at the waist, and she heard the distinctive slurping sound of their bodies disengaging. His energy ran out, though, and he rolled onto his back. 'Can't move.'

She chuckled. 'I'll get rid of them.'

'Make it fast.' He rubbed his tired eyes. The pounding was getting to him, too.

Brynn yawned as she padded to the door. She needed another good eight hours of sleep. Cody hadn't let her catch more than a few minutes at a time before he was on her and in her again. She smiled hazily as she lifted herself on tiptoe to look through the peephole.

Her eyes widened when she saw two familiar faces. Her cheerleaders! She quickly moved away before they saw her.

'What are they doing here?' she hissed. She ran a hand through her tangled hair and tried to figure out what to do.

'Let's break it down,' a muffled voice said.

'We can't break down her door.'

'We've looked everywhere else for her. She's got to be in there.'

'Then let's go convince the apartment manager to let us in. She'll kill us if we kick down her door.'

Oh, dear Lord! Brynn quickly reached for the lock. That was all she needed; her sweaty, overweight landlord letting Hannah and Trini in on her debauchery with Cody. She yanked open the door.

'I'm here,' she said. She poked her head out and used the door as a shield to hide everything else from prying eyes.

'Coach!' Hannah said with surprise. 'Are you OK?'

'We've been looking for you,' Trini said. 'You really had us wigging out.'

'Why?' Brynn said. She ran a hand through her hair to try to attain some semblance of order.

'You missed practice,' they said in unison.

Her eyebrows pulled together. 'What practice? I don't schedule practices on Sundays.'

'It's Monday,' Trini said bluntly.

The girl's observant gaze ran down her form, and Brynn pulled at the hem of Cody's white T-shirt. Darn it, she should have put on her robe.

'It can't be!' She frantically tried to piece together a timeline. The game had been Saturday night. She'd found Cody at her door the next day. It had been sunny when they'd gone to bed.

And then it had gotten dark.

And now it was sunny again.

'Oh no!' she whispered, horrified. She'd missed work and practice because of *sex*.

'That good, huh?' Trini said with a wink. 'Who is it? Not that creep from Palmer I hope.'

'Shhh!' Brynn hissed. She hastily looked towards the bedroom when she heard Cody rustling around. She bit the inside of her cheek and looked back to the women on her doorstep. 'I wasn't feeling well. I must have overslept.'

'By a day?' Hannah said.

'I'm much better now.' She began to close the door. 'You can tell everyone I'll be back tomorrow.'

'Oh, for God's sake, Brynn. Let them in.'

She spun around when Cody's voice sounded right next to her ear.

'If you missed practice, then so did I. It won't take a bunch of geniuses to figure that one out.' He hooked his arm around her waist and pulled open the door. 'Come on in, ladies. Are you hungry? We were thinking about finding something to eat.'

Brynn pressed her lips together tightly when she saw the stunned looks on her cheerleaders' faces. Hannah's eyes were wide as saucers, and even Trini's mouth hung open. Of course, the dark-haired girl was the first to recover. She grabbed Hannah's arm and stepped inside the apartment before the offer was rescinded.

'We're starved.'

Hannah's face broke out in a smile. 'Famished,' she agreed.

'Cody,' Brynn whined. Her reputation!

'Oh, come on, Goody. They're grown women. They've had sex before.' He closed the door and gave Hannah a considering look. He rubbed Trini's head affectionately as he walked past her. 'At least one of them has.'

All three women gaped at him as he strolled barefoot into the kitchen and opened the refrigerator.

'Mm-mm,' Trini murmured as her gaze ran down his backside.

Brynn didn't know what came over her, but she reached out and bopped the cheerleader upside the head. Trini let out a snort, and Hannah started laughing.

'It's not funny,' Brynn said, even though she fought a grin. She wrapped her arms about her waist and rubbed one bare foot on top of the other. She felt so exposed.

'Of course it's not funny,' Hannah said. Her voice dropped to a whisper. 'It's wonderful. He's soooo much hotter than that Palmer coach. What a creep.'

'Definitely the tastier of the two,' Trini agreed. She wiggled her eyebrows. 'Soooo ... how many points?'

Brynn tossed a glance at Cody. All he'd decided to throw on was his jeans. The muscles in his back clenched and relaxed as he searched her refrigerator. And that tight butt!

She sighed. 'How many points do you have?'

Trini and Hannah grinned and gave each other a high five before Cody turned around with a loaf of bread in his hand. Brynn felt his gaze land on her like a laser beam, and she quickly crossed her arms over her chest.

She'd tried to give the T-shirt back to him, but he'd decided it had looked better on her.

'I need to change,' she said. The reason he liked it so much was because he could see through it.

'Nonsense,' Hannah said. She wrapped her arm about her shoulders and walked her over to the breakfast bar. 'Sit down and relax. We're the ones who are intruding.'

Trini showed no shame. She hopped up onto the stool next to Brynn and stared dreamily at Cody. 'So you guys lost track of time, huh?'

Cody lifted one eyebrow. 'Huh.'

He set the bread, some butter and a packet of sliced cheese on the counter in front of him. 'If it matters, we're having grilled cheese sandwiches. Brynn apparently didn't make it to the grocery store during her shopping spree yesterday.'

'You cook?' Trini asked as she reached for the cheese. She started unwrapping the slices as Cody went in search of a pan.

'I do lots of things,' he said when he came up armed and ready to cook. He gave her a pointed look. 'With Brynn.'

'Oh, I know that,' she said, waving him off easily. 'I'm just checking you out.'

'She is our coach,' Hannah said protectively.

Cody smiled as he worked, and Brynn relaxed on the barstool. She'd gotten him to smile quite a bit last night, but it still made her go weak inside.

'Sorry about the Homecoming game,' Hannah said. 'It was rough.'

Cody just shrugged. 'You win some, you lose some.'

He glanced up from the frying pan. 'I heard you guys had a good night.'

Even if they hadn't already been under his spell, that was all it took to make the two captains fall in love with him. They braced their elbows on the counter and leaned towards him as they began to talk non-stop.

'We rocked!'

'Everything clicked. Karen even stuck the pyramid.'

'Dean Hawthorn told us how impressed everyone was.'

'The alumni said we looked better than we have in the past five years.'

Hannah looked at Brynn. 'Do you have the tape? We couldn't find it in your office.'

'Oh. Yes, I think it's in my bag.' She slid off the stool. Saturday night seemed like a year ago.

She walked over to the heap she'd dropped onto the floor when Cody had distracted her. She started to lean over for her bag, but remembered the shortness of the T-shirt. She kneeled instead. 'Here it is.'

'Can we watch it?' Trini asked, hopping off her stool.

'Sure.' Brynn combed her fingers through her hair as she walked across the living room to the VCR. Cody looked good enough to eat, but she needed a shower. Still, she couldn't believe how comfortable she felt having her cheerleaders in her home – especially at such an intimate time.

She stopped in front of the TV. 'That's strange.'

'Is the tape bad?' Hannah asked.

Brynn glanced absently at the tape in her hand, but her attention went back to the bookshelf next to the TV. It was bare. 'It's not that ... I must have taken the rest of the tapes to my office.'

Trini shook her head and planted her hands on her hips. 'There weren't any tapes there. We looked.'

Brynn's eyebrows drew together. 'Really? Then what did I do with them?'

'What's the problem?' Cody called from the kitchen.

'Nothing. I just seem to have misplaced our practice tapes.'

A look crossed his face, and he dropped the spatula onto the counter with a clatter. He strode into the living room with such purpose, all three women took an automatic step back. 'Let me see that,' he said as he took the remaining tape out of her hands.

He crouched down, plugged it into the VCR, and turned on the TV. The video of the cheer squad was crisp and clear. 'This is a game tape,' he said as he slowly stood. 'Do you use the same camera set-up for practices?'

Brynn looked at him. Why was he acting so strangely? 'Well, yes. Why?'

'The same angle?'

'I guess. Cody, what's wrong?'

'That fucking son-of-a-bitch!'

Hannah and Trini looked anxiously at Brynn, but she didn't have a clue what was happening.

'That's how he got our game plan,' he said, pointing at the television. 'Rex stole your tapes.'

Brynn's head swivelled towards the television. For a moment, she still didn't understand. When she looked more closely, though, things became clear. Bitterly clear. Her squad's performance wasn't the only thing on the screen. The football game behind them had been caught for posterity, too. 'Oh, no,' she whispered.

Rex had used her to get the tapes of Cody's practices. That fiend!

Her mind began churning. She *had* been missing a tape when she'd left Palmer College after the symposium.

Oh damn. Damn, damn, damn. No wonder Rex had done such an about-face. He'd screwed her in the trainer's room to get back at her, but when he'd seen what was on that tape, he'd decided to play her to get more.

She covered her face with her hands. She'd wondered about his change of heart when he'd shown up at Southern Trinity. She should have trusted her instincts. And darn it! She'd left him alone there, too. How could she have fallen for that phone call excuse?

She whirled towards Cody. His face was set, and his hands were clenched. 'I'm so sorry. I had no idea he could sink so low.'

'I did.'

'It *was* my fault,' she said, absolutely horrified. 'Your team lost because of me.'

Cody's throat worked. 'So he was here. In your apartment.'

Her stomach dove. She couldn't tell him about that! 'Yes – but I had no idea he stole from me. If I'd known, I would have told you.'

'He must have done a damn good job of distracting you.'

Trini and Hannah shifted uncomfortably, and Brynn fought not to squirm. She hated herself for what she'd let Rex do – both to her and Cody. What made it even worse, though, was how she'd gotten off on his sadistic treatment.

Cody looked away, and his Adam's apple bobbed. He didn't have to say it out loud. He knew. He didn't know the details, but he knew.

Brynn's fingernails bit into the palms of her hands. She couldn't believe she'd let this happen. She'd been so stupid. A sudden thought occurred to her, and her head whipped towards the bookshelf. The growl that came out of her throat sounded like a she-wolf. 'That bastard!'

She rushed over and began flipping through books and workout tapes. 'It's gone.'

Cody's chest heaved as he took a deep, cleansing breath of air. 'What's gone?'

She looked at him over her shoulder. 'Our tape.'

He raked a hand through his hair, and the muscles in his chest rippled. 'What tape?'

'*Our* tape – the tape of cheerleading practice the day you lifted me.'

His head came up, and Trini and Hannah gaped at her.

'I thought you were going to destroy that,' he said in a low voice.

She shrugged. 'I couldn't.'

A glint entered his eye, and the anger drained from his face. He crossed the room and caught her shoulders. 'No wonder that son-of-a-bitch was so vindictive. He saw it.'

Brynn's forehead scrunched. 'You think he was jealous? But why? That tape was pretty tame considering...'

Considering the other licentious things she'd done with Cody that would melt film.

'It wasn't tame,' Hannah said softly. 'It was personal and intimate.'

Trini shrugged almost embarrassedly. 'I wasn't there, but just the way you two look at each other makes me envious.'

'And that would be enough to make Rex blow his top.' Cody's hands tightened. 'Tell me you won't let him near you again.'

Brynn held his gaze steadily. 'If I never see that self-centred, vindictive snake again, it will be too soon. I hate him!'

'That makes two of us.'

Cody's fingers moved more gently into her hair, and she saw a familiar look enter his eyes. When he leaned down to kiss her, she lifted herself up on tiptoe to meet him. It was a kiss totally inappropriate for public display, but she didn't care. She opened her mouth for his tongue and scratched her nails down his back. They were both breathing hard when they came up for air.

'Whew,' Hannah said softly.

'Wow,' Trini agreed. 'Do you have any brothers?'

Cody didn't even look their way. He just stared down at Brynn with a satisfied look on his face. He patted her bottom softly and slowly stepped back from her.

At last, he looked at the cheerleaders. 'I'll feed you, but then you two have got to go. Your coach and I have things to do.'

'What about a cousin?' Trini pressed.

Brynn's face turned fuchsia. He was practically kicking them out so they could go back to bed.

Even Hannah got the point. 'We'll hurry,' she called as she rushed to the kitchen to find plates.

Brynn felt Cody's hot look level on her.

'We won't,' he promised.

12

'Where are they?' Trini asked as she burst into the office.

Hannah followed close on her heels. 'We heard that a bunch of boxes were delivered to you today.'

Brynn rested her elbow on her desk and propped her chin up in her hand. 'Have you two ever heard of knocking? We're in the middle of something here.'

Trini glanced at JJ as if she hadn't even noticed the big football player was in the room. 'Hey, Double J,' she said as she leaned over the desk to look at the computer monitor. Her face scrunched up like a prune. 'Comp Sci homework? Give me a break. We're here about something important.'

Hannah couldn't stand the suspense any longer. 'Come on, Coach. We've been waiting for a month. We want to see our new uniforms!'

Brynn lifted an eyebrow at the football star. 'See what I have to put up with?'

JJ laughed and began collecting his books. He stuffed them into his backpack and swung it over his shoulder. 'That's all right. I think I understand what I need to do.'

'Don't forget to give the users read-only rights to those group files on the server,' she said. 'We want them secure, but accessible.'

'I understand.'

She smiled at him. He was quickly becoming her star student. 'Call me if you have any questions.'

'I will. See ya, Professor Montgomery.'

Trini opened the door and shooed the big guy out.

Hannah was too busy visually scouring every corner of the room to say goodbye. 'There aren't any uniforms here,' she said in distress. 'They were supposed to arrive in time for the last game!'

'Bite your tongue,' Brynn said as she closed out of the computer script. 'Cody would strangle us if we said anything to jinx post-season play.'

Trini stomped across the room and planted her hands on the desk. 'Look, honey. We might be cute, but we have ways of making you talk. Where are our uniforms?'

'OK, OK,' Brynn laughed. She opened her desk drawer and grabbed her keys. 'They're in the dance hall. There wasn't enough room for them in here.'

The Latino girl swiped the keys and flew out of the room. Hannah hit the door behind her at a dead run. 'We'll meet you there,' she called.

Brynn chuckled as she locked her office door and followed at a more respectable pace. Scott Jetson was in the hallway, and she couldn't help but blush as she walked past him. Cody had been right. It hadn't taken the entire university long to figure out that they were now a couple. She still couldn't believe she'd lost an entire day in a sexual haze. Just thinking about it made her temperature rise.

She lifted her hair off the back of her neck as she walked down the stairs. There had been more nights like that. There'd been a few days, too, but Cody's schedule was getting too busy for them to take after-noon breaks anymore. With the football season coming to a head, nearly all of his time was consumed making game plans, conferring with his assistants, and getting his team ready for the post-season tournament.

She didn't mind. She had all his attention when he finally came to bed.

There was a nip in the air as she left the Clausen

building. It was a sharp contrast to her heated thoughts, and she hurried to the athletics centre. She rubbed the goose bumps on her arms as she skipped down the steps and turned into the dance hall. Her eyes widened when she saw the chaos inside.

Her cheerleaders hadn't waited for her. They'd already torn open the boxes and rummaged through the contents. Trini was working a skirt up over her hips and Hannah stood in the middle of the room topless. Brynn quickly closed the door behind her.

Hannah pulled on her top embarrassedly, but grinned as she smoothed the material over her stomach. 'Aren't they cool?'

'I love them!' Trini said as she skipped over to the mirror. She craned her neck to see behind her. 'Is my skirt too long?'

Brynn let out a snort. 'The question should be if it's too short.'

The dark-haired girl winked at her. 'That all depends on your perspective.'

Brynn rolled her eyes. She walked over to Hannah and tugged on the bottom of the girl's top. A good four inches of midriff were showing. 'These things weren't cropped so high when I was a cheerleader.'

Trini twirled and her skirt flew up to her waist. 'You should try one on!'

Hannah's eyes lit up. 'Hey! That's a great idea. You worked hard for these uniforms, too.'

'What?' Brynn held up her hands and backed away. 'Oh, I don't think so.'

Trini plucked a skirt out of a box and held it between her thumbs and forefingers. She jiggled it temptingly. 'You know you want to.'

She danced over with the skirt swishing in her hands. She held it up to Brynn's hipbones and then circled around behind her so they both could see in the mirror. 'What do you think?'

'They are cute,' Brynn admitted as she looked at her reflection.

Hannah dug a matching top out of a box. 'Here, this should fit. Put it on!'

Trini's grip tightened on her waist. 'You know if you don't, we'll put it on for you.'

'All right already,' Brynn said as she extricated herself from the girl's hold. She'd been tempted when the boxes had arrived anyway. With a defeated shake of her head, she unzipped her skirt and let it drop.

Trini whistled when she saw what was underneath. 'Sexy,' she said as she plucked at a garter belt.

Brynn jumped at the sting when the elastic snapped back into place. Cody liked the whole garter belt/stocking look. She stuck out her tongue at the cheerleader and undid the garters. She rolled off her stockings and replaced them with red cheaters and a tiny blue skirt.

'Here,' Hannah said as she passed her the rest of the uniform.

It was impossible to remain shy. Brynn pulled off her blouse and reached for her bra. She dropped it onto the chair with the rest of her clothes and pulled the top over her head. It was snug. She worked it down and felt the built-in bra plump up her breasts.

'Wow,' Trini said. She stepped up and straightened her crooked skirt. 'You've got awesome abs, and the close fit of that top makes your tits look huge.'

'Hey!' Brynn said when the girl reached out to feel her up. 'Go play with Hannah.'

Trini laughed. 'I played with her last night.'

Brynn threw the blonde a startled look, but she just sputtered as the dark-haired girl flounced by.

'Oh, give it up,' Trini said as she picked out a new set of pompons. 'I made you come three times.'

'You came twice,' Hannah blurted. Her hand flew up to cover her mouth when she realised what she'd just said aloud.

Brynn didn't know whether to laugh or be embarrassed for her. But really, there was no harm in experimentation. That was what college was for – and these two definitely needed to work out the friction between them. She hadn't considered sex, but if it worked, all the more power to them.

Trini threw her a wink. 'Don't worry. She wouldn't let me use the strap-on, so she's still technically a virgin. She wants a real cock for her first time. We're looking for a real big one.'

Brynn's mouth dropped. OK, now she was embarrassed.

'Is that my cue?' Hawthorn said as he walked into the dance hall.

Brynn spun around, but her horror was nothing compared to Hannah's. The girl turned the oddest shade of pale red. When the dean's gaze ran speculatively down her pert figure, she nearly fainted.

'Good. We have models,' he said. He rubbed his hands together in anticipation. 'I invited Mr Clausen over to see the uniforms. It only seemed fitting since it was his generous kick-off donation that got the ball rolling.'

Trini took a playful pose in front of him. 'Think he'll like them?'

'How could he not?' The dean threw the cheerleader an intimate look. 'They're very flirtatious.'

Brynn tugged at her top. The cut of it came to a point somewhere over her belly button. She couldn't help but notice that it pointed right down at her skirt, as if giving directions to what was hidden underneath. Her face flushed. 'You must think I'm silly. I couldn't resist trying one on.'

'"Silly" isn't the first thing that comes to mind.' Hawthorn's gaze slowly ran over her. After a moment, his head came up, and he caught his arms behind his back. When he looked at Hannah, he was once more the proper university dean. 'I assume you'll be wearing these for our last game tomorrow night?'

'Last game of the regular season,' Hannah corrected. 'And of course, we'll be wearing them!'

'Then I'll send out an email notice to the donors who made contributions. It will give them an added incentive to come to the game.' Hawthorn glanced at his watch and lifted an eyebrow. 'Girls, could you go watch for Mr Clausen? He's a bit late, and I'm not sure if he knows his way around this building. It isn't his, after all.'

'No problem,' Trini said. She rustled her pompons experimentally. 'I saw some football players in the weight room anyway. I want to try these puppies out.'

Hannah shook her head. 'I'll make sure he gets here,' she said responsibly.

'Thank you, dear.' The dean watched as the cheerleaders bounced out of the room. 'Ah, youth. The energy never ceases to amaze me.'

'You must think I'm trying to recapture it,' Brynn said with a self-conscious laugh. She headed to the chair with her clothes. 'I feel so ridiculous wearing this in front of you.'

'But why?' His blue eyes twinkled, and her stomach sucked in tightly when his hot gaze brushed her skin. 'You look sexy – just like you did when you were captain of the squad.'

Her stomach did a flip. God, she loved it when he

talked like that, even if it was inappropriate. His British accent just got to her. 'Thanks, but I'm not the captain anymore, I'm the coach.'

'Clausen won't mind.'

'But I do.' She turned to look at herself in the mirror. 'I'm not sure I have the legs to carry off this skirt anymore.'

Hawthorn stepped closer. 'Oh, you've got the legs – and the pert little ass.'

Brynn's spine snapped straight when he reached out and patted her backside. She twirled around and smoothed down the back of her skirt. 'That's very ... sweet of you.'

'Ah.' He steepled his hands together and bowed his head. 'I've overstepped my boundaries. I do apologise. It's just that seeing you dressed this way brings back so many fond memories.'

Brynn relaxed and smiled understandingly. 'I do miss those days.'

He pressed the tips of his fingers against his mouth. 'I'd only been a professor a few years when you showed up in my class.'

'I enjoyed World History. You were my favourite instructor.'

'And you were my favourite student. Your eyes had such a sparkle whenever you learned something new.' He shrugged. 'You put a sparkle in my eyes, too. I probably shouldn't admit this. You were so young, and it would have been improper, but ...'

She went still.

He trapped her with that piercing blue gaze. 'I've always considered you the one that got away.'

Brynn's jaw went slack. The professional side of her was affronted by his admission, but the cheerleader side of her felt a little thrill.

Red stains coloured Hawthorn's cheekbones. 'I shouldn't have said anything.'

She reached out and touched his arm. 'It's all right. I had a crush on you, too.'

A trickle of moisture collected in the crotch of her panties when she saw desire flare in his eyes. His tongue moistened his upper lip, and she snapped out of her reverie.

'But I'm with Cody now. We're very happy together.' She took a deep breath. She couldn't believe that she'd started to fall under his spell again. She'd thought she was over her juvenile fascination with him.

The dean dropped his hands and self-consciously pulled at the sleeves of his business jacket. 'Yes, I know. I'm thrilled you took my suggestion.'

Suggestion? She pressed her legs together more tightly when she remembered. He'd told her that opening her legs could open her options.

'A lot has changed in ten years,' she said.

'Time does have a way of moving on.' He ran a hand over his silver-tinged hair. 'You must think me an old fool to be panting after a gorgeous young thing like you.'

'No,' she said, taking pity on him. 'It's flattering. You're an attractive man.'

'Oh, now. Don't talk like that. It makes me wonder about what might have been.'

He stepped closer, and she felt the ballet barre press at her lower back.

'Just tell me, did you ever picture the two of us together when you had your schoolgirl crush?'

Heat made her flush. She'd been young and naïve, but her tame little daydreams still stirred her. 'Maybe we shouldn't talk about this.'

His eyes glazed over. 'I did. My fantasies were very ... *arousing.*'

Brynn caught the ballet barre with both hands. Her ears were scorched from his naughty words, but she was entranced.

She tried to fight the fog clouding her brain. She knew she couldn't let this happen. She was in a committed relationship with Cody. Just because the embers of an old crush were heating up didn't give her reason to forget that. She couldn't.

She shouldn't.

'If only you'd told me about your feelings then, we might have been able to explore them.' The dean smiled lazily and leaned forward. She felt his fingers brush against hers as he braced himself against the barre. 'You probably didn't realise, but your innocence was such a turn-on for me. I can't tell you how many times I tried to get you alone in my office, but you were immune to all my hints. Of course, that only made me want you more.'

Her mouth went dry, and she swallowed hard. What would have happened if she'd been more experienced? Would she have followed up on his silent offers?

The puddle of moisture slowly seeping through her panties and cheaters told her 'yes'.

'You were always so prim and proper.' He reached out and traced his finger along the hemline of her cropped top. 'I couldn't wait to bend you over my desk and hump you until you couldn't walk.'

Her breaths hitched. 'Dean Hawthorn –'

'Call me Darren.'

She inhaled sharply when his hand suddenly slipped under the hemline and covered her breast. The built-in bra provided no barrier to his skilful fingers. She reached up and grabbed his forearm. 'Dean!'

'Just one touch,' he crooned. 'For old times' sake.'

Her fingernails bit into his skin, but she couldn't make herself stop him. His fingers were too skilful. Long and thin, they knew just how to touch her. She bit her lip and let out a whimper when they began plucking at her nipples.

'No!' she said when he began rolling her sensitive tip between his thumb and forefinger. She dragged his hand away from her breast, but he was stronger than his thin frame let on. He spread his hand on her heaving belly and refused to break the touch.

She stared up at him, breathing hard. 'I'm with Cody.'

'But you still want me,' he said gently. 'Don't feel guilty, Brynn. You're a sexual woman. It's natural to be attracted to more than one man.'

'That doesn't mean I should act on my feelings.' She swallowed hard. This was wrong. She knew it was wrong.

'Of course it doesn't,' he said sympathetically. The fluorescent light in the room caught the silver hair at his temples when he leaned down. 'I understand completely.'

Tension was thick in the air. He was still too close. 'Thank you,' she said uneasily.

'You're welcome.'

She started to sidestep away, but went dead still when he leaned down and touched his tongue to her lips.

Her pussy contracted with a pang.

Oh, dear Lord. What was he doing?

They shared breaths as they stared at each other. His boldness stunned her, and she didn't know how to react. His tongue felt hot and wet as it pressed against her lips. Suddenly, she began to shake. His tongue moved, and her mouth rounded in a surprised 'O'. Her eyelids fluttered closed. Hesitantly, she opened her mouth.

His kiss was luxurious. There was no haste as he Frenched her. His tongue pressed in deep and rubbed intimately against hers. At last, his lips sealed against hers. When his arms swept around her, her reluctance vanished.

Oh, he knew how to kiss.

She leaned her head back into the crook of his arm as their mouths mated. When his hand slipped over her breast again, she covered it to hold it in place.

'Ah, yes,' he whispered as he ran soft kisses down to her neck. Her head fell back further to allow him access. 'I always knew there was a soft sex kitten underneath all that armour.'

One last bit of resistance caught her in the chest. 'Cody,' she whispered.

'Coach Jones will never have to know,' he said into her ear. 'This is unfinished business between you and me.'

'I can't.'

'Then allow me.'

She was in a near trance as he turned her around. When he gently pushed her forward, she offered no resistance. She caught the ballet barre and bent at the waist. Goose bumps collected at the base of her spine when he flipped up her skirt and caught the waistband of her cheaters.

'So pretty,' he said as he caressed her bottom. 'I knew that red would look best.'

Her thighs clenched when he began tugging them off of her. He chuckled when he saw her white lace panties. 'You're wet.'

Brynn squeezed her eyelids together when he cupped

her. With that evidence she couldn't deny her attraction to him anymore. 'Just once,' she said. 'To get it out of our system.'

'Yes, well, we'll see if once is enough.'

His knees bumped against hers, and she heard the rasp of a zipper. She tensed when he peeled down her panties and bared her. She risked a glance at the mirror and saw him staring at her pussy.

It was too much.

She closed her eyes and felt the knob of his cock press against her. He rubbed her lower back, but she couldn't relax. She'd been fantasising about this for too long. She couldn't believe that she was really splayed out like this before him, ready to take him.

'Sexy little Brynn,' he said as his hands wrapped around her waist. 'I'm going to give you what you've been asking for.'

'Ah!' she cried out in surprise. Her fingers clenched at the barre.

He didn't thrust into her in one smooth swoop. Instead, he entered her by jerks that dragged out the penetration and made it feel hotter and more invasive. Her fingers were white by the time he seated himself deep inside her.

'Oh yes,' he said roughly. 'You were definitely worth the wait.'

Brynn stared at their reflections in the mirror. They looked like they were role-playing with him as the sharp-dressed history teacher and her as the naughty cheerleader trying to improve her grade. She creamed. She shouldn't have made them both wait so long.

His hands clasped her waist tightly, and he began to pump. His cock was sturdy, but it felt foreign. It was odd to be taking someone other than Cody. Guilt snuck up on her again, and she bowed her head.

'Such a sweet girl,' he panted as he worked inside her.

He pushed her hips forward, and she rocked up onto her toes. He reversed directions and was almost out of her when he pulled her back onto her heels. His cock pierced her deeply, and she moaned. Unable to help herself, she ground herself onto him.

'That's my little cheerleader,' Hawthorn rasped. He reached under her top and caught her breast. 'Again. For old times' sake.'

Something inside of Brynn clicked. Old times. Like when she'd dated the wrong boy for all the right reasons. Like when Cody had been ready and waiting and she'd held him at arm's length. Like when she'd shied away from her professor because her attraction to him had been too scandalous.

Those days were gone. Scandal had found her anyway, and she refused to miss out on anything ever again.

She rocked her hips back, and her lungs worked like bellows as he juddered into her. He went deep – as deep as he could go. She ground onto him again and began to pump ferociously.

'Oh, sweet thing,' Hawthorn groaned. His hands pawed at her, trying to find a better grip. 'Come on, little cheerleader. Show me what you've got.'

Cody strode into the dance hall with a smile on his face. 'Hey, Brynnie. There's a rumour that you're wearing a cheerleading uniform. Let me see . . .'

The familiar gleam of blonde hair caught his eye, but he nearly doubled over at the blow that hit him in the gut.

God, it was like time had been turned back. She was dressed in a cheerleading outfit with a tiny top and a flouncy short skirt – only someone else had flipped her skirt up to her waist.

And someone else was nailing her.

Her panties stretched tight across her thighs as the dean pumped his meat into her. Harsh breaths filled the room as their bodies undulated together.

Fury spread through Cody's body like venom. 'Hawthorn!' he bellowed.

The dean's head snapped to the side. Brynn's eyes flew open, and she stared at his reflection in the mirror. A look of horror crossed her face.

Hawthorn yanked his dick out of her, but it was red and covered with her juices. It was enough to send Cody over the edge. He charged forward as the man stuffed his stiff cock back into his pants.

'Now, Mr Jones,' Hawthorn said uneasily. He held up his hands and backed away. 'Let's talk about this.'

'Let's not.' Cody pushed a chair out of his way, and it clattered noisily to the floor.

Brynn spun around and pushed down her skirt. She was reaching for her panties when he let go a right cross at her boss. 'Cody!' she yelled.

The punch caught Hawthorn right on the chin of his hoity-toity face and sent him stumbling backwards.

Cody glared at Brynn and saw surprise, fear and regret all jumbled on her face. The look caught him right in the chest and, for a moment, he couldn't breathe.

He'd seen that look once before – when Rex had walked in on them.

He turned on Hawthorn.

'You slimy son-of-a-bitch,' he growled. The man was just catching his balance, but he put him down with a body blow and stood over him with his hands fisted. 'What gave you the idea you could touch her?'

'Cody, please.' Brynn stepped towards him, but stopped when she saw the look on his face.

'I'll have your job for this,' Hawthorn said as defiantly as a man flat on his back could. He reached up to cup his sore jaw, but made no move to get to his feet.

'Just try,' Cody growled. 'Because I'll take you down with me.'

Suddenly, the door to the dance hall banged open. Trini and Hannah spilled into the room, along with three football players.

'What's going on?' Hannah called.

Nobody else needed an explanation.

Cody bent down and caught Hawthorn by the lapels of his suit jacket. If the coward didn't have the guts to defend himself, he deserved to get his ass kicked. He pulled his fist back, but his players bolted across the room.

'Come on, Coach,' Jets said as he caught his arm.

'It's not worth it,' said JJ. He pried the dean's jacket out of his hand and pushed him away.

'The hell it's not!' Cody growled.

'You're right about that, son.'

His gaze snapped to the door. Old man Clausen was standing there, looking like the powerful alumni donor he was. 'It's about time somebody smacked that smart ass down for all the diddling he's done.'

'Mr Clausen!' Hawthorn rolled onto his side on the floor and groaned. He weakly pushed himself to his knees. 'I'm sorry you had to see this. There's been a misunderstanding of sorts between the coach and myself.'

'No misunderstanding, Darren.' Clausen's chest puffed out with indignity. 'We all know you'll stick your prick into anything that wiggles. It was only a matter of time before one of your conquest's men took exception.'

The dean reached for his ribs. He was still having problems breathing. 'It was nothing like that, I assure you. You need not worry yourself over this.'

'I won't. Seems to me you deserved what you got. Now, get on your feet and return to your office.'

Hawthorn got to his feet unsteadily, and Cody lunged again. JJ stopped him with a shoulder to his belly. Jets grabbed him from behind, and they held him immobile as the Brit limped out of the room.

'Let him go, Mr Jones,' Clausen said calmly. 'The man might be a pest, but he does good work for the university. I doubt you'll have any more problems with him.'

'And if I do?'

'Then you have my full permission to clean his clock. Now,' the old man said as he rubbed his hands together, 'would you girls like to join me for a cup of coffee? Those fancy uniforms need to be shown off.'

'Um . . . I'll go,' Hannah said. Wisely, she led the donor out of the room.

JJ and Jets finally let go of Cody. He shrugged them off and straightened his sweatshirt. He felt like going another ten rounds.

'Take it easy, Coach,' they told him as they backed towards the doorway.

Trini didn't want to leave, but she threw her coach a sign that she'd be just outside if she needed her.

Cody stalked around the room until everyone was gone. At last, he turned on Brynn. 'What the hell is wrong with you?'

She looked at him remorsefully. 'I'm sorry. I never meant for that to happen.'

'So it was an accident? He tripped and his dick popped into you?'

She closed her eyes.

'Did he force you?'

She twisted her necklace until the links almost popped. 'No,' she said weakly.

'Goddammit, Brynn. What the fuck has gotten into you?' He stepped towards her, and she bumped up against the mirrored wall. 'It used to be that a guy couldn't pry your legs open with a crow bar. Now you're spreading for anyone that looks at you sideways.'

Her face went white. He didn't care. He wanted something out of her. An explanation, tears ... *something*. He reached out and caught her by the chin. 'I thought we were making something together, Brynnie.'

'We were.'

'Then why did you just throw it out the window?'

'I didn't. I mean, I didn't think. Cody, please. I never wanted to hurt you.'

His head snapped back, and his eyes opened wide. Oh, that sounded a little too familiar. He felt sick. For the first time ever, he had an inkling of what Rex must have felt like when he'd stumbled across the two of them. But then again, Rex hadn't cared for her. He closed his eyes against the pain. 'For not wanting to, you did a pretty damn good job,' he said tightly.

'I'm sorry,' she said, reaching for him.

He batted her hand away. 'No, I can't hear this now.'

'Let me explain.'

He pulled back. He couldn't deal with any of this. He had a game to prepare for – an important game. In the scheme of things it was probably insignificant, but football was the only thing he'd ever been able to count on.

He certainly couldn't count on her. After all, he'd always been her second choice. He just hadn't known that Hawthorn had been in the running.

'I've got to go,' he said. It was hard to breathe with

the lead weight sitting on his chest. He backed away to the door and yanked it open. He was halfway out before he stopped and looked back at her. 'And stay away from me until football season is over. I won't let you destroy that, too.'

13

Brynn rolled off the couch when she heard a knock on the door and pushed herself to her feet. She wiped her runny eyes with a Kleenex and tossed it into the overflowing wastebasket. She wasn't in the mood for company, but she had a feeling she knew who it was.

And they weren't likely to go away.

She ran a hand through her hair and tried to smooth out the creases in her pyjamas. It didn't help. Dejectedly, she padded over to the door and opened it. As she suspected, Trini and Hannah were on her doorstep. Both were still wearing their cheerleading uniforms.

'We came as soon as we could,' Hannah said. She juggled the things she carried until she had an arm free. She used it to give her a hug.

'We had to stop off for the four major "man problem" food groups,' Trini said. She patted her on the back as she walked into the apartment.

'How are you doing?' Hannah asked quietly.

Brynn shrugged. She knew she looked like hell. She hadn't made it off the couch in twenty-four hours, and she was on her second box of tissues. She hadn't realised the human body was capable of storing so much water.

Hannah gave her shoulders a squeeze and kicked the door shut with her foot. She set a pizza box on the breakfast bar, and Trini put a bottle of wine beside it. She pulled three pints of ice cream out of a brown grocery bag and opened a drawer to find spoons. Brynn's gaze fell on the white sack that Hannah dropped onto the kitchen counter. It was Kettle Korn. She felt her eyes well up again.

'I'm sorry,' Hannah said. She reached out and rubbed her arm. 'I didn't mean to upset you.'

'You didn't,' Brynn said. She grabbed another Kleenex and blew her nose. 'You're both so sweet.'

'Hey, don't spread that around,' Trini said as she took the lids off the ice cream. She jammed a spoon in each. 'Butter pecan, chocolate peanut butter, or Rocky Road?'

Brynn looked at the choices listlessly.

'You're still in the chocolate peanut butter stage.' Trini passed her the pint and took the Rocky Road for herself. She walked back to the living room and looked at the radio. It was playing alternative rock and roll, but she recognised the station. 'You listened to the game.'

'I had to,' Brynn said. Wearily, she plodded back to the living room and dropped onto the couch. She was embarrassed to have them here. They both knew why Cody had banned her from the football stadium. They'd been there. They'd seen what she'd done.

Or more aptly, whom she'd done.

'How is he?' she asked quietly. 'The radio announcer made it sound like he was in a bad mood.'

'Bad? Try rotten,' Hannah said as she sat on the couch beside her. 'His players were trying their best not to make mistakes.'

Trini parked her butt on the coffee table. 'Jets got his ass chewed more than once.'

Brynn looked away. Poor kid. He'd taken flak because of her. 'I can't imagine what you must think of me.'

Hannah wrapped an arm around her shoulders. 'Come on. We still love you. You're the best coach we've ever had, and we wouldn't be your friends if we turned away from you now.'

Trini gently combed Brynn's hair back from her face.

'We know all the stress you've been under. You're only human.'

'But Cody.' Brynn's breath hitched as she said his name. 'I can't believe I did that to him. What was I thinking? It was so unlike me.'

'It was Hawthorn. The man can be amazingly seductive. I should know.'

Brynn looked at the pretty dark-haired girl through watery eyes. 'But things were going so well. I should have said no more forcefully. I should have meant it.'

Trini shrugged. 'The dean is your boss, and he knows how to use that power. Ever think of what might have happened if you hadn't bent over for him?'

The colour drained from Brynn's face. It sounded so base when put that way. 'He wouldn't have done anything. I've always rejected him. There were times when I didn't even know he was asking and I refused him.'

'But he never stopped asking, did he?'

Hannah pulled another Kleenex out of the box on the end table and passed it to her. 'I don't think he'll be asking again – not after what Coach Jones did to him.'

Brynn wiped the tears from her face. 'Is Hawthorn OK?'

Hannah shrugged and sampled her butter pecan ice cream. 'Rumour is that he had X-rays taken, but his jaw wasn't broken. We don't know how he looks. He didn't show up tonight.'

Brynn made herself take a bite of ice cream, simply because she couldn't remember if she'd eaten anything all day. It was probably good that Hawthorn hadn't gone to the game. If Cody hadn't wanted her there, she could only imagine how he would have reacted to seeing the dean in the stands.

'We have worse news,' Trini said gently. She set her pint to the side and laid her hands on Brynn's knees.

'Palmer won tonight, too. We have to face them in the first round of the tournament in two weeks.'

Brynn felt the two-ton weight hit her in the chest. 'Palmer? No!'

'Yes. Fate has a sick sense of humour, but this might be the best thing that could have happened.'

'Are you nuts?'

Hannah took away her ice cream before she could drop it onto the sofa. 'Just listen to us,' she said. 'This might be your chance to show Coach Jones how much he means to you.'

Brynn caught her necklace and twisted it into a knot. What chance? She had been trying to think of a way to make Cody forgive her, but this wasn't it. If Rex were thrown in his face at such a fragile time, he'd never take her back.

She closed her eyes. How had she managed to screw things up so badly? And so quickly?

'Look at me,' Trini said firmly.

'He doesn't want anything to do with me.'

'Yes, he does, but you have to get off your duff and make the first move.'

Brynn blinked and sat back.

'We're not trying to be mean,' Hannah said. 'We just want what's best for you.'

A half-laugh/half-sob escaped Brynn's throat. 'And what is that?'

'Coach Jones,' Trini said with a steady gaze. 'Or don't you want him back?'

'Of course, I do. I want him more than anything!'

'Then you're going to have to do something to make him believe that. He's hurting because he doesn't think you've ever chosen him.'

Brynn stiffened. 'Yes, I have. After Rex –'

'Exactly,' Hannah said sharply. 'It was only after

Coach Stanton played that nasty trick on you that you turned to Coach Jones.'

Brynn looked at the cheerleader with wide eyes. She could understand Trini coming down on her, but it was jolting to hear innocent little Hannah's tough love.

'The coach thinks he was your fall-back position,' Trini said unflinchingly. 'The rebound guy.'

Brynn cringed. 'Oh, God, I never thought of it like that. To him, it must seem like Rex always came first. Then when he caught me with the dean ... He must hate me.'

'Don't even think that,' Hannah said. She leaned her head close. 'Trini and I have seen the way he looks at you. We'd both give up our left pompons to have a guy look at us that way.'

Trini shrugged when Brynn glanced her way. 'It's true. I'd hop right down to one side of the fence if I had a guy like Coach.'

'He's more than a hottie,' Hannah said softly. 'He's a keeper.'

Brynn closed her eyes again when the tears began to stream down her face. 'I threw him away.'

'No, you didn't,' Trini said. 'You had a weakness, and Hawthorn kept poking at it. No pun intended.'

'You were curious.' Hannah squeezed Brynn's shoulders comfortingly. 'I, of all people, should understand that.'

Brynn tossed her tissue into the wastebasket and wrapped her arms around her knees. 'Cody doesn't. How could I expect him to?'

'All right, enough of this,' Trini said as she came to her feet. 'It's time to stop feeling sorry for yourself. You've let these men run all over you for so long, you've forgotten how to take charge of your life. Aren't you tired of playing the patsy?'

'The what?' Brynn said, looking up with a stunned expression on her face.

'The patsy. The toy that these guys are passing around. It seems to me that Coach Jones is the only one who's treated you like a real woman. He never lied about what he wanted. He wanted you.'

Trini threw up her hands. 'Meanwhile, this Rex guy and Dean Hawthorn are using sex as a weapon. Well, two can play at that game.'

'What are you talking about?' Brynn said numbly.

'We play Palmer in two weeks. That gives you four-teen days to turn the tables on that creep Stanton. He's your real problem. Hawthorn was just an extenuating circumstance.'

Hannah nodded. 'Trini has already talked to Coach Jones about him anyway.'

'Hannah! Shush!'

'You did what?' Brynn's head snapped towards Trini. 'What did you say to him?'

The Latino girl rolled her eyes. 'Blabbermouth wasn't supposed to say anything.'

'Trini,' Brynn warned.

'I had a chat with Coach Jones. I just thought it was time we had a little one-on-one. In a perfectly platonic way,' she quickly assured.

'Oh my God. What did you do?'

Trini crossed her arms over her chest. 'I simply told him how the dean coerced me into bed. Heck, if the guy could seduce me, you didn't stand a chance.'

Brynn twisted her necklace. She couldn't believe what she was hearing. 'What did Cody say?'

'Not much. Trini and I had to blockade the door to get him to listen to me.'

'Did he say anything about me?' she asked hesitantly.

'He didn't have to. The guy is crazy about you. It's as

plain as that cute Roman nose on his face. He's just insecure about your feelings towards him.'

'Cody's never been insecure in his life.'

Trini pointed a rigid finger at her. 'He is when it comes to you. If it came down to him and Stanton, he's not sure who you'd choose.'

'Him. I'd pick him.' Brynn pulled at her necklace. Not so long ago, she wouldn't have been so sure of her answer. Now, she knew it to the depths of her being.

'You need to show him that,' Hannah said. Brynn's head snapped to the side, but the cheerleader's blue gaze was steady. 'Prove to him that Rex isn't a problem and this whole thing with the dean will just fade away.'

'And how can you be so certain?'

The girl shifted on the cushion. 'Trini's taught me a thing or two.'

'And believe me, she's a quick learner.' Trini planted her hands on her hips. 'I know what I'm talking about. You have to go after Rex.'

Hannah nodded in agreement. 'And you have to use whatever weaknesses he has to get what you want.'

Brynn looked at them. Their faces were so full of determination, she couldn't help but fall in line. 'You're right,' she said.

She needed to take charge of her life – and that meant getting Cody back. It was time she to get rid of the Rex problem. Forever.

Hunger pangs finally hit in her belly, and she reached for her ice cream. For the first time since she'd stumbled out of the dance hall, she felt hope. 'What should I do?' she asked as she carved out a chunk of peanut butter.

Trini's eyes lit up, and she snatched up her Rocky Road. She began pacing like an evil genius as she began eating. 'OK, here's the plan.'

* * *

Brynn was full of steely concentration as she walked down the hallway of the Patterson building on the Palmer College campus. It was late in the afternoon. The last classes of the day were coming to an end, and most students had already returned to the dorms. She wasn't looking for a student; she was looking for a football coach.

She passed Julie's office and was happy to see it dark. She didn't need any distractions today.

She looked for Room 148. The directory had listed it as Rex's office. She hoped he'd be there. She wanted to finish this off quickly.

'Damn,' she muttered when she found the room locked.

The light was still on, though. She turned on her heel and considered where he might have gone. Her backbone stiffened when she thought of the training room. She really didn't want to go back there, but if things had to go full circle, so be it.

Her high heels clipped along the linoleum floor, but she heard the distinctive sound of steel clanging as she passed the weight room. She hesitated and opened the door. She fully expected to find a bunch of college athletes, but instead, she found her prey.

She leaned against the doorway as she watched Rex. He was flat on his back doing bench presses. The bar was laden down with three big discs on either side. He'd stripped off his shirt, and she could see the muscles in his arms and chest bulging as he lifted and lowered the bar.

His strength should have intimidated her. It didn't.

Cody had been right all along. The man was a spoiled bully. He thought because of his physical strength and Stanton money, he deserved more than anyone else.

Her temper flared. He deserved something, all right.

She'd been so stupid. He'd carried a grudge against her for ten years, not because she'd hurt him, but because she'd embarrassed him and his family name. She'd fallen all over herself trying to get back in his good graces, but he'd never had any intention of forgiving her. He didn't want to forgive her. She'd wronged him, and that was that.

He finally finished the set of exercises. The barbell clattered to a rest above his head, and he dropped his arms to his sides. His head came up when he sensed her presence, and she wiped the angry expression from her face.

'Hello, Rex,' she said silkily. 'May I come in?'

His eyes narrowed. 'What are you doing here?'

She traced her finger down the doorframe. 'I missed you. You haven't called since the last time we ... made love.'

She had to clear her throat in order not to gag on the words.

'We didn't make love. We fucked.'

The muscles between her shoulder blades clenched, but she let her eyelashes drop demurely. 'Please don't be crude. I wanted to congratulate you on your team making it to the post-season tournament.'

'Southern Trinity made it, too.' He sat up on the bench, and his body language was tense. 'Spying on me won't work, Brynn. I would have thought you'd learned that the first time.'

She looked at him through the slit of her eyes. She'd spied? He was the one who'd stolen her videotapes.

He ripped open the Velcro at his wrist and tightened the fit of his leather weight-lifting gloves. 'Don't be so coy. I know that's why you came to Palmer the first time. Cody sent you.'

'I came for a computer symposium.'

'Nice cover story. You said you weren't with him, but I knew you were. And hell, he confirmed it on the radio after the Midwestern Texas game.'

Brynn set down her purse. She'd known Rex was sneaky, vindictive, underhanded, and a million other reprehensible things. She'd just never pictured him as paranoid.

'Believe what you want, but I'm not with Cody anymore,' she said.

She took off her coat and draped it over the stack of free weights. His expression changed when she turned. Perfect. She and the girls had shopped for two days before they'd found what they'd wanted. The dress was silk in a muted grey that hinted at silver. Dashes of red gave it colour and drew attention to the lines of her body. With the way the shimmering material skimmed over her, every dip and curve was there for the world to see.

She fingered her necklace deep into her cleavage. The low cut of the dress's neckline and the thin spaghetti straps didn't offer much coverage at all. 'He caught me with another man,' she said bluntly.

That, at last, got Rex's attention. His gaze bored into hers as he searched for the lie. 'Cody walked in on you banging another guy?'

'The dean.'

His jaw dropped.

She toyed with her necklace and shrugged. 'You know how I am. Hawthorn aroused my curiosity, but Cody caught us in the act. He threw me out before the last game of the season. I would have thought you'd heard by now.'

A smug expression settled onto Rex's face. 'Oh, that's just too perfect to be true. You and the dean. I wish I could have been there to see Jones' face.'

Disgust gelled in Brynn's gut. She needed to finish this. Much longer around this pig, and she'd be ill.

She looked about the room until she found what she needed, but hesitated when she glanced at his powerful body. Could she do it? What if Trini was wrong? She let out a slow breath. *Stick to the plan*, she told herself.

'Take me back, Rex,' she said in a husky voice. 'You were the best lover out of all of them.'

He sneered at her with distrust, but she'd scored a direct hit to his ego. His sweaty chest puffed out with pride, and he rudely clutched his crotch. 'I screwed you like a low-class whore.'

'And I liked it.'

'Damn right you did. I'd never seen anyone take it up the butt with such enthusiasm.'

Brynn wanted to grab one of the free weights and knock the cocky expression off his face. Instead, she pulled up her skirt and dropped to her knees in front of him. She laid her hands on his knees. 'You understand me better than anyone.'

'You like to play the innocent, but you're at your best when it's down and dirty.'

She stroked her fingers up his thigh to the bulge in his shorts. His stomach muscles worked when she opened her hand and covered his cock. She squeezed and felt it thicken. 'I was a fool to betray you. Let me show you I'm sorry.'

'How sorry?'

'I'll swallow this time.' She boldly reached up and splayed her hands across his muscular chest. 'Lie back.'

He was like a rock. 'This isn't like you, Brynn. So help me, if you're playing me again . . .'

She froze. She'd taken things too far. She'd told Trini she wasn't a good actress. 'So don't act,' the girl had said.

Don't act. Brynn let her hands quiver against Rex's chest, and her gaze shied away. 'Am I not doing it right?' she whispered.

'Doing what right?'

'Seducing you.'

He stared at her for a long hard moment and then let out a wicked laugh. 'Shy little Brynn has come to seduce me. All right, baby. What have I got to lose? Playing me or not, I still get a blow job.'

With a wink, he dropped onto his back and folded his hands on his chest. The bastard wanted her to service him.

Easy, Brynn reminded herself. Just a few more minutes, and she'd have him where she wanted him.

Her stomach rolled, but she lowered her head and rubbed her cheek against his stiff ridge. He grunted, and she caught his shorts. He lifted his hips to help her, and she stripped him down to his tennis shoes. She had to bite back a laugh when his stubby cock reared upright like a fat little boy wanting attention.

'Get to it,' he demanded.

The jerk. He wanted it? Well, he was going to get it.

She dipped her head and licked the underside of his cock from the base to the tip. It wasn't very far. His hips rolled, but she latched onto him and began to suck for all she was worth. Using both hands, she caressed his balls. She held nothing back as she tongued him. She suckled and pumped until he was writhing on the bench.

She winced when his hands caught her head. 'Ow!' she complained.

She lifted her head and flung her hair over her shoulder. This time, she didn't have to hide her cunning look. It fitted the moment too well. 'I won't do this if you're going to pull my hair.'

A look of distress crossed his face when she caught his thighs and pushed herself to her feet.

'Hey,' he said as he reached out and caught her wrist. 'Get back down there.'

'We're going to do this my way,' she said.

Her heart thudded as she walked over to the open cabinet she'd spied earlier. She let out a calming breath as she picked up a roll of athletic tape. She twirled it around her finger as she strutted back to him. His hot gaze swept down her figure and stopped on her red shoes. Her footsteps slowed. She'd worn them because she knew he'd liked them – but 'liked them' didn't come close.

She was playing with fire here.

'What's the tape for?' he asked, his eyes narrowing.

Trini, you'd better be right.

'I'm going to tie you up.'

'Tie me up?' The look on his face was incredulous – yet vaguely intrigued. He covered it quickly and reared upright. His cock was so small, she couldn't see it anymore for the thick tree trunks of his legs. 'Fuck that, if anyone is going to get tied up it will be you. I'll truss you up like a pig and screw you from behind.'

If she hadn't seen the look of curiosity on his face, she wouldn't have been so brave. But she had seen it. She just needed to shake him up a little more, and he'd be putty in her hands.

She reached for the straps of her dress. Watching him through the curtain of her lashes, she pulled them over her shoulders and let them skim down her arms. Gravity did the rest. The dress slid down her curves and fell to the floor. It pooled around her red shoes, leaving her wearing nothing but a teeny leather thong.

Rex went still. 'Turn around,' he said hoarsely.

Brynn glanced nervously at the door. She'd been

caught too many times not to be wary. This time, she wanted him to get caught, but not quite yet. She slowly pivoted.

'Ah!' she said in surprise when he caught her ass.

She forced herself to stand still as he fondled her butt cheeks, but she jerked when his thumbs traced the thong to where it disappeared into her crevice.

He made a tsking sound. 'Damn. It wouldn't do much good to put this up a flagpole. It's so tiny, nobody would be able to see it up there.'

Brynn's blood turned to ice in her veins even as his thumb rubbed suggestively against her anus. The flagpole?

Her breaths went shallow in her chest. *He'd* run her cheaters up the flagpole? 'I did deserve that,' she said hoarsely.

'Of course you did,' he said. He pulled back on the waistband of her thong and let it snap back into place. 'You were a slut. Everyone needed to know.'

Brynn felt sick. She'd been horrified when all those football players had seen her with Cody, but the rumour could have been denied. She would have hung her head for the rest of the school year, but she might have been able to stay and graduate.

That flagpole, though. She hadn't been able to hide from the proof that flew so proudly the next day. Everyone knew that cheaters were part of the cheerleading uniform. Combine that with the rumour, and she'd had to transfer to another university.

She couldn't believe she'd blamed Cody all these years.

The embers of rage in her stomach exploded into a four-alarm fire.

She schooled her face and turned to face Rex. She caught his wrist and lifted it towards one of the vertical bars supporting the barbell. She ripped off a chunk of tape with her teeth. 'Stop stalling,' she purred. 'The sooner you let me tie you up, the sooner you'll feel my tongue.'

He stared at her belligerently for a long moment, but then lay back.

Trini had been right. For such a big bully, his secret desire was to have someone dominate him.

He wrapped his leather-clad hand around the pole, and she secured him with the thick tape. She made several figure eights until she was sure he couldn't get free.

'Very nice,' she cooed.

She strode around to the other side of the weight bench, but jerked when he jabbed his hand between her legs. She let his fingers play as she ripped off another strip of tape, but then lifted one eyebrow. Little blotches of colour stained his cheekbones as he obediently lifted his arm over his head. She bound him to the weight bench and glanced at his cock. It was thicker than ever and straining towards the ceiling.

He was hornier than she'd ever seen him.

Good. It served him right.

She tossed the tape towards the cabinet and leaned over him. 'Are you comfortable?' she asked.

He lifted his head and nipped at her breast. She pulled back from the sharp sting.

'Get down there,' he growled. 'I'm about ready to blow.'

She let her hair stroke his chest as she turned her head. 'I can see that.'

She caught him in her hand, and his hips bucked as she pumped him.

'God! Enough! Your mouth, Brynn.'

She swirled her thumb around his tip, but then

slowly stood upright. 'I don't think so,' she finally declared.

She planted her hands on her hips and rocked one red shoe back onto its heel. 'That stubby little prick isn't worth it.'

A choked sound erupted from Rex's throat. The red that had stained his cheekbones spread. His face was nearly purple as his head snapped up off the bench. 'You bitch!'

Brynn smiled as she caught his cock again. She wrapped her fist around him and tilted her head as if considering it. 'You know, I can use two fists on Cody and still not cover him.'

She tossed her hair over her shoulder. 'Forget this. I'm going to go apologise to him.'

She strutted around the weight bench with her breasts bouncing proudly. Rex tried to kick at her, but she neatly avoided him as she picked up her dress. She threw him a hard smile. 'You must think me heartless, but then again, I learned from the master.'

With a calm expression on her face, she let the dress slide over her curves. Rex squirmed and cursed from the weight bench, but the tape held well. Every time he twisted, it only adhered to itself more tightly. Brynn picked up her coat, purse, and the keys she'd spied next to his water bottle. As a last thought, she bent down and gingerly picked up his sweaty underwear between her thumb and forefinger. 'Goodbye, Rex.'

'You can't leave me here!'

'Relax,' she said as she opened the door. 'I'm sure someone will find you in the morning.'

His violent swearing was muffled when the door swung shut. Brynn held her head high as she walked down the hallway to his office. She wasn't exactly proud of herself, but she certainly felt better. The girls had been right. It was high time she took charge of her love life. Now, it was on to Step 2 of 'The Plan'. She could only hope that it went as well as Step 1.

Cody slammed his beer onto the table when someone began knocking on his door. He wanted to be alone, but whoever was out there seemed determined to stay until he answered.

What the hell did it take for a guy to have a meltdown in peace?

Angrily, he stomped across the room and yanked open the front door. 'What do you want?' he growled.

He never saw the sledgehammer that hit him square in the chest. Brynn was standing on his doorstep.

'Hello, Cody,' she said softly.

He folded his arms over the pain and leaned against the doorframe for support. 'What are you doing here? I thought I told you to stay away from me.'

'I know, but I had to see you.' She looked at him cautiously. When he didn't answer, she began digging in her purse. 'I brought you something.'

She thrust a CD at him, but he made no move to take it. What he wanted from her couldn't be put on a computer disk.

Her hand shook as she hooked her blonde hair behind her ear. 'It's the Palmer playbook.'

Now that was a kick in the ass. He came right out of the house onto the porch and grabbed the CD from her grip. He glared at it. It wasn't even labelled. 'Where did you get this?'

Her face turned pink. 'From Rex's computer.'

Cody's throat went tight, and he nearly snapped the CD in two. He didn't want to know how she'd gotten access to that bastard's computer.

She began playing nervously with her necklace. 'He

used me to get videotapes of your practices. I had to make things right.'

'And this is right?'

'I just wanted to level the playing field.'

'That's already been handled,' he said in short, clipped words. 'We've changed everything since our last game with Palmer. We'd be stupid to keep running the same offence when Rex could be sending copies of those tapes to every team on our schedule.'

'Oh,' she said, her face crestfallen.

'Go home, Brynn,' he said tiredly. 'It's late, and Southern Trinity doesn't need to cheat to win.'

'I didn't mean it like that! I just wanted you to know that I'm on your side.' Her blue eyes were liquid as she looked at him. 'I care about you, Cody.'

He took two steps back and banged into the railing when he saw tears start to roll down her cheeks. He looked at her in disbelief. He'd wanted to hear her say that, but how was he supposed to believe it now? She'd obviously just come from being with Rex. Did she really think that this made up for everything?

She wasn't playing fair, but he couldn't stop his hungry gaze from sliding over her. She looked so beautiful, even with the long dark coat covering her. He hadn't been able to sleep without her beside him in bed. His gaze hit her shoes and stuck.

On cue, his cock started fighting with the zipper of his jeans.

'I don't want this,' he said firmly. She pushed her hands behind her back when he tried to give the CD back to her. Instead, he caught her purse and slipped it inside. 'I don't need it.'

She caught his arm. 'Wait. You need to know that I just turned in my resignation to Dean Hawthorn.'

He flinched at the name.

She hurried past it. 'I'll finish my classes, but after the semester ends, I'm done at Southern Trinity. I know I've made mistakes, Cody, but I'm trying to put things right. Do you think you'll ever be able to forgive me?'

Damn, he wanted to. He ran his hand through his hair. His arms were aching to grab her and pull her to his bed. He wanted to just shut out the world, but he knew that would be a mistake. His brain wasn't that fogged by alcohol.

He turned away, but she hurried after him as he stepped into the house. He started to close the door on her, but she used both hands to push it open.

'Please,' she said. 'Just one more thing.'

His pulse was pounding in his ears. He couldn't take much more of this.

'I knew it was you, Cody.'

The sledgehammer wasn't giving up. He knew what she was talking about.

'That night in college. I think I knew all along, but didn't want to admit it.' Her cheeks were wet with tears as she looked up into his face. 'You called me "Goody". Nobody ever called me "Goody" but you.'

Cody fought for air. Damn it, he wanted to believe her more than anything in the world. His hand shook as he grabbed the doorknob. 'And no one ever will again,' he said as he shut it.

He turned the lock and dropped his forehead against the door.

And he'd thought he'd been having a meltdown before.

He hadn't even been close.

14

Brynn tried to stay away from the big Southern Trinity/ Palmer College game. She really did, but listening to the radio alone in her apartment nearly drove her crazy. The broadcast only offered a glimpse of what was happening in that football stadium, and she needed more. She wanted to hear the gasp of the crowd when Trini did a twisting dismount from a scorpion lift. She wanted to see Hannah do her trademark high split at the top of a pyramid. She wanted to feel the crisp night air, taste Kettle Korn, cheer for Jets' tackles, and yell when JJ made a mad dash for the end zone.

Most of all, she wanted to see Cody.

She knew he didn't want her there, and she respected his decision. Her attempt at reconciliation had been too little, too late. She'd hurt him too many times for him to forgive her. She understood.

She just wanted to be there when he destroyed Rex and the Palmer Patriots.

It was well into the second half when she walked through the gate. The tunnel was empty as she hurried down its long corridor to the field. The noise of the crowd drowned out the echo of her boots against the concrete. This time, the Southern Trinity fans were getting their money's worth.

She came to a stop in the shadows. It was the perfect place to hide, yet get a good view of the field. A quick glance at the scoreboard showed that the Trojans were still ahead by two touchdowns. She hadn't missed anything on the long walk in from the parking lot.

She searched for Cody and found him pacing up and down the sidelines. The highlights in his brown hair were fading now that fall was turning into winter. The concentration on his face was clear even from a distance. He was focused on the game – and Rex.

Brynn followed his glare. This game was personal.

She toyed with her necklace and leaned tiredly against the wall. She was all cried out. The tears had simply dried up. Looking at Cody still hurt, but Rex? He was nothing to her.

A timeout was called, and she automatically looked at her cheer squad. That, at last, pulled a half-smile out of her. 'Amazing,' she said softly.

They were unrecognisable as the rag tag team she'd assembled at the start of the season. Their new uniforms were as sharp as their moves. The squad had piggybacked on the energy of their captains and everyone looked happy and excited. Soon, they had the crowd clapping along with their chants of S-T-U, S-T-U.

Brynn's eyes widened in delight when Steve and Mark pushed Trini and Hannah into liberty lifts. Jimmy did a tumbling run in front of them that ended with a back layout so high, it made even her gasp. She pressed a hand over the ache in her chest when the crowd came to its feet.

They weren't standing for the football team; they were applauding her cheerleaders.

'Oh,' she gasped when Hannah suddenly looked her way. She quickly stepped back into the shadows, but it was too late. She'd been caught.

'Hey!' Hannah said as she trotted over.

Trini wasn't far behind. 'You made it.'

'Yes, but nobody's supposed to know.' Reaching out,

Brynn caught her captains and pulled them into the tunnel. 'Cody doesn't want me here.'

'He's busy,' Trini said. She looked at the field as she tried to catch her breath. Lifts took more out of the flyers than people realised. 'He won't notice if you stay.'

Brynn turned her attention back to the battle being fought on the field. 'We look pretty good tonight.'

'We should,' Hannah said. 'Jets told me that Coach Jones worked them to the bone this week.'

That didn't surprise Brynn. 'There's no way he's going to lose to Rex again.'

Trini plopped her pompons on her hips. 'And why do you think it matters to him so much?'

Brynn waved her off. She wasn't going to get into that again. She was here for the football game. Nothing more. 'It hasn't got anything to do with me. Those two butted heads even when they were on the same team.'

'Haven't you ever wondered why?' Hannah asked. She brushed her hair back, but jumped up onto her toes when Jetson made a hard tackle. 'Fumble!'

Brynn craned her neck to see. The crowd was already screaming. 'Did we get it? Can either of you see?'

'Southern Trinity's ball,' Trini said when the official signalled the possession.

For a while, the three simply watched the game. It gave Brynn so much pleasure to see the Trojans slowly dismantle the Patriots' defence. Cody had been right. He hadn't needed any help to win this game.

'Number 69 looks sluggish,' she noted. The Patriot player had left them shaking in their shoes at the last game.

Trini let out a snort, and Brynn looked at her sharply. The girl was laughing too hard to explain. Instead, she pointed at Hannah. The blonde's face was red hot.

Trini gasped for air and swung her arm around

Brynn's shoulders. 'You weren't the only one who planned a bit of subterfuge for this game, honey. Number 69 should be tired. Our little Hannah kept him busy all night and most of the day.'

Brynn's eyes widened, but Hannah wouldn't meet her flabbergasted stare. The cheerleader's pompons swished around her skirt as she traced patterns in the dirt just outside the tunnel.

'She said she wanted a big dick, so we found her one,' Trini said.

'Hannah,' Brynn gasped. She clapped a hand over her mouth, but it didn't hide her surprise. 'You didn't have to do that. Not for me.'

The girl looked at her shyly. 'It wasn't for you. It was for me. I . . . I kinda like him.'

'Kinda?' Trini said. 'What would you do if you really liked a guy? I mean, I took on the quarterback, but we couldn't keep up with you two. How many times did he hump you?'

'I don't know,' Hannah said, staring at the floor. She grinned self-consciously. 'I stopped counting.'

Brynn grinned with her, but this was serious. A girl only had a first time once in her life. She walked over to her captain and bent her head close. 'How do you feel?'

Hannah blushed, but there was excitement in her eyes. 'I won't be doing any spread eagle jumps tonight.'

Brynn remembered her all night and day ride with Cody and totally understood. 'Sore?'

'A good sore,' Hannah confided. 'He did things I never imagined – and I just let him.'

'Did you come?' Brynn asked gently.

'Of course she came,' Trini said. She threw her arms around her two friends' shoulders. 'All you have to do is flick her clit and she comes. I should know.'

Hannah blushed a thousand shades of red, but she couldn't stop smiling.

Brynn's chuckle caught her unexpectedly. 'So tell me,' she said. 'How many points does he rate?'

Trini let out a hoot of laughter.

Hannah's mouth gaped open, but she knew she'd never get away until she dished. 'Well, I . . . I don't have anything to compare it to, but I'd rate it about a hundred.'

'Details, honey. How big is his cock?'

Hannah ran a hand over her embarrassed face. 'A fifty? Maybe? I don't know. It felt huge.'

'A fifty? Wow,' Brynn said.

'What about his stamina?' Trini prompted.

'Another fifty.'

'I love his gold eyes,' Brynn said, getting into the game. It was fun when somebody else was under the gun. 'They're so unique. They're worth ten on their own.'

Hannah lifted her hands and curled her fingers. 'His chest is a thing of marvel. Twenty-five right there.'

Brynn could imagine. Those football pads could only emphasise a physique so much. 'So are you going to see him again?'

'We've got plans for after the game.'

'Plans? Oh, you make it sound so pretty,' Trini said. 'Admit it. You're going to hop back into the sack.'

Hannah bit her lip. 'Eventually, I hope he takes me to a movie or something.'

Brynn patted her on the shoulder. 'Make him take you to breakfast. It's a good time to talk.'

Trini cocked her head to the side. 'Maybe you should try that with Coach Jones. He'll be in a good mood tomorrow morning. Take him some coffee and dough-nuts. Who knows? Maybe it will lead to something even sweeter.'

The laughter trailed off. Brynn knew her cheerleaders' intentions were good, but they didn't understand how bad things were. 'Doughnuts aren't going to fix what's wrong between Cody and me.'

'They could be a start,' Hannah said. 'We still have hopes for you two.'

Brynn shrugged. Her hopes had died on Cody's doorstep. She took another deep breath and looked at the field. The game was turning into a rout. 'You should get back out there. The crowd is getting too quiet.'

'Are you sure? You shouldn't have to hide like this. You're our coach.'

'I know, Hannah, but it's what Cody would want. I have to respect that.'

The cheerleaders looked at each other and, suddenly, Brynn found herself caught in a group hug. 'We're glad you came,' they said.

She hugged them tightly. They didn't know that she'd turned in her resignation, and now wasn't the time to tell them. They were too excited about the game, the squad, and newfound love. She'd wait until football season was over before she broke the news, but she was going to miss them so much.

'Make me proud,' she said.

'We will.' They lifted their pompons and ran back to their positions. Soon the crowd was clapping along with them.

'Hello, Brynn,' said a low voice. A low English voice.

Brynn spun around and found Dean Hawthorn hiding in the shadows behind her. 'How long have you been standing there?'

'Long enough to know that Hannah is now on the market.' The smile slipped from his distinguished face, and he frowned. 'I apologise. Under the circumstances, that was in poor taste.'

He stepped forward into the light, and the purple bruise along his jaw line became more apparent. Humbly, he folded his hands in front of him. 'How are you, Brynn?'

Brynn tugged the belt of her leather jacket tighter. She hadn't expected to run into the dean here. They'd had very little interaction since Cody had knocked him flat on his behind. She looked at tips of her boots. 'I've been better,' she admitted.

He took a step closer. 'I would hope that you've had time to reconsider your resignation.'

She didn't look up. 'I think it would be best for all of us if I left.'

'I disagree.'

She glanced at him through her lashes. 'It would certainly be best for you. You've got to be looking over your shoulder every time you step into the hallway.'

'If you're referring to Coach Jones, I believe we've come to an understanding.' Hawthorn reached up to straighten his tie. 'I was referring to your students. You've proven to be an excellent teacher and an outstanding cheerleading coach.'

Brynn looked away and blinked back the moisture. And she'd thought she'd been numb. 'I haven't set a very good example.'

'Your personal life is your own business.' Cautiously, he reached out and caught one of her hands in both of his. 'I apologise that I forgot that rule.'

She sighed and patted the back of his hand. Finally, she looked up into those ever-piercing blue eyes. An unspoken communication ran between them. He still wanted her, and she still wanted him. Their connection was elemental. It just wasn't meant to be. 'It wasn't entirely your fault. I was receptive to your advances.'

And withdrawals and advances. She glanced away again. 'I just can't stay here.'

'I am truly sorry that things didn't work out for you and Mr Jones.'

Her throat tightened, so she just nodded.

The roar of the crowd had them both turning towards the field. JJ was streaking down the sidelines.

'He's going deep,' Brynn said. She went on her tiptoes to see over the people who stood in her way.

'He's open.'

The quarterback let the ball fly. It soared through the air and dropped into JJ's open arms. He didn't even have to break stride as he cruised into the end zone.

'Touchdown!'

Brynn turned to smile at Hawthorn, but he was gone. She glanced down the tunnel in time to see him walking out the other end.

She sighed. Another time and another place, they might have stood a chance.

She turned back to the field and saw Cody. He was walking down the sidelines towards her. He didn't see her, but she could see his face. There wasn't even a hint of a smile after the touchdown. He was too focused on the time clock.

She sagged against the wall. Her and Cody Jones ... Another time and another place ... She brushed away a lone tear that dripped from her eyes. There was less than two minutes left in the game and Southern Trinity was ahead by twenty-four points. By all rights, she should go.

She just couldn't make her legs move. She wanted to see him win.

The clock took forever to count down. When it finally did, the crowd erupted onto its feet. Students poured onto the field as security tried to keep things to a contained bedlam. Southern Trinity was continuing in their quest to repeat as national champs, though. People were going to celebrate.

Everything inside Brynn told her to go, but she crept just outside of the tunnel to catch one last look at Cody.

He was meeting Rex at mid-field for the final handshake. That, finally, brought a true smile from her tired soul. Even from a distance, she could see how much it pained Rex to shake the winning coach's hand.

She was still standing there smiling when Cody turned around and looked straight at her.

'Hunh!' Brynn inhaled sharply, but it was too late. He'd seen her.

Feeling terrible, she darted down the tunnel. She hadn't wanted to spoil his night. A clatter of footsteps pounded after her. She looked over her shoulder and came to a stop when she saw her entire cheerleading squad.

'There she is,' Hannah called.

'Get her!' Trini ordered.

Brynn took a surprised step back, but couldn't escape when Steve and Mark caught her and lifted her onto their shoulders. 'Put me down,' she ordered.

'Coach wouldn't like that.'

'I *am* your coach.'

'He meant Coach Jones,' Scott Jetson said as he met them at the corner of the field. He passed his helmet to Trini. Brynn felt like a sack of potatoes as her cheerleaders handed her over to the football player.

'Jets,' she said firmly. 'This isn't a good idea.'

She started to struggle. She felt ridiculous having her student manhandle her. She kicked her feet, but he wasn't putting up with it. Her stomach dropped when he flipped her over his shoulder to carry her fireman style. 'Scott,' she screeched as she smacked his back.

She let out a yelp when he swatted her on the butt.

'Stay put,' he ordered.

The swarm of people was thick. Brynn's head bobbed up and down with every step Jets took, and she looked past his waist. Everything was upside down, but even she could see that the crowd was parting like the Red Sea.

'Oh no. Scott! You don't know what you're doing!'

'Yes, I do.'

'He doesn't want to see me,' she moaned. 'Don't do this. Not tonight.'

The defenceman didn't listen to a word she said. He just strode through the pandemonium as if he carted his computer science professor around on his shoulder every day. It took him an amazingly short time to make it to the eye of the storm.

Brynn's world spun when he set her on her feet and, for a moment, she caught his shoulders to steady herself. 'Uh, you're going to get me in trouble,' he said uneasily as he pried her hands away from him.

Another body stepped into his place and strong hands caught her by the waist. Brynn slowly opened her eyes. She closed them again when she saw Cody standing in front of her. 'I'm sorry,' she said plaintively. 'I tried to leave, but they caught me. They thought they were doing something nice.'

'They were.'

Her eyes flew open when his lips suddenly pressed against hers. She stood frozen as another roar echoed throughout the crowd.

'Come on, Goody,' he said, pulling back an inch. 'You can do better than that.'

He watched her closely as he moved in again, and Brynn's heart began to thud against her ribs. Her legs went weak, and she clutched at his sweatshirt. When he kissed her again, she began shaking.

He bundled her closer, and she knew she had to be dreaming. This couldn't be happening. Someone bumped against her, and she let out a short cry when someone stepped on her foot.

It wasn't a dream.

She looked at Cody uncomprehendingly.

'I'm the one who's sorry,' he said. He leaned closer to talk in her ear so she could hear over the din. 'I was such an idiot. My male pride almost let you walk away again.'

Her heart skipped a beat. 'But what about –'

'I was drunk,' he said. 'We'll talk about it later. Now kiss me, damn it. I'm like a starving man here.'

She didn't care that thousands of people were watching. All she knew was that he was on a high, and this might be her last chance to touch him. She wasn't going to waste the opportunity.

Reaching up, she wrapped her arms around his neck, and he groaned when their bodies came into full contact. His hands caught her ass, and his head dipped. The kiss jolted her all the way down to her toes. It went on and on until –

'Ahhhh!' Brynn yelped when cold water doused her.

'Damn it, you guys,' Cody said as he jumped.

JJ and Jets took two steps back, but were laughing too hard to hide the water cooler they carried between them. 'Cool your engines, you two,' Jetson howled.

'Yeah, get a room,' Trini piped in. The smile on her face was blinding.

JJ held up his hands when Cody took a mock threatening step towards them. 'It's tradition!' he squeaked.

'Get her a towel,' Cody said. He ran a hand through his wet hair and poked his finger in his ear. 'Get *me* a towel. It's fucking freezing out here.'

Brynn shuddered as he pulled her close again. They were both sopping wet, but soon they joined in the laughter. She wrapped her arms around his waist. 'Congratulations on the win.'

'It felt good,' he admitted. He dropped his head to nuzzle her ear. 'I heard that someone else recently got revenge on Rex, too.'

Her excitement dampened. She didn't want to get into the details of that.

'The underwear hanging from the flagpole was a nice touch,' he said with a grin.

He was all right with it.

Relief made Brynn go limp. She hugged him tight. 'I thought so, too.'

'Coach! Coach Jones.' A reporter and his cameraman elbowed their way through the crowd. 'Can we get a word with you?'

'Just a moment, boys.' He glanced down at her and wiped a droplet of water from her chin. 'Wait for me? You can warm up in my office while I get these interviews out of the way.'

She didn't want to let him go, but she forced her arms to drop. 'I'll be there,' she promised.

His eyes were hot. 'Be ready. I'm taking you home as soon as I can shake everyone.'

Hannah wrapped a towel around Brynn's shoulders. She hugged it to her, but walked backwards as the cheerleader pulled her away. 'Hurry,' she mouthed.

They were tearing at each other's clothes before they even made it inside the front door of Cody's house. He was frantic for her, and Brynn was desperate for him.

'We could have been doing this the other night if I weren't such a fool,' he said. He tossed her Southern Trinity sweatshirt to the far corner of the living room and reached for the clasp of her bra. 'You told me everything I wanted to hear, but I was too hammered and depressed to listen.'

She didn't want to talk about that. She didn't want to talk at all.

'Brynnie?' he said. He caught her chin and made her look at him.

'Make love to me, Cody.'

One eyebrow lifted. 'Yes, ma'am.'

He backed her into his bedroom as she reached for the zipper of his pants. Together, they tumbled onto the bed. Squirming and twisting, they tugged at each other's clothes. By the time they were both naked, the room looked like a clothes hamper had exploded.

Brynn was breathing hard when Cody's hand cupped her breast. 'I've missed you so much,' she said.

Her back arched when he caught her nipple with his mouth. He set up a suction that had her writhing underneath him. She clutched his shoulders to hold him against her and raked her other hand down his back.

He caught her hand and brought it around to his cock. 'That's how much I missed you.'

She moaned. He was hot and hard as he overfilled her hand. Her legs dropped open, and she wriggled her hips into position. Thrusting upwards, she pressed her aching pussy against the tip of his cock. 'Hurry, Cody.'

He thrust into her, and his shoulders sagged in relief. He dropped his head into the crook of her shoulder and began pumping his hips hard and fast. Brynn wrapped her legs around his waist and lifted to meet every thrust.

It had been too long, and they were both too needy

for it to last. The orgasm hit them both hard. Their joined bodies stiffened as one, then collapsed against the mattress. It was a while before either of them could move or even speak.

Cody's breaths were harsh in her ear. 'Did you really turn in your resignation?' he asked.

Brynn idly raked her fingers through his thick brown hair. 'Yes.'

'Do you have any plans?'

'No.'

'Come with me,' he said as he propped himself up onto his elbows. His gaze was intense as he stared down at her. 'I'm leaving, too.'

Her air came out in one, long exhale. It would kill her if she'd ruined his career. 'Because of me?' she said weakly.

'Because you won't be there anymore. Because I can't stand looking at that bastard Hawthorn's ugly mug. And because I've accepted an offer from the Cowboys. They want me to be their offensive coordinator.'

Her fingers bit into his sides. 'Dallas? You're going to the pros? Your old team?'

He nodded, but didn't take his eyes off of her. 'As a coach. I want you to go with me.'

He waited for a moment. When she didn't answer, he added, 'You could try out for the cheer squad.'

The Dallas Cowboy Cheerleaders? They were only the most famous cheer squad in the world. For a moment, Brynn couldn't think. When she realised she was getting everything she wanted, she crumpled into an emotional heap. 'Yes,' she choked out.

He dropped his forehead against hers. 'Good. Kidnapping's not high on my list, but I was going to resort to it if you said no.'

She chuckled and kissed him. 'We might have a problem, though. I know the Dallas cheerleaders aren't allowed to consort with the team.'

His brow furrowed. 'That's the players. They'll have to change the rules for the coaches, because we, by God, are going to do a lot of consorting.'

His hips moved, but her thighs clamped around him to stop him from leaving her.

'I got you something,' he said by way of explanation.

She reluctantly let him go, but he only moved so far as to pick his pants up off the floor. He dug into a pocket, but his eyebrows drew together when he came up empty. He looked at her sheepishly as he searched the other one. He sighed in relief when he pulled out a jewellery box.

'This is for you,' he said as he opened it. It was a bracelet.

He caught the silver chain and tossed the box aside. With purpose, he crawled back onto the bed and settled on his haunches above her.

Brynn reached for him, but he caught her wrist and concentrated on the bracelet's latch. Her attention was torn between the gift and the cock that lay heavily on her stomach as he straddled her. 'You shouldn't have,' she whispered.

'I gave you a hard time,' he said. He turned her hand over and kissed her palm. 'I thought about a necklace, but you're too damn hard on those.'

Brynn lifted her wrist so she could see. It was a charm bracelet. Her lips trembled when she saw a kernel of popcorn. He'd chosen the charms himself.

'Cody,' she sighed. There were a set of pompons, a football, a computer monitor, and a heart.

He caught that one. 'This is mine,' he said softly. 'You've had it since I was twenty-one.'

She swallowed hard and reached up to cup his face. 'I wasn't ready for you then. I knew there was something between us, but it was too raw. It scared me.'

He ran his finger down her cheek. 'Does it still scare you?'

'Some,' she admitted.

'Think you're ready for me now?'

She shivered convulsively when his touch left her face and trailed down her arm. He watched closely as he reached behind him and pressed his fingers between her legs.

'I think you are,' he said as he slowly penetrated her.

Automatically, her legs pulled up.

'Uh-uh,' he said as he crawled off of her. He caught her by the waist and rolled her onto her stomach. 'There's just one more thing we need to finish before we can move on to the next chapter of our life.'

'What's that?' she asked, looking over her shoulder.

'I think you know,' he said as he took his position between her spread legs.

'Ohhhh,' she gasped when he caught her thighs and lifted them into the air as if she were a wheelbarrow.

'Does this feel familiar?' he asked slyly. 'This was how our first night was supposed to end ten years ago, Goody.'

Her fingers caught at the sheets when she felt his big cock poking at her. He pressed in deeply, and her toes pointed hard at the other wall. 'Oh, God,' she moaned.

The position made him feel huge inside her. She didn't know if she would have been able to handle it as a virgin. He lifted her legs higher until her cunt was at the right angle for his hips. Her breasts swung freely as he held her suspended in mid-air, and she caught hold of the headboard as he began to thrust.

'And it's Jones nailing one right between the uprights,' he said hoarsely.

'Cody,' she moaned.

'Too much?' he asked, immediately pulling back.

'No. No,' she panted. Rolling her head on the pillow, she looked at him over her shoulder. 'Go deep, Jones. Go deep!'

Visit the Black Lace website at
www.blacklace-books.co.uk

LOOK OUT FOR THE ALL-NEW BLACK LACE BOOKS – AVAILABLE NOW!

All books priced £6.99 in the UK. Please note publication dates apply to the UK only. For other territories, please contact your retailer.

Coming in April

HOT GOSSIP
Savannah Smythe
ISBN 0 352 33880 6

Suzy Whitbread packs in her job and returns to the village where she grew up. She was frowned upon as a teenager for the close friendship she had with Clifton McKenna, a successful horse trainer with an overbearing wife. Now, Suzy finds that Clifton has recently been confined to a wheelchair after a riding accident, and she is determined to help him recover. But with Clifton's son Jem also having designs on Suzy, father/son rivalry becomes the catalyst for some very hot gossip. **Sizzling sexual tensions in small-town England as a secret affair becomes public.**

LA BASQUAISE
Angel Strand
ISBN 0 352 32988 2

The lovely Oruela is determined to fit in to a lifestyle of opulence in 1920s Biarritz. But she has to put her social aspirations on hold when she falls under suspicion for her father's murder. As Oruela becomes embroiled in a series of sensual games, she discovers that blackmail is a powerful weapon that can be used to obtain pleasure as well as money. **An unusual, erotic and beautifully written story set in the heady whirl of French society in the 1920s.**

Coming in May

BLACK LIPSTICK KISSES
Monica Belle
ISBN O 352 33885 7

Sultry and mischievous Angela McKie loves dressing up in fetish clothing inspired by Victorian decadence. Perfecting an air of occult sexiness, she enjoys teasing men to distraction. She attracts the lustful attentions of two very different guys: Stephen Byrne is a serious young politician with a bright future; Michael Merrick is a cartoonist for a horror comic. Both want her, and set out to get her, but quickly discover they have bitten off more than they can chew when they allow themselves to be seduced by Ms McKie. **A witty, well-crafted, naughty story set in the fashion-conscious London Goth scene.**

THE HAND OF AMUN
Juliet Hastings
ISBN O 352 33144 5

Marked from birth with the symbol of Amun, the young Naunakhte must enter a life of dark eroticism as a servant at his temple. She becomes the favourite of the high priestess but, when she's accused of an act of sacrilege, she is forced to flee to the city of Waset. There she meets Khonsu, a prince of the Egyptian underworld whose prowess as a lover is legendary. But fate draws her back to the temple, and she is forced to choose between two lovers – one mortal and the other a god. **Highly arousing and imaginative story of life and lust in Ancient Egypt.**

Black Lace Booklist

Information is correct at time of printing. To avoid disappointment
check availability before ordering. Go to www.blacklace-books.co.uk.
All books are priced £6.99 unless another price is given.

BLACK LACE BOOKS WITH A CONTEMPORARY SETTING

☐ IN THE FLESH Emma Holly	ISBN 0 352 33498 3	£5.99
☐ SHAMELESS Stella Black	ISBN 0 352 33485 1	£5.99
☐ INTENSE BLUE Lyn Wood	ISBN 0 352 33496 7	£5.99
☐ THE NAKED TRUTH Natasha Rostova	ISBN 0 352 33497 5	£5.99
☐ A SPORTING CHANCE Susie Raymond	ISBN 0 352 33501 7	£5.99
☐ TAKING LIBERTIES Susie Raymond	ISBN 0 352 33357 X	£5.99
☐ A SCANDALOUS AFFAIR Holly Graham	ISBN 0 352 33523 8	£5.99
☐ THE NAKED FLAME Crystalle Valentino	ISBN 0 352 33528 9	£5.99
☐ ON THE EDGE Laura Hamilton	ISBN 0 352 33534 3	£5.99
☐ LURED BY LUST Tania Picarda	ISBN 0 352 33533 5	£5.99
☐ THE HOTTEST PLACE Tabitha Flyte	ISBN 0 352 33536 X	£5.99
☐ THE NINETY DAYS OF GENEVIEVE Lucinda Carrington	ISBN 0 352 33070 8	£5.99
☐ DREAMING SPIRES Juliet Hastings	ISBN 0 352 33584 X	
☐ THE TRANSFORMATION Natasha Rostova	ISBN 0 352 33311 1	
☐ SIN.NET Helena Ravenscroft	ISBN 0 352 33598 X	
☐ TWO WEEKS IN TANGIER Annabel Lee	ISBN 0 352 33599 8	
☐ HIGHLAND FLING Jane Justine	ISBN 0 352 33616 1	
☐ PLAYING HARD Tina Troy	ISBN 0 352 33617 X	
☐ SYMPHONY X Jasmine Stone	ISBN 0 352 33629 3	
☐ SUMMER FEVER Anna Ricci	ISBN 0 352 33625 0	
☐ CONTINUUM Portia Da Costa	ISBN 0 352 33120 8	
☐ OPENING ACTS Suki Cunningham	ISBN 0 352 33630 7	
☐ FULL STEAM AHEAD Tabitha Flyte	ISBN 0 352 33637 4	
☐ A SECRET PLACE Ella Broussard	ISBN 0 352 33307 3	
☐ GAME FOR ANYTHING Lyn Wood	ISBN 0 352 33639 0	
☐ CHEAP TRICK Astrid Fox	ISBN 0 352 33640 4	
☐ ALL THE TRIMMINGS Tesni Morgan	ISBN 0 352 33641 3	

☐ ARIA APPASSIONATA Juliet Hastings	ISBN O 352 33056 2
☐ THE RELUCTANT PRINCESS Patty Glenn	ISBN O 352 33809 1
☐ WILD IN THE COUNTRY Monica Belle	ISBN O 352 33824 5
☐ THE TUTOR Portia Da Costa	ISBN O 352 32946 7
☐ SEXUAL STRATEGY Felice de Vere	ISBN O 352 33843 1
☐ HARD BLUE MIDNIGHT Alaine Hood	ISBNO 352 33851 2
☐ ALWAYS THE BRIDEGROOM Tesni Morgan	ISBNO 352 33855 5
☐ COMING ROUND THE MOUNTAIN Tabitha Flyte	ISBNO 352 33873 3

BLACK LACE BOOKS WITH AN HISTORICAL SETTING

☐ PRIMAL SKIN Leona Benkt Rhys	ISBN O 352 33500 9	£5.99
☐ DEVIL'S FIRE Melissa MacNeal	ISBN O 352 33527 0	£5.99
☐ DARKER THAN LOVE Kristina Lloyd	ISBN O 352 33279 4	
☐ THE CAPTIVATION Natasha Rostova	ISBN O 352 33234 4	
☐ MINX Megan Blythe	ISBN O 352 33638 2	
☐ JULIET RISING Cleo Cordell	ISBN O 352 32938 6	
☐ DEMON'S DARE Melissa MacNeal	ISBN O 352 33683 8	
☐ DIVINE TORMENT Janine Ashbless	ISBN O 352 33719 2	
☐ SATAN'S ANGEL Melissa MacNeal	ISBN O 352 33726 5	
☐ THE INTIMATE EYE Georgia Angelis	ISBN O 352 33004 X	
☐ OPAL DARKNESS Cleo Cordell	ISBN O 352 33033 3	
☐ SILKEN CHAINS Jodi Nicol	ISBN O 352 33143 7	
☐ EVIL'S NIECE Melissa MacNeal	ISBN O 352 33781 8	
☐ ACE OF HEARTS Lisette Allen	ISBN O 352 33059 7	
☐ A GENTLEMAN'S WAGER Madelynne Ellis	ISBN O 352 33800 8	
☐ THE LION LOVER Mercedes Kelly	ISBN O 352 33162 3	
☐ ARTISTIC LICENCE Vivienne La Fay	ISBN O 352 33210 7	
☐ THE AMULET Lisette Allen	ISBN O 352 33019 8	

BLACK LACE ANTHOLOGIES

☐ WICKED WORDS 6 Various	ISBN O 352 33590 0
☐ WICKED WORDS 9 Various	ISBN O 352 33860 1
☐ THE BEST OF BLACK LACE 2 Various	ISBN O 352 33718 4

BLACK LACE NON-FICTION

☐ THE BLACK LACE BOOK OF WOMEN'S SEXUAL   ISBN 0 352 33793 1   £6.99
FANTASIES Ed. Kerri Sharp

To find out the latest information about Black Lace titles, check out the website: www.blacklace-books.co.uk or send for a booklist with complete synopses by writing to:

Black Lace Booklist, Virgin Books Ltd
Thames Wharf Studios
Rainville Road
London W6 9HA

Please include an SAE of decent size. Please note only British stamps are valid.

Our privacy policy
We will not disclose information you supply us to any other parties.
We will not disclose any information which identifies you personally to any person without your express consent.

From time to time we may send out information about Black Lace books and special offers. Please tick here if you do not wish to receive Black Lace information.   ☐

Please send me the books I have ticked above.

Name ....

Address ....

....

....

....

Post Code ....

Send to: Virgin Books Cash Sales, Thames Wharf Studios,
Rainville Road, London W6 9HA.

US customers: for prices and details of how to order
books for delivery by mail, call 1-800-343-4499.

Please enclose a cheque or postal order, made payable
to Virgin Books Ltd, to the value of the books you have
ordered plus postage and packing costs as follows:

UK and BFPO – £1.00 for the first book, 50p for each
subsequent book.

Overseas (including Republic of Ireland) – £2.00 for
the first book, £1.00 for each subsequent book.

If you would prefer to pay by VISA, ACCESS/MASTERCARD,
DINERS CLUB, AMEX or SWITCH, please write your card
number and expiry date here:

....

Signature ....

Please allow up to 28 days for delivery.